PARADISE

Koji Suzuki

Translated by Tyran Grillo

VERTICAL.

Published by Vertical, Inc., New York.

Originally published in Japan as *Rakuen* by Shinchosha, Tokyo, 1990.

ISBN 1-932234-23-3/978-1-932234-23-7

Manufactured in the United States of America

First American Edition

Vertical, Inc.
1185 Avenue of the Americas 32nd Floor
New York, NY 10036
www.vertical-inc.com

PARADISE

CONTENTS

Part One

Legend

1

Long ago, in prehistoric times, there lived a cattle-raising Mongolian tribe called the Tangad. They roamed the northern rim of the Gobi Desert along the Altai mountains in search of grass and water for their horses, cattle, and sheep. They never cultivated the land or settled down in one place for too long. Although they raised cattle, they did not really know how to control animals, and it was fair to say that they simply chased after their herds. The requirements of mobility did mean that they were expert horsemen.

Lakes appeared unexpectedly in the distance ahead, only to disappear as the riders dozed off on horseback during their journey. Pursuing a vanished lake was futile. In fact, if it was ever found, it was seldom recognized as the same lake, its new locale having altered the shape dramatically. These lakes were, in their transience, more akin to puddles. Yet in due time their waterside would turn a lush green.

The Tangad had no writing system. Instead, speech and spoken promises were treated with the utmost importance, and every member of the tribe was expected to keep one's word. A man could be killed for breaking even the simplest of pacts.

When boys came of age at thirteen, they went out hunting alone, bringing back the spirit of their first kill as their own. A man was to protect that spirit for his entire life. If the spirit's power was feeble, the man was destined to die prematurely. If strong, he would be saved by this endowment alone in any life or death situation. With that first kill, his fate was written. The age of thirteen was therefore a milestone in every man's life.

The men rode horses whenever they went out hunting. As children, they learned to ride on sheep, which allowed them to ride swiftly and surely in pursuit of their game when later on they switched to horses. While only birds and rabbits normally fell prey to their arrows, in times of conflict the men donned armor and hunted down human foe instead. All the men were strong, and they thundered across the plains kicking up dust storms. Given an opening they penetrated deep into enemy lands, killing every man while stealing women and livestock. While, at first, the newly acquired women mourned the loss of their families, after a few years they forgot their former life and grew accustomed to that of the new tribe, giving birth to children with slightly different features. There were the occasional few, however, who refused to let go of their husbands' memories.

Bogud was a boy born of one of those plundered women. Wars were either won or lost. Defeated tribes simply dwindled out, while the victors grew stronger, assimilating other clans and dominating the desert.

His upbringing was typical, as were his height and skin color. But his face was chiseled, and compared to the other boys, whose faces seemed wedged into their broad shoulders, his jaw line was somehow more delicate. He had strong arms, but his fingers were long and slender, which perhaps explained the rare dexterity he began to exhibit from the age of ten. Bogud drew pictures of animals on the ground with sticks and sharpened stones. His vibrantly rendered horses and cows were so alive, they seemed ready to jump from the dirt at any given moment. His cave drawings in particular were rumored to play host to spirits and the thought of erasing them never even crossed the tribespeople's minds. As for one drawing of a horse, which seemed to change expression in the torch light that filled the caves, it was said to slip out secretly from the wall to graze by the lake when everyone was asleep. This peculiar ability won Bogud much attention from the elders.

When he was thirteen, having reached the most important year of his life, Bogud began to consider carving designs into stone as he had done on the earth. Soil was susceptible to rainfall and wind, distorting the original image beyond recognition. Bogud wanted the impulses that welled up in him to remain as something permanent. The desire to carve a lasting image onto a rock had come to him together with a desire to draw people. He believed that if he could create a permanent portrait, the thought, too, would last.

Bogud had drawn mostly animals in profile and never anything inanimate. Not a single rock or tree. As for people, he could not draw them. It went against tribal law.

......Never make a picture of a person.

No one had ever thought to question why this was so. There were only a few among the Tangad who could draw, and so most had forgotten there even was such a law. And so, coming of age as he was now, the impulse to draw people overtook him, making him the first to think it strange that something so trivial was considered taboo.

In truth, there was only one person he wanted to draw. She

was Fayau, daughter of the fourth most powerful chief among the Tangad's twelve tribal leaders. A fetching girl with long black hair, Fayau was a year younger than Bogud. While there were others who rivaled her in beauty, none surpassed her in charm. Her appeal was beyond description. Just being at her side made even the most grizzled men feel relaxed and carefree. No one could explain how the girl's merely average physique, and mildly lovely eyes and lips, could hide so much power within.

If Bogud was not preoccupied with his drawing, his sights were on her. There were times when he watched her from afar, others when he was close enough to feel her hair grazing his cheek. Just a few words between them was enough to set his heart afloat with joy. This joy was reflected in his bearing, and so the Bogud that Fayau knew was always cheerful and manly.

Bogud had yet to touch her body and left unspoken his yearning to make her his wife and leavc behind their descendants in this world. To do this, he would first need to be recognized as a strong and able man by everyone in the tribe. His coming-of-age quest was still six months away. It was tribal law that a boy could not take a wife, as a full man, until at least a year after his journey.

Bogud awaited it eagerly. Though unsure of how to make Fayau his future wife, he had no doubts that he would. He wanted nothing more than to take her in his arms and hold her close. Bogud decided to act on what had only been a vague desire: to carve a life-sized image of her. He had never before broken any of the laws of his people, so this required some serious determination.

No one could find out about it, so he snuck away from the camp when everyone was asleep. Carrying a little food and water with him, he quietly rode a sheep towards a tributary of the

Selenge River. When, at last, he reached the bottom of a deep terra cotta ravine, he found a suitable rock for his carving. Concealed by the shade of the crag, it was hardly noticeable from the river bed. Bogud stood there, contemplating the stone which, by his own hands, would soon become Fayau. He concentrated on the hard surface, overlaying her image in front of it. In his mind's eye, she posed for him as if deep in thought, turned around and smiled at him, talking while her charcoal hair swayed in the wind. Through squinting eyes, he compared an imagined Fayau with the very real stone before him, and when her hovering image fixed itself into the most captivating form imaginable, Bogud's eyes shot open. He cried out, his voice echoing down the ravine, and worked his canvas with a stone tool crafted with hard minerals.

For three days and three nights, he chiseled away without rest. Adding an ochre pigment to the delineated image, he at last finished a portrait that could easily have been mistaken for the real thing. Bogud studied the carving from various distances, voicing admiration for the quality of his work. Ignoring his fatigue, he stood dazed for a long time, speaking to the image as it changed expression in response to the sunlight. He approached Fayau timidly and caressed her, spreading his hands wide to embrace the stone. And, for that one moment, Bogud forgot about the offense he'd committed in violating a cardinal rule of the tribe.

However, since this was the first time he'd ever acted against his people, it was impossible for him not to worry over it. He left his masterpiece at the bottom of the ravine and, spurred on by a mixture of both fear and satisfaction, made the journey home, ignorant of the enormity of the punishment he and the Tangad would endure as a result of his transgression.

2

When Bogud returned to the settlement, he immediately ran to the elders' camp to ask why they were not to draw people. Whenever anyone was faced with something they didn't understand, they sought the council of Tafune the Elder. Tafune was also a shaman and therefore held a special status among the tribesmen. Able to communicate with ancestral spirits, he embodied all that the Tangad believed in. Bogud was convinced that Tafune was the only one who knew the ways of the world.

Tafune tied a length of stiff black hair behind his back. His eyes, sunken in furrows of aged flesh, looked up at the young man entering the camp. When he met Tafune's gaze, Bogud was slightly intimidated, feeling as if the elder were looking straight into his heart.

"And what have you drawn today?" Tafune mumbled.

Bogud couldn't quite make out the words, and only assumed this was what the old man had asked.

"Horses, cows, and a few rabbits just now," Bogud lied, breaking away from the elder's drowsy stare. When Bogud met his eyes a few moments later, he might as well have confessed to his act of violation.

"Was there something...you wanted...to ask me?" the elder inquired, pausing between each phrase. Bogud could never get anything past Tafune, a man with a wealth of life experience.

There was no use in wasting words.

"Why are we not allowed to draw people? I want to know the reason."

Tafune stopped himself in mid-yawn, emitting a strange noise from his nostrils.

"Tell me you have not already done this?"

"N-no, I have done nothing of the sort."

"Good, keep it that way. The law is the law and we must uphold it."

Bogud crouched down and brought his face closer.

"Won't you tell me why then?"

Tafune grew visibly annoyed and clicked his tongue.

"I cannot."

"Would it upset me to hear it?"

"Yes, I believe so."

Bogud knew he should just give up on the matter. Unable to leave, however, he could only look down at Tafune with a weary face. After thinking it over for a moment, Tafune flared his nostrils and sighed, then said in his husky voice, "All right, sit down."

Bogud sat cross-legged on the mat.

"You think that I will tell you anything if you just ask me, don't you?" said Tafune almost mockingly.

"Well..."

"So, how many has it been now?"

"What?"

"Years, I mean."

"Thirteen."

"Thirteen? So your spirit-seeking quest isn't too far away

now. Just don't let it get to your head. Your life has yet to begin."

"And how old are you, elder?"

"I've forgotten. I can't recall how many seasons have come and gone in my lifetime," said Tafune gravely, his face shaded by remembrance. "Look, Bogud. You are wrong to think that you can learn anything if you just asked me. My knowledge is only slightly more than yours, and even I do not know the reasons behind our customs. Ever since I was born, the law has always been the law. You, on the other hand..."

Tafune touched his fingertip to the ground and drew a simple shape. He seemed lost in thought, unsure of what to say.

"You are the most talented artist of the clan. And as such, this particular rule weighs on your mind more than any other."

Bogud nodded and Tafune was beginning to think that, as long as Bogud could be trusted with a secret, it might be okay to tell him.

"As for what happens if you break this rule, you cannot repeat this to anyone else. Promise me. If this should get out..."

"You have my word. I won't tell anyone."

They exchanged glances by way of assurance.

"Okay then. If you draw someone, you will lose that person."

Bogud's eyes went blank and his breath cut short.

"What do you mean, lose?"

"Death, lifelong separation...it could be either."

Bogud wanted to change the subject in a way that wouldn't alert Tafune to his seething agitation, but he got carried away by his anger and leaned in even closer.

"Why? Why is there such a law?!"

"You can question it all you like, but it will not change a

thing. If I ask you why you were born into this world, could you answer it? This is no different."

"Then why must I keep it a secret?"

"Think about it. If this became widely known, the land would soon be overrun with those exiled in hatred. Because everyone has enemies. It would destroy our clan."

"I understand. You have my word, I will protect this secret."

Bogud held his head in confusion and made to leave.

"Hold on. I am thinking your gifts might be useful to us."

"How so?"

"Your art is a haven for spirits. Such power could be used to protect our ancestors. From now on, I want you to work in stone. Stand the stones on the earth where the dead sleep to watch over their souls."

"Of course, I would be honored."

Thinking only of Fayau, however, Bogud was barely paying attention to Tafune's words. He agreed to it only halfheartedly and left the elders' camp. Bogud suddenly felt dizzy stepping out into the early spring sunlight and fell to the ground.

There was a thick forest near the camp. He glimpsed Fayau walking among the trees.

......Am I really going to lose her?

Bogud's breath trembled with rage. He could see her right there before him, only this time it did nothing to calm him. For a moment, Fayau disappeared behind the tree trunks. The next, her profile was visible briefly between them. Bogud silently cursed the entire tribe for their laws. Fayau slipped out of sight once more. The way she materialized and vanished, Bogud couldn't help but liken her to the fleeting lakes in the desert that shifted and faded into nothingness.

That's it! Bogud shouted in his heart. *I'm making my own rules now. What is tribal law anyway? I don't need reasons. If I draw the woman I desire, then I will have her. That's a rule of my own making, and I will live by it!*

Just then, Fayau slipped out of the woods, walking eastward with a cool countenance. Unaware of Bogud's gaze upon her and of the intense desire welling up in his heart, she stepped elegantly into the meadows. If only he could convey his burning passion, she would yield to him without hesitation, yet there was no way he could express his thoughts in speech, no way to exchange words of love with this abyss between them.

As Bogud followed Fayau with his eyes, she suddenly stopped. Her body half-hidden by the trees, she turned around as if looking for something until she caught sight of Bogud. A smile came to her face and she extended a hand towards him. But Bogud, unable to smile back, merely glared at her in despair.

3

Summer came and Bogud prepared for his spiritual quest. He took great care in choosing just the right horse and shot at trees to hone his hunting skills. As his fate would be decided by whatever he killed first, practicing on animals was not an option. There was no exception to this. Were he to miss and fell an animal, he would have to take on its spirit for the rest of his life. Consequently, he chose as his training ground a prairie without so much as a single wild hare. A hare's spirit was considered to be the weakest of all. If he killed one, even during target practice, his dreams of having Fayau would be just that.

His determination was so fierce, it manifested itself in body and mind alike. As the days went on, he began to shed his slender, boyish frame for one of noticeable prowess. And once Bogud reached the point where he could shoot a twig right in half from a hundred paces away without fail, summer had ended: his time had come at last. His body would continue to mature during the journey, which could last anywhere from six months to a year, making him an even better hunter. These physical changes seemed nothing less than the result of an intense desire to see his wish fulfilled. And so, where others might have encountered frustration in their training, Bogud found utter joy.

That morning, he intentionally did not call out to Fayau, though she would be the only thing on his mind until the earthen

Tangad encampments disappeared into the lower steppes behind him. If only he could obtain a powerful enough spirit, then he would have Fayau for his own! She was the sole source of his distending passion. He was aiming for a red deer of legend which no one had ever brought down. Countless people had lost their lives in pursuit of it. Of all the animals, the red deer chambered the most powerful spirit, and finding it was so difficult that no one living among the Tangad had ever even seen it. The sole exception was Koriko, a young man whose life had ended three years before, at the age of seventeen. At the time of his coming-of-age quest, he was a hero among the clan, on his way to becoming a chieftain someday. He set out upon his journey with everyone's highest expectations. He then encountered the legendary red deer at the foot of Mount Mowanna and gave it chase before losing sight of it. The deer never showed itself again. By then, Koriko's provisions were depleted. Ironically enough, the land around him was replete with wildlife. Wild hares hopped all around as if to tease him, but he knew that if he killed and ate just one of them, his journey would be over once the animal's feeble spirit became his own. While battling with this frightful irony, he persisted after the deer but, in a moment of hunger-induced derangement, shot a hare with red eyes. Until he bit into its meat he believed he had slain the deer. His discouragement, when he discovered that it was a hare, was so immense that everyone saw him return a changed person, the heroic shadow of his earlier days forever tainted. Four years later, he died from a high fever, so fragile had the rabbit's spirit rendered him.

While this important journey did shape a growing man's destiny, it was his attitude towards his own life which ultimately decided the outcome of the quest itself. If there were those who put their lives in danger for the sake of gaining more powerful spirits, there were also those who, from the very outset, were content to settle on lesser ones. But Koriko's ambitions were so great that he ended up chasing after his own delusions, ultimately succumbing to his body and putting his reputation to shame.

I'm different from Koriko, Bogud vowed to himself as he turned his horse to the northwest, where the red deer was said to live. He was willing to go all the way in pursuing this animal, even if it meant starving to death. Bogud believed that obtaining its spirit would be enough to absolve his violation of tribal law.

Fayau was praying for his safe return as she watched him fade from view into the northwestern horizon. However, Bogud knew nothing of her feelings. Fayau herself did not know exactly what she felt for him. Bogud's presence did always make her feel protected. A woman could never feel fully at ease without a man who was ready to stake his life over her; this was the necessary condition for any inkling of love. Even so, the two of them had never expressed their feelings in words. Had Bogud known how Fayau felt about him, his eagerness to find the red deer would not have been nearly as strong. There was little reason to put his life on the line for something readily obtainable.

Bogud made his way to the upper regions of the desert and spotted a bear as he entered a heavily wooded forest. These were also considered to be of high spiritual rank. They were easy to find, difficult to bring down. Paying no attention to the bear, Bogud made his way westward where the evergreens and deciduous trees blended along the borders of the plains. He couldn't afford to get lost in the woods, as it would be nearly impossible to tell which way was which. He'd learned from Tafune that the boundary between the woods and steppes continued straight to the west and the forest trees bore fruit, allowing him to economize his rations of dried meat packed in cow innards.

Though summer was only just over, the air was already cold in the high plains. Snow was a rarity here, even in winter, relegated to higher elevations in the south. The snowcapped peaks of the Altai mountains were in Bogud's sight.

4

He steered his horse south now, riding straight through the wide open plains towards Mount Mowanna and its neighboring peaks, where the red deer of legend made its home. It was well into autumn by the time he arrived at the base of the mountains, where the climate was growing colder by the day as it welcomed the long winter ahead.

Searching for signs of the red deer, Bogud wandered for days on end through the trees, consuming grass roots and river water to sustain himself. All the while, Fayau was the only thing on his mind. Were it not for that, he would easily have lost sight of the purpose behind his journey. Traces of any deer having thrived here were nowhere to be found. Would any animal ever have inhabited such a place? A feeling of utter lifelessness permeated the hushed, bleak air. Fearless though Bogud was, he found himself gripped by a feeling of terror, thinking he might be lost in some sacred space where human presence was unwanted. He took a moment to clear his head, knowing that Koriko must have been overwhelmed by this same unearthly atmosphere. It was an oppressive place to a young man who knew only the world of the Tangad, and it gave him the feeling of being on a different plane of existence entirely.

Bogud scoured the snow-dusted mountainside, overlooking the chestnut-colored fields, for any signs of life. After much careful searching, he finally came across some deep holes at the foot of the mountain, dug by tarbagans for their hibernation. The holes were plugged up with droppings for camouflage, but the color difference was enough to give the land a noticeably speckled appearance. Bogud was relieved. The presence of marmots meant there would be all kinds of animals in the vicinity.

Picking up on the sound of flowing water, he followed it deftly to a heavily wooded ravine, where he made a fire by rubbing two dry sticks together and warmed himself. At the riverbank, he stuffed his cheeks with what little cured meat he had left and thought of what lay ahead for him. His eagerness in pursuing the red deer hadn't wavered in the least; the problem was finding the deer itself. Weary of his own naivete, he searched for an answer in his own brief experience, when he suddenly remembered a technique the elders used often while wolf hunting. Wolves had been observed during winter to call to other members of the pack to assist in catching their prey. The elders used this knowledge to their advantage by hiding among the rocks and mimicking the howling of wolves to lure them out within shooting range. Still, how was Bogud supposed to do this when he didn't even know what the red deer sounded like? There had to be another way.

That's it! he thought.

Why not make use of his own talents? If animals could be lured by voice, then a decoy should work just as well. He only thought of it because the riverbed vaguely resembled the Selenge tributary where he carved his effigy of Fayau. Only this time, he would be acting within the law.

He found a suitable rock that was easily visible from both

the mountain ridge and the slope leading to the ravine's edge. As he set to work, he tried his best to evoke Koriko's description of the legendary deer.

Bogud remembered lying beside him in the night, looking up at the Tangad firmament. The deer he now rendered into art was still inlaid among the glittering of stars that adorned the dome above them then. Koriko, who by that time had become a weakling, spoke of nothing to Bogud, seven years his junior, but that red deer. From Koriko's account, Bogud could paint a clear picture of the deer in his mind, and as he gazed at the sky, invisible lines connected a group of bright stars that stood out to him to form a magnificent portrait of a deer across the night. While the constellation may have been a far cry from the real deer, it was the only model he had to go from. Its antlers branched out elegantly, longer than the body from which they grew, and though its legs were slender, they imparted a feeling of great power. As he progressed with his carving, Bogud recaptured the sensation he'd felt when making Fayau's portrait by the Selenge. Plagued by hunger and fatigue, he put all his affection for her into his work. Soon, he could hardly tell whether he was drawing her or the deer as they blurred together in his mind's eye.

As he neared completion at last, he backed away for a moment like he always did for a final check of his work. Because it was an image direct from the heavens, the deer appeared animate, poised on its hind feet, about to leap from the stone. It was not, however, a deer running across the night sky, but one ready to soar into the sun.

Whereas Bogud had colored Fayau's portrait with ochre, he had no such pigment with him now. Imbedded as it was in the ashen stone, it would hardly be conspicuous from a distance. It had to be red, in accordance with its namesake. Bogud cut his left arm and, gathering the blood in his right hand, quickly painted the deer's image, breathing life into it with every stroke.

Bogud dug a hole into the earth big enough for him to hide in and went through the most tedious process of building a bonfire next to it. After leaning a number of body-length branches against a rock, he crossed two foot-long sticks inside and rubbed them with all the strength he could muster. It was backbreaking work and he had to continue until that moment when friction turned into flame, lest all the effort be for naught.

Once he had a fire going, Bogud tossed some fair-sized stones into the blaze. When they were red hot, he used them to line the bottom of the hole he'd dug earlier, covered them with damp grass and soil, and crouched over them, waiting for the deer to show itself. This way, he could stay warm without the fear of smoke betraying his presence. This was yet another survival tactic he'd learned from Tafune the Elder.

Unsure of how many days had passed, the prospect of getting buried in the earth was starting to seem like an acceptable end. Spirits flew around him in Fayau's guise, beckoning him repeatedly to the netherworld. More than once he caught himself just short of sticking an arm into one of the tarbagan holes. Bogud nearly lost his mind when, gnawing on some grass roots one day, he had a sudden desire to eat his own flesh. It was only after he'd nearly cut off part of his thigh that he came to his senses. His conscience reminded him of why he was there and he vomited once he was aware of the grass he was eating. Tafune had once told him that certain roots were toxic and could greatly cloud one's judgment.

As winter was reaching its end, the red deer appeared at long last. It was a quiet morning. Bogud opened his eyes vacantly and saw the creature's shimmering reflection. In the flow of melted snow, its figure swayed across the riverbed stones. Knowing it couldn't be his carving, Bogud started before opening his eyes wide. The legendary deer stood at the water's edge in all its refinement, gazing at the image Bogud had created. Its magnificent antlers reached from between its ears for the heavens exactly as the constellation had depicted it. The resemblance was uncanny.

Once Bogud was keen to the reality of what he was seeing, he reached for his bow.

......It's really here.

Joy and excitement tingled in his chest as he prepared to shoot.

What could it be doing, I wonder? It's as if the deer is communicating with my picture.

For a brief moment, he felt as though they had exchanged words somehow through the medium of his portrait. As Bogud released his arrow, the deer turned in his direction and their gazes met. Its eyes were beautiful and entirely devoid of terror. It was unclear whether or not they'd spotted him in the shade of the trees.

The arrow flew straight and true, piercing the deer's neck. The magnificent animal reared up on its hind legs and collapsed, not a trace of pain in its expression. Confident now that Fayau would be his, Bogud cried out her name with a voice that filled the ravine.

He scaled the riverbank, looking down at the dignified beast, now dead. Some of the strands of its red fur glittered like gold in the sunlight. Bogud nimbly tore off the hide, ripped open the stomach and gutted it, then placed the entrails onto sunlit rocks to dry. The remaining meat would be for food. He fed on venison and awaited spring's arrival, packing what he couldn't finish in the deer's dried intestines for his homeward journey.

He looked northeast and saw a vast green of short grass. It was spring. Hoisting the hide and antlers onto his horse's back, Bogud set out for the wide pastures. He stopped many times to partake of the deer's flesh along the way. It wasn't long before he finished everything, making the legendary deer's spirit his own.

In the spring of the following year, Bogud took Fayau as his wife. When he was fifteen, he got his own camp, and by seventeen fathered a son. As the only one to have ever brought back the red deer's spirit, Bogud came to hold a prominent role in the sacred rites of his people. To protect the purity of departed souls, he carved red deer on stones for every passing. As the days went by, he worked continuously with Fayau at his side. Whatever design he carved, each contained a deer with front legs raised high, jumping towards a large, round sun. Fayau was fond of the red deer running across the sky. Sitting at Bogud's side, she watched her husband carefully and copied him until she could faithfully render the image herself.

From all this work, Bogud climbed steadily in status, prompting rumors that he would soon take the rites to become chief. His future was bright. His son was now three years old and, unknown to both parents, a second child was on the way. Bogud always paid proper respects for his blessings. However, there was one thing that bothered him: his violation of tribal law seven years ago. He was content with his life now, but that only sharpened his worries. Fayau was no longer just an object of his adoration. She was his wife, and also the mother of their child. Losing his family would be no different from losing the world. No sooner had Bogud resolved to confide in Tafune than the land trembled with dust clouds on the horizon. His fears were about to become a reality. A tribe from the north was on the move.

A few days before this, a young chief by the name of Shalab of the same northern tribe was crossing the Selenge tributary with a shaman and a group of his followers in tow. There, he happened upon Bogud's carving. Unaware that it was a portrait in stone, Shalab rode his horse up the riverbank and called to the figure. When she offered no response, Shalab dismounted and walked up to the silent stranger, only to realize she was carved in rock. Less taken with its splendid craftsmanship than he was with the beauty of the woman it depicted, Shalab gently touched Fayau's cheeks, his voice filled with wonder.

"This woman. Where does she come from?" he asked the shaman. This was not an image created blindly, but one that surely had a model. The shaman carefully inspected the features of Fayau's garments and head ornaments.

"It appears to be a Tangad woman."

"These Tangad, are they strong?"

The shaman's eyes shone in what was otherwise a face scorched dark by the sun.

"What are you thinking?"

"I'm going to take this woman for my own."

There was no doubt in Shalab's voice. He, too, held a firm resolve behind his tough exterior. Destroying everything in his path and stealing women along the way was the only life he knew.

"The Tangad are unyielding."

"As far as I'm concerned, this will be my last battle. I will bring this woman to the New Land."

The New Land. It was an ancient legend among Shalab's people:

When the snow on Jinst Uul peak does not melt for an entire cycle of seasons, in the following year the northern corridor leading to the New Land will appear from the depths of the ocean. When the sun is at its highest, we will cross this corridor to more fertile land, where water and endless pastures abound.

Now was their only chance, as the corridor leading east would soon again sink into the sea. Throughout all of last year, the snow on Jinst Uul had not melted. As summer was still a hundred days away, they still had time. There wasn't one among the northern tribe who objected going to the New Land. The regions in the far reaches of the north were buried in ice; the crunch of frozen earth beneath their feet urged them towards more fertile soil. Of course, no one had actually ever seen the New Land, yet the northern tribe spoke of it as if they'd witnessed its abundance and bright skies firsthand. Neither Shalab nor the shaman could explain the legend's existence and would have been at a loss for words to explain it. Even so, they were determined to make it their reality.

The shaman was fond of Shalab, but always regarded him with apprehension, knowing his penchant for impulsive action. He only wished Shalab would learn to act with more foresight.

"Stop this nonsense," said the shaman, shaking his head.

"Always fighting..."

"Forecast for me. Will I win or lose?"

The shaman cast his animal bones.

"You will not lose," he answered frankly.

Shalab was satisfied with this and turned to his followers. Had the augury been negative, his determination would have been no less unwavering. His boastful attitude often contradicted fate, and he was adept at putting his words into action. The shaman was well aware of this. And so, even though it belied his hatred for war, it only made sense for him to predict a victorious outcome for his leader.

"Tomorrow morning, we attack the Tangad. We will destroy them and take their women. Let us return quickly and prepare."

Shalab and his army rode at once into the northern plains and gathered the strongest of their clan. Shalab felt that fate must be smiling down on him. Just before crossing to the New Land, he'd chanced upon the perfect woman. This was the last battle he would ever need to fight. Shalab closed his eyes, imploring the spirits for victory.

5

In desert warfare, the initiating side always had the advantage, so Shalab advanced his army windward and raided the Tangad unawares just before sunrise. The landscape trembled with the coming of dawn as the Tangad rushed out of their tents, squinting out into the northern horizon to see a cloud of dust bearing down upon them like a tornado. Realizing an enemy was approaching, Bogud mounted his horse. Wielding a spear and a bow, he rode through the camps to sound a distress call. When he returned, Fayau looked at him in fear and took her son by the hand.

"Don't worry. The red deer's spirit is with me."

With that, Bogud left and rushed straight into the oncoming fury.

Shalab's advance guard caught the Tangad riders unprepared, splintering the defense into small groups. Situated as they were downwind, the Tangad could hardly see through the billowing sands. Men and horses fell to swift arrows, accompanied by the sound of skulls cracking under stone axes, and soon the sands were steeped in blood. Though Bogud wove nimbly through the arrows and spears, he could do nothing but defend himself.

Here were his people at the hands of the ruthless Shalab, who waged war like a child might play, and Bogud was helpless to protect them. Spears snapped, arrows ran out, and the Tangad were soon completely surrounded by enemy riders.

Bogud fell off his horse trying to dodge a spear and lost consciousness. At the moment he blacked out, he knew the punishment for his indiscretion had befallen him at last. A number of horses rushed past his body rolling along the ground.

As the sun peaked above their heads, Shalab lined up all of the Tangad women and scanned the crowd for the visage he'd seen at the Selenge. He didn't have to look very hard, however, before he felt a pair of remarkably radiant eyes upon him. He turned in their direction to see Fayau's pretty face burning with palpable hatred. For the first time in her life, a woman whose eyes had always imparted tranquility with their gentle charm flared with hostility and sheer malice.

Shalab rode his horse up to her. Nonplussed by her indignation, he asked her calmly, "What is your name?"

Fayau shut her mouth tightly and gave no answer. Her three-year-old son had just been murdered and, aside from Tafune, all the men must have been killed as well. She was convinced that her husband was also dead. It was the only moment she ever cursed herself for being a woman. Were she a man, she would have fought bravely to the end. But, as things stood now, she had no means for revenge. As for this robust man, who blocked the sun atop his horse, how could she ever stand up to him?

"I've seen your portrait by the Selenge River, but you are even more beautiful in person," he said in good spirits, as if he'd just successfully hunted down some elusive prey. Tafune was the only one who understood the meaning of these words. He looked up to the heavens.

......What have you done to us, Bogud? Why did you violate

the law of our people?

Shalab turned to Tafune. "Who drew that portrait?"

"...Bogud."

"A member of your tribe?"

Tafune gestured with his chin towards the battlefield, still warm with Tangad blood, indicating that Bogud was among the fallen.

"And his relation to this woman?"

"Her husband."

At this, Shalab's face grew sober.

"From hereon, this woman is to be my wife. She will live with me in the New Land."

"The New Land?" Tafune repeated.

"Yes. You know of it?"

There was no such legend among the Tangad, though Tafune had heard of it in passing. According to the myth, once every few hundred years, a land bridge called the "northern corridor" appeared from the sea.

Taking the spoils of his conquest, Shalab headed for the northern steppes. All that was left behind were dead bodies, burned camps, and Tafune, a man now reduced to a living corpse. Because he was a shaman, the elder had been spared for fear of bringing a curse upon any who laid a hand on him, though Tafune himself would rather have died than endure the aftermath. Everything dear to him was now ravaged or gone.

Listening to the sound of the wind, he surveyed the damage once more. Tafune had lived with the Tangad people for nearly sixty years. He cherished the earthen camps where he was reared. No matter where his occasional wanderings had taken him in life, he always recognized the value of his tribe whenever he returned. He had no wife or children. The tribespeople were his family. Now, the wind was all he could hear, its voice keening over the flattened land. Scraps of burned-down tents fluttered pathetically in the gales. Tafune searched through the rubble, hoping he wasn't the only man to survive. He would have been happy with anyone. He didn't even care if it was a newborn, as long as it was alive. He staggered along with his walking stick, calling to the dead bodies in hopes of a response.

The winds stopped, and the fields were blanketed by stillness. Bogud awoke with sand caked on his face. His body ached all over, and blood had clotted wherever he felt pain. Luckily, however, he had suffered only minor injuries. He got to his feet and looked around, but was hardly able to accept what his eyes were seeing. The scent of blood was still fresh in the breeze. His head throbbed. Bogud walked towards his camp, faltering around the fallen, but once he saw the mountains of corpses ahead, he ran as fast as he could, shouting his wife and son's names.

Upon seeing Bogud running towards him on the plains, Tafune cried out to him. He was relieved not to be the only one left and it gave him at least some hope in his despair. Tafune's voice echoed across the plain, tinged with neither joy nor sadness.

But Bogud was too focused on his family to worry himself over Tafune's troubled heart. He continued towards the camp and looked everywhere for Fayau and the child. Just ahead, Bogud's camp was reduced to ashes and next to it lay his fallen son with head split open. Fayau was nowhere to be seen, nor did she seem to have been killed. She'd been abducted. It was the same everywhere.

All that Bogud had ever lived for had been destroyed in a flash. He held his son's body and cried like a wolf into the sky.

As Tafune quietly watched Bogud, whose grief most surely surpassed his own, he gradually regained something of his self-composure. Gathering the dignity befitting his position as elder, Tafune approached Bogud. Yes, Bogud was to blame for bringing this calamity upon them... Yet it was useless to blame him now. He was already suffering his punishment. Still, Tafune figured Bogud needed to know the truth.

"Why did you break the law of our clan?" he said sadly.

These were the last words Bogud wanted to hear.

"I know it was you who drew Fayau at the Selenge tributary."

"Why do you say such things?" replied Bogud. Tafune's statement was shocking to him. Was this how retribution worked? This wasn't castigation from the wrathful heavens, but the result of some man's wish to have Fayau for himself.

Bogud stood up and looked for a horse, yet these, too, had been stolen. Urged by despair, Bogud made to run towards the northern plain in Shalab's wake.

"Where are you going?"

"To take back Fayau, of course. She and I will restore our people."

If this was indeed divine punishment, Bogud would probably have given up on Fayau. But if it was only the deed of this man Shalab, then he wouldn't accept this reality without protest. Perhaps the gods had used Shalab to reprimand him indirectly, but he had to make sure of it.

"Impossible. You cannot expect to bring down the northern clan all by yourself."

"That's not my intention. Fayau is all I want."

"It is the same thing."

Bogud started running.

"Wait! There's something you must know. The northern clan is heading for the New Land."

Bogud stopped and turned back. Tafune's wisdom was not to be neglected.

"It is said that when the snow on Jinst Uul does not melt, the northern corridor will appear from the sea."

"Northern corridor? What is that?"

"A path to the New Land."

"So you're saying that the northern clan will take Fayau to this 'New Land'?"

"Yes, and you're already too late. The northern corridor appears only for a brief span of time."

"Then I must hurry!"

There was no time to lose. With every word they spoke, Fayau and her captors were fading into the north.

"Just let her go, Bogud. What is to be done about those left here?" Tafune made a sweeping gesture towards the scattered bodies. "They will fall prey to the spirits of mice and hares."

Bogud heard voices inside him, the murmuring of his people, fallen to the earth and dusted with windblown sand. But he would not let himself be moved.

"I promise you I will return. Please let me go. I will get Fayau and come back to give the dead proper rites and to rebuild our clan."

Bogud ran. The sun was setting. He had to catch up with them before it got dark. Then he would trail them and wait for his chance.

Fine, thought Tafune as he watched Bogud's receding figure. *He's sure to return.* Restraining a hot-blooded youth was like trying to hold back the ebbing tide. The tide always rose again, and just so would Bogud return. He heeded no words now.

As he watched Bogud turn into a dot on the northern plains, Tafune's heart ached for the past he would never recover. He held no resentment towards Bogud for bringing this ill fate upon them. Looking beyond his sadness, Tafune was in fact envious of Bogud's youth and zeal, for he too had once been like that, long ago.

Despite the fact that Bogud was out of earshot, Tafune shouted:

"Bogud! It is no use going north. You are walking into certain death. You do not know yet about the world..."

When Bogud vanished into the gloom, Tafune tasted true loneliness for the first time in his existence, passing a sleepless night through long fits of weeping.

6

Night fell. The desert was so cold, it seemed as if the intense daylight had all been a lie. The northern tribe had set up camp near a small lake. The warriors feasted on the cattle they'd pillaged and enjoyed the night in leisure, basking in the afterglow of their victory. Shalab quickly retired, returning to his tent to sleep with Fayau. Surprisingly, she showed no signs of resistance. Mindful of the anger that emanated from her body, of the possibility that she might make an attempt on his life, Shalab was on guard as he had his way with her, until the very moment he finished. Yet Fayau's body had opened up to him with unexpected ease. True, Shalab didn't feel that her heart was his. He felt the sheer loathing welling from deep inside her. Though slightly irritated by the secrets of the heart, which managed to keep itself closed while offering up the body, Shalab finally just went to sleep feeling happy enough. He was totally unaware of the change taking place in Fayau's body.

What was once a flicker inside her was now a growing flame. Listening to the men rejoicing outside, she'd realized what was happening inside her. It was a sensation she'd experienced before, and all the womanly signs seemed to point to it. She was carrying new life. Her intuition as a mother had alerted her to the fact. This child was without a doubt Bogud's. Knowing this, Fayau decided it best not to resist Shalab. Feigning the passivity of a blade of grass, she would allow him to have her as soon as possible. Under no circumstances could she let on that the child was Bogud's. If Shalab found out, he was sure to kill the baby the moment it left her womb. If she allowed Shalab to believe it was his own, then the child was sure to be raised well. Fulfilling her maternal instincts was more important to Fayau than clearing the grudge. The quiet motherhood she possessed was a rarity among warring nomads. Her first priority was to preserve the line of her beloved Bogud in this world.

She turned onto her side and placed a hand on her belly, imparting warmth to the tiny cell divisions beneath. She thought of her fallen husband. She remembered the sheer joy she felt when carving together with him and knew that their comfortable life was gone. Tears flowed from one eye into the other, drawing a line down her cheek before trickling through the mat beneath her into the cold earth. Fayau pressed both hands to her mouth to stop herself from screaming, asking herself how she would ever hide her insurmountable sadness, when she suddenly noticed Shalab's battle ax hanging from a crossbeam in the tent frame. He was fast asleep and it would have been easy to kill him right then and there. The temptation crossed her mind, but she thought about it logically. How would she ever live on after that? How would she ever provide for the child inside her? While it pained her to no end to realize it, Fayau would need to rely on Shalab's protection. There was no other way of surviving, in this desert.

And so Fayau suppressed her rage all night with her back to Shalab, and wept quietly, shedding tears that shook her frame.

Legend

Bogud stood on a hilltop, straining his eyes and ears in the darkness, searching for burning fires and voices of celebration, for any tribe was bound to celebrate on the night of battle and eat whatever livestock they'd taken. He saw no fires, but heard a snatch of raucous singing. Carried up from the valley by the gentle evening winds, its source was hard to determine. The voices swelled and faded all around him, and just when he thought he'd located them, they came from a completely different direction. He imagined that the wild hare spirits, known for trickery, were teasing him with false hope. Bogud made as if to brush them away and concentrated on what he was hearing. The sounds glided over hills and ravines, where they were deflected into the sky and fell like rain into his ears. He was sure of one thing, at least. Fayau was hardly a day's journey away. He looked up in exasperation and saw the Big Dipper shimmering in the sky before him. The night was growing even colder.

The following morning, Bogud awoke by a lake. Though still in need of food, he was at least able to quench his thirst. Having suffered through far worse conditions than this during his spiritual quest, there was no reason to think the outcome this time would be any different. And above all, Bogud told himself, he had the protection of the exalted red deer's spirit.

He saw a single horse drinking from the opposite bank. Unable to tell whether it was wild or domesticated, he approached quietly for a closer look. If the horse was wild, taming it was out of the question. When the horse saw Bogud coming nearer, it lifted its head elegantly without fear and made no effort to run. Bogud then noticed the plaited harness around its neck.

......What luck!

Bogud praised the spirits. The horse was one of the Tangad's, separated and lost from the herd.

It wasn't long before he tracked down remnants of the victory feast he'd failed to find the night before. The embers were still smoking. Meat still clung to the scattered bones and Bogud indulged in whatever he could salvage.

Shalab's clan wasn't heading due north, but north-northeast. Knowing this made it easy to move on. Bogud tracked them late into the afternoon, waiting until nightfall to make his move. The terrain here was much different than the steppes, overgrown with evergreen forests so dense that even sunlight on a midsummer day hardly found its way through the foliage. The cold was unbearable. However, compared to the bare plains he'd left behind, the large tall trees provided the perfect cover for sneaking in the dead of night. Bogud slipped through the trees, searching for Shalab's tent in the clearing. His would be a splendid tent worthy of a chief, easy to pick out from the rest. While the men were busy enjoying themselves in their continued celebration, Bogud would simply take Fayau and escape. There was nothing complicated about it. Exacting his revenge on Shalab wasn't his main objective, but he would gladly do it if the opportunity presented itself. Failure would mean certain death.

Bogud crept up to a conspicuous tent, lifted the hem, and peeked inside. A small fire pit glowed faintly in the center. Beyond it was a shadowy heap on an animal skin mat. Was it Fayau? He couldn't make out her face from where he was. He slipped into the tent and edged his way over without a sound. His suspicions were confirmed once he saw her close up. But there was a man with her. Shalab was sleeping with his body bent over her. The men continued their ruckus outside.

Bogud looked down at Shalab, wondering why he hadn't joined in the festivities. Here before him was his mortal enemy, and it set his blood to boiling. He looked up from his beloved Fayau's face and somehow calmed himself.

Bogud took the stone ax into his hands.

He thought of waking Fayau first, but didn't want to risk stirring Shalab from his slumber.

He aimed for Shalab's head, raising the ax high above his own.

At that moment, Fayau felt she was dreaming that an ax was being brought upon her. The dream then turned into a nightmare once she realized it was her dead husband who was wielding the ax. She screamed and turned over. A warrior to the very core of his being, Shalab awoke with a start in response to her cry and jumped quickly to his feet to dodge the weapon coming straight for his head. The ax cut through the mat and lodged into the soil.

"Who are you?" said Shalab, crouching low in readiness.

There was no need to answer him; a pause now was exactly what his adversary wanted. Bogud brandished his fists and charged. He struck Shalab's right shoulder, but he did not so much as budge and his expression was one of total confidence. In the same way that Bogud possessed artistic genius, Shalab was blessed with mastery in battle. Putting Bogud into a headlock, Shalab threw him down and jumped onto his back as onto a mount. Bogud's life was in Shalab's hands now. Unable to watch any more of this, Fayau cried out Bogud's name. Shalab looked at her. Hearing the genuine emotion in her voice, it all came together.

"This man, is he your husband?"

Fayau lunged for Shalab's head and clawed at his face, but in the blink of an eye she was thrown to the ground.

Right next to her face was Bogud's. She couldn't believe that the husband she took for dead was actually here. She was happy to see him again, even if only for these brief moments, but the possibilities of what now lay in store for him terrified her.

......But you have the spirit of the red deer with you.

Knowing this helped to alleviate her fears. She extended a hand to Bogud and touched his cheek. She hardly had time to feel the warmth of his skin when she was snatched away by the tribesmen who showed up after hearing the commotion.

With this, the dwindling bonfire was made to flare up again. Having already eaten their fill, the men turned their attentions to the entertainment Bogud's capture would provide. Bogud was covered with oil, tied up with leather cords, then dragged out before the fire. The men cheered and spat at him, musing crudely about the various ways they might kill him. Bogud felt the flames lick his back, while his face dripped with sweat. His body glowing deep red in the firelight, he prayed fervently to the spirits. Were he to be finished off like everyone's exhibition, his spirit would shadow this tribe until they were destroyed. Bogud didn't want to die alone. Still unaware that his child was growing inside Fayau, he wanted her to join him in death as she did in life.

Shalab was forced into an aggravating dilemma. Despite being the hero of his people, he was only concerned with Fayau's reaction to all of this. If he killed Bogud here and now, Fayau would despise him for the rest of her waking life. He would gladly show mercy just this once if it meant that her feelings for him might grow as a result. If Bogud died here tonight, Shalab would never win her over. Shalab had kidnapped many women in his life, but this was the first time he'd ever felt this way about any of them. He wanted not just her body, but everything that she was. Nevertheless, any display of leniency now might lose him the faith of his clansmen, as they wanted nothing more than to see this man struggle and die.

Shalab sought the advice of the shaman, who spoke with welcome dignity.

"This man is not to be harmed. He carries a most powerful spirit with him. If we take his life, he will become a demon and kill off the entire clan."

No matter how powerful Shalab might have been, he couldn't oppose such wise words. The men's cheers dissipated into heavy silence.

"We must bring him north with us and throw him to the waters once we reach the coast," the shaman continued. "If fate is kind to him, he will wash up onto shore. If not, and if he dies at sea, his spirit will wander the waves forever, never to bring us harm."

Shalab promptly laid down his decision.

"We will do as he says."

He glanced at Fayau, who placed a hand on her chest with a sigh of relief. It was obvious her heart was still with her husband. Still, Shalab didn't think badly of Bogud. He rather admired him for surviving the assault, for his courage in tracking them this far, and above all for the strength of his convictions. He saw no need to kill him. By the time they reached the New Land, Bogud would be lost at sea, never to be seen again. Shalab pitied him only because of the love they shared for the same woman.

The terrain changed as they went north. Once they were high enough above sea level, the evergreens were gone, and the land was covered instead with alpine vegetation. One hundred sunsets later, summer had, by their reckoning, arrived.

Before long, they came out onto an ashen landscape, a veritable wasteland without a single tree or shrub to be seen. Though the surface soil was damp and bearded with moss, the earth was frozen a meter down. Despite the lack of rain, the landscape was dotted with pools of water from melting ice, dully reflecting the long, weak rays of the sun. It was a season of short nights and long days. Bogud was still bound, leashed to a horse as they continued north. He struggled to keep up and tried his best not to lose his footing in the water holes.

Summer passed its peak and the air grew colder. The only indication of autumn's imminence was the waning arc of the sun's daily path. Shalab picked up speed, for when summer was gone, the northern corridor would go with it.

Suddenly, the scenery opened. As they trekked through rolling hills, the corridor gradually came into view, obscure in the haze beyond: a stretch of land jutting out from the cape into the wintry sea far into the east. The end was nowhere in sight, but if the legend was true, it would lead them to the fertile land they sought.

The northern tribe arrived at the cape's tip and shouted joyously when they saw the corridor stretching straight into the ocean. By now, the frigid conditions didn't bother them anymore. Unable to hunt, they had consolidated their rations so as not to go hungry. But they knew the corridor would take them to another realm entirely. A paradise without hunger or cold. A new, unseen world awaited them beyond the open waters.

"We're just in time!" Shalab said. "Let's cross while we still can. We haven't arrived in the new world yet."

At his command, everyone set out single-file down the long and narrow pathway.

"Time to say farewell."

Shalab undid Bogud's straps and floated a dug-out canoe that the shaman had built. Fayau was in tears as she watched, certain this was their final parting. She placed a hand on her stomach, then gestured to Bogud. The meaning was clear to him.

......My child is in there.

He narrowed his eyes and looked at her as if to say, *I'll win you both back*. Then, unnoticed by Shalab, Bogud let a flat stone fall from his hands. Fayau picked it up as he was pushed into the canoe along with some cured beef and water. On the stone was an image of Bogud's deer. In the hundred and some odd days it had taken to get this far, he'd managed to carve the deer, despite being tied by the wrists in such an awkward position, out of sight from his guards. The single deer had its front legs raised high, jumping towards the sun. She felt his strength of will in this image. Fayau clutched the deer to her heart, watching as Bogud floated far off into the tide, and started to believe this wasn't the last she'd see of him after all. Bogud *would* come back to her. She knew it as clearly as if the deer on the stone had whispered it into her ear.

Bogud had no way of getting off the canoe. He could only let the current take him where it may. Having known only the desert all his life, the thought of swimming never even entered his mind. Still, had he been able to swim, the speed of the current and icy waters wouldn't have permitted him to reach land. The boat was pulled south along the frigid current, and Fayau soon disappeared beyond the waterline.

On his twentieth day out at sea, Bogud awoke to find a change in the ocean. The canoe was hardly moving and the scent of land was in the air. He stood up. He couldn't see out very far through the morning fog, but the sea was calm. Once the sun climbed its way into noon and burned the mists away, he finally realized why: he was floating into an inlet. Crags came into view and the soil's familiar odor was immediately pungent. There was plenty of greenery along the coast and it was just as warm as his homeland. Had he gone west from here, he would have come out into the desert.

Bogud climbed up onto the rocks. With no time to spare, he followed the same route north after Fayau. As it was now well into autumn, the conditions were harsher. Fearful of getting caught in the snow, he hurried his pace.

He stood again on the same hill, that very cape where Fayau watched him float out of her life. The corridor was no longer visible, covered by a threatening ocean across which chunks of white ice drifted quickly southward. He could see nothing else. He was too late. His greatest fear had become a reality. The mythical northern corridor had disappeared into the depths of the sea, completely severing him from the one he loved.

He knelt on the ground and looked skyward.

Where could this new world possibly be?

While his heart continued north, his feet carried him in the opposite direction one step at a time, thinking only that some great power beyond human understanding was barring his way.

This must be heaven's wrath. I should never have broken our law. I must return to the homeland.

He then remembered the Tangad warriors still sleeping in the desert and his promise to Tafune. He would return temporarily to tend to the souls of his brethren and seek Tafune's council.

Bogud still knew little of this world. But he was sure of one thing. He was never going to give up Fayau.

7

Tafune had aged considerably in the past six months. If he had any purpose in living, it was to bury the Tangad's fallen and nothing more. The corpses weighed somewhat less due to weathering, but it was still hard work for an old man like him. When Bogud stood before him, many of the bodies were still rotting upon the fields.

Bogud assisted him with the burials and spent nights carving deer glyphs into large stones by firelight. He made one for every man and placed each on the earth where a body had been interred to protect its spirit. Bogud conducted his work in earnest and used the time to ask Tafune to share all he knew. As Tafune imparted his wisdom, there was only one thing he neglected to address, only one thing he would not answer, and that was how to bring Fayau back. Were he to reveal this, Bogud was sure to run away again and leave their task unfinished. Tafune therefore decided to put this question aside until every Tangad soul had been given proper rites.

As the days went on and Bogud carved pictures of deer leaping across the sky, he couldn't help but see Fayau in them. He never would have drawn her again, of course. It was only because he was putting all he had into these deer that thinking of Fayau was inevitable. He knew there was no such thing as a flying deer; yet, every one he carved was soaring towards the sun. The reasons for this were beyond him.

Three years went by and their work was nearly complete. Though they passed the days in serenity, Tafune was well aware of the tenacious will burning in Bogud's heart. He couldn't possibly keep him back forever. Bogud himself was like one of his deer, prepared to leap into the sky at any given moment. No one could stop him. Tafune had one last bit of knowledge to offer and beckoned Bogud over.

"Please, sit."

Once he was aware that Bogud was kneeling at his bedside, Tafune propped himself up on his elbow. As his vision was failing, he groped the ground until his fingers curled around a thin piece of wood. He used it to draw a faint circle in the dirt. He then placed scraps of animal hide on both ends of it.

"Okay, imagine this is the world. Right now, we are here."

He pointed the stick to the left.

"This is the new world," he continued, moving the stick to the right.

"And between them is the great dividing sea."

Just as Tafune had said, most of the circle between the hide scraps marking this land and the new world was filled by a void. He drew a thin line across it.

"This is the northern corridor that you saw. According to legend, it appears only once every few hundred years. Crossing it would bring you into the New Land, but it has already receded into the waters."

Bogud listened to the elder's words and said nothing. Tafune was truly the only one who understood everything. He had encountered and intermingled with the northern tribes, the peoples of the mountain and of the sea—in essence everyone who surrounded this desert—and had gathered knowledge from all of them along the way. Bogud listened intently so as not to miss a single word.

"The New Land is brimming with sunlight and warmth. The fields abound with wildlife. The earth is lush and laden with grains. It's a green land, you see. There's no wandering deserts in search of lakes. And, what's more, tribes never kill one another."

He spoke as if he'd seen it himself. Perhaps because he was dying, a scroll depicting his personal utopia was unfurling across his mind—the place to which he would wander after he breathed his last. A new world unto itself.

Bogud grabbed the elder's arm tightly. He didn't care what kind of place the new world was. He only wanted to know one thing.

"I must get there somehow. Is there a way?"

The question brought Tafune back to reality. With a twitch of the cheek, his eyes opened slowly like clam shells and looked again at the map he'd drawn. He moved the tip of the stick below it.

"South, you go south," he said.

"You mean to tell me that if I go south, there is a corridor leading to the New Land?"

Bogud was eager for a positive answer, but Tafune shook his head weakly.

"Not quite. No one has ever seen it. However, you are the one who wields the spirit of the red deer of legend. So if anyone has a chance...it is you."

Bogud wasn't satisfied with this. At the same time, he couldn't deny the clarity of the elder's map. If he went due east, he would be met with only endless seascape, and since the northern corridor was completely flooded over, it left only the south by a simple process of elimination. He couldn't think of any other way. The more Bogud knew, the more this world seemed to be against him. The future was never certain. Tafune knew this. Bogud, however, did not; he was sure that Tafune knew everything.

Bogud studied the map. Fayau had crossed from the northern cape to the other side of the ocean. And now, the only hope lay in the opposite direction. He would be going *farther* away from her. Bogud wanted proof that going south would bring him to the New Land. He kept silent as Tafune spoke with heartfelt sympathy.

"Well, do you plan on waiting for the northern corridor to show itself from the sea again? That won't be for another few hundred years... Can you wait that long? Go south! It's the only way."

Tafune's voice grew stronger with every word. Having changed his mind about being strict with Bogud, he was realizing in his old age that the world worked in truly mysterious ways. There was no need to understand anything before doing it. If a man confronted his obstacles and was open to whatever the future held in store, then the world was bound to be shaped by his desires. Only from such an unaffected point of view did Fayau's retrieval become possible.

Bogud made up his mind. He would do as Tafune bade him.

My life's been defined by my actions. I've shaped my destiny through my battles. I would rather keep chasing after my dreams until I crumble into dust than sit around waiting for fate to show me mercy.

"Okay, then. I will go south."

Bogud placed a hand on Tafune's. Even now, with the inner flame of his life dwindling to its final flicker, Tafune explained to Bogud how to reach the south. Starting with the Big Dipper, he explained how to use constellations for navigation, how the sun changed position as one went south, and how the Southern Cross would appear in the night sky. He also told Bogud how to use the seasons to estimate his location.

"The sun and the moon and the stars will guide you on the right path."

Tafune's body grew still with these final words.

Bogud spent the night carving a stone through his tears. It was the first time he ever cried. Even when Fayau was kidnapped and his son murdered, he felt more anger than sadness. But now, grief streamed down his face unfettered, for at last he was all alone.

By dawn, he'd finished carving a red deer in offering to Tafune. He buried the elder in the ground and placed the stone above him before preparing for departure. When Bogud first moved to this area, the lake was spread out to the west of the hills. Now, it had grown smaller and was receding into the west. He would probably never return to this land. Countless grave stones lined the hills. Half of them were those carved together with Tafune, the rest with Fayau. He longed for those days long past, remembering fondly the time he spent carving stones, Fayau always at his side, watching his hands closely and copying him. He would do anything to have that life back again. Bogud set off for the south as the sun climbed in the east, rising from where his love awaited.

8

On the other side of the sea, daylight was ending in the new world. Fayau knelt in the light of sunset, offering silent prayers. This had become a daily ritual for her. And at her side, mimicking her gestures, was Wolib, daughter of Fayau and Bogud.

In the desolate, hilly landscape, Wolib drew pictures in the dirt. Cradled in her left hand was the stone—the deer still clear upon its surface—that Bogud had given to Fayau before their separation at the northern corridor. Wolib looked back and forth between the stone and the sun and copied the design onto the ground: a deer jumping after the setting sun. Its antlers were large and the deer seemed to be flying with them. Fayau was in awe of Wolib's drawings. Her deer were imbued with something intangible, just like Bogud's. The images were hardly refined, but this did nothing to diminish their power. Wolib was truly her father's daughter.

Thanks to the spirits, Fayau and Wolib had managed to live peaceably so far in this new world. The dry landscape reminded Fayau of her homeland. By no means did this new world guarantee a safe and comfortable life, but she found the land oddly relieving. Easily a thousand suns had risen and set since her separation with Bogud.

After they crossed the northern corridor, the terrain was not at all what they'd hoped for. A thick, silvery bed of ice slowed their progress considerably. Shalab's tribe was hit hard, losing almost half of its number to hunger and cold. The cliffs of ice that impeded their way were overwhelming to a desert people. Some lost hope and collapsed to the ground. Was there no path to the south, or was it just that they could not find it? They had no way of knowing. The shaman, who could commune with spirits, had not been able to withstand the frigid climate in his old age and had perished. Mourning hung over the tribespeople's heads, but the real despair had yet to come; an even greater misery befell them.

It all started when one of the men blurted out, "If I knew it was going to be like this, I would never have left the homeland in the first place..." The moment these words reached Shalab's ears, he killed the man for all to see.

"From here on, we go my way. There's no use in crying over it now. From here on, there's no turning back. You can die or move forward, it's your choice. Those who want to stay, stay. As for me, I'm going on."

These words were enough to renew their enthusiasm.

Then, after three years of wandering, Shalab and his people at last discovered what they were searching for: towards the east end of a long mountain chain that ran from east to west, an iceless trail. They owed its discovery to the three-year-old Wolib.

Aside from her artistic talents, this little girl was also blessed with keen hearing. She could pick out the sounds of running herds from far away and even tell which direction they were coming from. She therefore had not one, but two roles to fulfill in serving the tribe. Shalab, believing that Wolib was his own flesh and blood, adored her more than anything. The others also treated her with respect.

As people collapsed from the cold and Shalab's leadership showed signs of faltering, Wolib sensed a change in the wind as it slid across the ice. This wasn't the woeful whistling she normally heard woven through the gales. It rolled over stones, caressed dampened soil, and dried out the land. This wind was weighted with life, like a breeze blowing through the grass in early spring. But Wolib had never once experienced the coming of spring. She had only her intuition to go on.

She pointed southeast. Shalab asked her why.

"Because, that's where the wind is singing."

In spite of the dire circumstances, Wolib hadn't lost her innocence. To her, the wind was melody. Shalab and Fayau had total faith in her and guided their people in the direction she indicated. And after walking for a number of days, they'd come upon that narrow pathway along the foot of the mountains. At first, they doubted that the corridor would lead them to more temperate land, but as they continued on, their fears faded as increasing numbers of reindeer and musk oxen traversed the fields ahead of them. Before they knew it, the ice had faded into emerald fields, and for the first time they discovered truth in the legend that had guided them.

Though life had been hard, and, at times, indeed, Fayau had seemed to be at death's door, she had remembered Bogud and called upon the red deer to help face her hardships. Regardless of the distance between them, she felt his protection vividly at every moment. She did not know that it was the spirit of the red deer, and Wolib's heaven-sent sensitivity to sound, that would help reunite them in the far distant future. She did know to wait, as long as necessary, for that day. She felt an immense will that moved the sea and raised waves and rolled on east as a towering tsunami. Its presence grew stronger as the sea grew ever brighter as they descended the mountain southward.

The climate grew warmer as they continued on. Throughout the long journey, the tribespeople banded together and chased after animal herds. At first, they hunted only a head each, but eventually devised a way to kill their animals in great numbers by running them into holes and ditches. This, coupled with the growing abundance of edible plants, meant hunger and cold were but a memory.

However, their life would be far from tranquil, for an unexpected pitfall lay ahead.

At one point of their journey, one of the tribespeople dug up some grass roots and cooked them for food. The bulbous roots were fragrant and soon many had tried them. About half of those who ate them broke out in brown sores and died of high fever. Shalab subsequently ordered everyone to avoid eating the root. Unfortunately, this did little to quell the epidemic, for it had nothing to do with eating the roots themselves, but with the deadly spores released into the air when they were pulled out from the ground. This silent disease spread from one person to the next, and in the blink of an eye many of them were dead. Shalab could do nothing but watch as his tribe wasted away. Painfully aware of his own powerlessness, he cursed the heavens. Now, more than ever, he wished for the wisdom of his shaman, long dead back in the icy steppes. Not a holy man himself, Shalab knew nothing of appeasing the powers that be.

Tribesmen were falling one after another and turning into the dust from which they were created. The unceremonious death of his brethren struck Shalab as shamefully anticlimactic. Even he, who had survived countless battles, and who had led his people from the cold into this vast, open land, became debilitated by the effects of the disease. Knowing he was doomed, he beckoned Fayau and Wolib to his side with a wave of his hand. Seeing him like this gave Fayau a queer feeling. This was hardly a worthy punishment for Bogud's archenemy, a man who'd killed their treasured son. Almost too easily, Shalab curled inward into a fetal position, and died. Fayau neither rejoiced at his death nor mourned it. If she didn't still love Bogud, her grief might have been more acute.

The epidemic raged on, even after Shalab's passing. When, at last, Wolib contracted the disease, Fayau could only look up from the brown spots covering her daughter's body and offer prayers toward the western horizon, to Bogud's red deer spirit. She could not lose Wolib if she were to do right by Bogud's devotion. Waiting was her task. It would be a daunting span of time, raising Wolib well, waiting for Bogud's arrival. Endless days. Too many seasons to count stretched out before that moment. But Wolib, daughter of Fayau, would birth a child of her own someday and have descendants. It didn't matter how many generations it took. Yet if Fayau lost Wolib now, Bogud's determination would wander the sky forever, unrequited.

Day after day, Fayau prayed to the west. Whether or not this had any effect, Wolib struggled bravely with her illness. She held out longer than anyone and began to show signs of convalescence. She was the first of many who managed to recover, and, for whatever reason, the seemingly invincible disease disappeared as quietly as it had come. The tribe's numbers had dwindled to a fifth of what it had been at the northern corridor.

Fayau and Wolib became the new leaders by succession. They continued moving everyone south and came upon a place that filled Fayau with longing. The terrain resembled almost exactly that of her Tangad homeland. Desert. It was far hotter than the one she knew so well, but its contours and colors were exactly the same. The rare rainfalls came in more plentiful doses, however, and the puddle they left in the sands was large. Edged by a smattering of greenery, it was a rather favorable place to live.

With her authority as chief's wife, Fayau decided this was where they would end their long journey. It was incredibly ironic. After countless days, suffering many fatalities along the way, their destination was hardly any different from the world they'd left behind...

Fayau had Wolib draw the red deer on earth and stone every day, so that Wolib's own children may feel their grandfather's strong will too someday. Fayau's wish to bequeath the image down the generations had an effect on her daughter who, mimicking the calls of fowl and fauna, threw herself into the task. Wolib never forgot to sing as she drew. The air around her was pregnant with beautiful sound; it seemed to arise from the earth itself. If the blood coursing through her veins was after something, all she could do was hone her senses to approach it.

Fayau stood with her daughter on a hill, looking out into the western horizon. Fayau spoke to the setting sun, as if she knew that it was the rising sun in Bogud's eyes. The sun was a worthy messenger of her words. When at last it dipped out of sight, Wolib stopped drawing red deer upon the earth. Fayau took her by the hand and returned to their tent. That was how their days ended.

9

The soil changed color as Bogud continued south. From chestnut to dark brown, then to red. The sun grew higher, the lush grass greener. There was no shortage of food, no freezing cold to endure. The journey south was far more comfortable than the one north. According to the Tangad calendar, winter was approaching, yet the temperature was gradually rising. Bogud was urged on by his undying optimism and he was sure to reach a southern corridor, so long as nothing stood in his way.

Winter ended, making way for spring. Sweat dripped from Bogud's naked body. He'd never experienced heat like this, even in the desert. It coiled about him causing terrible discomfort. Even so, it was far better than starving in the cold.

The scent of salt water was present in the air. In the many days he spent drifting in the ocean, Bogud had come to know it well. There was no mistaking it for anything else. He rode his horse up onto a hill where he could get a better view. Looking into the eastern horizon, he saw, vaguely, a strip of reflective surface. Bogud sped down the hill. He lost sight of the ocean, but when it came into view again, it was vivid with color, and he could even hear the sounds of waves from the distance. He had at last reached the southern sea. With the shore on his left, he scaled another hill to scout out the corridor leading to the New Land. He thought he'd see it then and there.

Three days passed, and he didn't espy a single island. The water's hue was completely different from the north; the bright, clear ocean here instilled optimism in the viewer. The northern corridor had extended from a distinct cape on the shoreline, but here there was no such formation to be found. The even rock line stretched on with no end in sight. Still, the beauty of the sandy beach and white-capped waves washing along the shore were enough to quell Bogud's desperation. He continued south along the coast.

Ten days passed. No change in the landscape. Bogud realized something was wrong when he noticed the sun sinking right where the land met the sea. He had a bad feeling about this, but he kept going.

Twenty days passed. By now, the sun was setting in the center of the ocean and rising from behind the land. Bogud eventually stopped his horse and thought of how this could be. It was obvious. He had merely been trying not to see it. He thought the coastline only went south, but at some point it must have veered west and hooked around, which meant he was now going north. North, where he'd started. In other words, where he was now was already the edge of the south. Bogud dismounted.

How could this be? There is no southern corridor.

He drew Tafune's world map once more upon the sand to check his direction, confirming that he'd passed the southern cape. Bogud decided to retrace his steps, if only to get a little closer to Fayau in the New Land. As he swayed left and right on the horse's back, Bogud appealed to Tafune many times.

......Elder, isn't there a corridor anywhere?

Then Bogud paused. Had Tafune even spoken of a southern

corridor? No, he'd only urged him to travel south. Bogud wanted to know the answer. What should he do? What would let him have Fayau for his own again? Maybe the corridor would appear if he waited long enough. Bogud scanned the open sea as he skirted the beach. In the north, the cape had jutted out proudly into the dark waters, filled with possibility. There was, however, nothing like that here. He could wait for thousands of years and see no changes in the vast depths. Bogud even felt the force of some will that resisted change, and his breathing became ragged.

What should I do? he asked himself over and over. *Fayau is right there on the other side of the ocean, and I'm helpless to do anything about it. Tell me, spirits. What can I do to overcome these waters?*

A single piece of driftwood floated onto the beach and lingered for a moment before being drawn back into the sea. The salty breeze caressed his face. Suddenly, he heard Fayau call out his name—or was the voice that of the spirit inside of him? A flicker of intuition—

Why didn't I think of it before?

He fell to his knees, clawed at the sand, and laughed.

......The ocean isn't an obstacle. It's a gigantic corridor!

Bogud thought back to his unwelcome canoe ride in the north. It had taken him a few hundred days to get here by land, but only a fraction of that for the current to whisk him along a comparable distance. Moreover, the ocean continued to carry him onward even while he slept at the bottom of the canoe.

Bogud searched the land far and wide for large trees, marking his path along the way. He would make a raft much larger than the vessel prepared for his exile. Whatever the cost, he had to get across the vast plain of water that extended before him.

Bogud watched the ocean carefully in the coming days, and in doing so grew keen to a fundamental fact. He observed a natural rhythm in the ebb and flow of the tide. It reminded him of something Tafune once told him:

The ocean breathes slowly.

He had never said why. The pull of the Moon and Earth, the position of the Sun and the stars... Neither Bogud nor Tafune understood the causality behind what was clear to the eyes—certainly not the force called gravity that affected the lives of all men.

Bogud made an important discovery by observing the tide's cycles. Making a large raft was all well and good, but he couldn't drag it all by himself far enough into the ocean. This dilemma had been tearing at the fringes of his mind for some time, but the tides now gave him his answer. Once the waters receded, he would assemble the parts on the beach and just wait for the tide to roll in.

Day after day, Bogud trudged through the dense forest in search of raw materials for his raft. The way he envisioned it, he would need two large, durable pieces of lumber as the vessel's backbone. Having only a stone ax for a felling tool, it took him a number of days just to cut down one tree, but he was patient. If he went out to sea in a crude raft and ended up dying, all would be lost.

He used his horse to drag logs to the shore, lining two of them lengthwise before laying the other logs across them. He checked his work from all angles to ensure that the spacing was perfect. Bogud jumped on the logs to test their strength until he found the sturdiest configuration, notching them accordingly to facilitate assembly later on.

By the time he was finished with the framework, a hundred days had come and gone. In the interests of survival, he had shed his desert habits and become a man of the sea, catching fish and clams from the water to satisfy his hunger. When everything was ready, he waited for the tide to recede. Once it did, he transported the parts and put the raft together as quickly as he could. He'd practiced these movements so much, he could have built it with his eyes closed. When the tide came back, the oblong craft was lifted onto the water's surface. Just before Bogud was carried out into the open sea, he hitched the raft to a stake lodged in the sand. He had a few more things to see to.

On the floating raft, he built a deck and erected a small hut on top of it, similar to those of a Tangad encampment. This was to be his home for however long his voyage took. After finishing the hut, Bogud slept in it at night and hunted in the daylight hours. He captured wild boars and other animals and took them on board alive. These, together with whatever fish he managed to catch, were to be his sole source of food. As for drinking water, he would have only the river water he took with him. Once it ran out, he would have to resort to rain water. But Bogud was fearless. The closer the vessel approached its final form, the closer he felt to Fayau. It had been no different during his pursuit of the red deer.

After exactly one year on the southern shore, he was fully prepared for his voyage.

Bogud hopped aboard the raft and drove a thick pole into the sand to push himself out to sea. The palm leaf sail crackled as it swelled with wind. Bogud was confident. He truly believed that the vessel would carry him to Fayau. If the currents shifted and steered him in the opposite direction, he would paddle the raft himself, as simple as that. The animals screeched in their cage while Bogud fixed his gaze eastward, where Fayau awaited. And so he never noticed the land disappearing behind him; Bogud had no idea the earth was round. Even when he finally realized there was nothing but water around him, his courage never faltered.

......I am the hero who gained the red deer's spirit.

This confidence was bringing him closer and closer to Fayau. He plunged a flat piece of wood into the water, steering the prow eastward.

The morning sun seemed to beckon him as it peeked above the horizon. Bogud himself was turning into the red deer of legend.

Part Two

Paradise

1

As the prehistoric era made way for the historical age, the world at last began to reveal itself. Even so, it had taken thousands of years for humanity to realize the Earth was round. In the sixteenth century, Copernicus advocated his heliocentric theory and was succeeded by Kepler, who in the following century discovered the law of planetary motion, proving that the Earth did indeed revolve around the Sun, in an elliptical orbit. Rather earlier than that, however, among certain literati, the Earth was said to be round.

In the fifteenth century, the Italian astronomer Toscanelli drew up a world map based on a spherical model, and a German geographer by the name of Behaim even produced the first terrestrial globe. Toscanelli's map, however, was far from perfect, as it delineated only the Old World of Europe, Asia, and Africa, with the New World nowhere in sight. For these men, the world was what they knew, and outside of it no "world" existed. Toscanelli believed that sailing west would have landed one in India. And so, when Columbus, an acquaintance of Toscanelli who held the Italian's theories in high esteem, set sail across the Atlantic from Palos harbor in 1492 and landed on the island of San Salvador, he naturally thought he was in India. This was hardly surprising, given that the maps he had to go from had nothing to indicate otherwise, and it was a belief he carried with him to the grave.

Others embarked on epic voyages with this assumption in mind, discovering many lands both large and small. They called it "discovering," which gives the impression that no one lived in these places prior to their arrival. Since in truth these lands were inhabited by natives with their own cultures, we must say the expression betrayed a one-sided arrogance. Europe's ships ventured across the globe, installing governorships at key locations for trade. After three hundred years of this, Captain Cook and other like-minded sailors had explored nearly every island in the Pacific.

The brown-skinned people of the Polynesian islands welcomed these newcomers with mixed reactions. Some resisted their arrival, others embraced it, but none were immune to the bewilderment of it all. There were even those who prostrated themselves before them, believing their gods had at last manifested themselves in the flesh. The islanders had legends and myths, but nothing akin to established religion. The Europeans therefore easily subverted what they saw as deviant spiritual beliefs in favor of spreading Christianity through the missionaries who accompanied them.

Where did the Polynesian people come from? The countless coral reefs and volcanic islands dotting the vast ocean are inhabited by a people with the same cultural thread. They must have a common ancestor, for they simply could not have developed separately on their respective islands. Some say there was once a large continent in the Pacific Ocean that was home to a developed culture; that, because of some major cataclysm, it sank into the sea; and that this upheaval made islands out of mountain ranges, where the survivors subsist today. What happened to their advanced civilization? In a sunny environment where fruits were plentiful, there was no need to maintain such a civilization and so it perished... So goes the theory. Yet, nowhere in the Pacific is there any sign of a former continent. Perhaps it never existed in the first place.

If, in actuality, no continent was ever lost, this leaves only one possibility: namely, that the Polynesians migrated across the waters from another part of the world. There is much speculation as to wherefrom. While some believe these ancestors to be South American Indians or even Jews, the consensus is that a tribe from the Mongolian steppes wandered south and set out on a great sea journey from the China coast, sailing to the Philippines first, and from there island-hopping across Melanesia, to Fiji, to Tonga, to Samoa. Due to the lack of historical accounts to support this, it is a purely hypothetical explanation, based only on linguistic clues and observation of folk customs. After establishing a foothold in Tonga, Samoa, and other islands, they presumably set out on additional voyages, colonizing all the islands of the South Pacific. But this leaves many unanswered questions. Why would Mongols leave their homeland in the first place? And why travel into southern China? Most puzzlingly, why would a desert-faring people who knew nothing of the ocean take it upon themselves to embark on some reckless voyage, seemingly without hesitation, across a vast and foreign seascape? It would have required unparalleled determination, the source of which is a mystery. It is likely to remain a mystery forever.

Now, by the end of the eighteenth century, America had gained its independence, while France was in the throes of revolution.

PARADISE

In England, the Industrial Revolution was well underway and China was dealing with peasant uprisings. In that hectic era, a solitary boat was drifting in the South Pacific towards Talofa, a small island with a twenty-four kilometer radius that still had a Stone Age culture. This island, located north of Tahiti, had no coral reef and didn't belong to any archipelago; even from the summit of its volcano, no other islands could be seen from it. Because it was a distant, solitary island, European and American ships had never visited it. The people of Talofa were, of course, Polynesians, but the island had its own culture as well, and a mythology that differed somewhat from that of the other islands of the South Pacific. Perhaps the gods there were an offshoot of Polynesian spiritualism; or perhaps in Talofa, the gods who'd crossed into this new world could remain pure. A ravine gaped like an open wound at the foot of the volcano, cradling a river into an inlet on Talofa's eastern shore; wild with greenery, heavily shaded, it looked like an ideal place for worship. Maybe a god could survive without changing form in such a sanctuary.

A bluish-white light hovered in the air where ocean blurred into sky. The sun had burrowed through the guts of the tar-black beast.

The inlet was still, punctuated only by the single boat. No one could be seen on it, obscured as it was by a limp sail that fluttered pathetically from its crude mast. The boat crept through the morning gloom, slowly but surely towards the shore. It was May, 1800.

2

Laia stepped into the sea without a sound. A new moon climbed high above her, outlining her naked body, half-submerged. She looked up at the sky, then to the crescent reflected on the water's surface. Its shape reminded her of the fishing hooks the men took with them out to sea. Laia felt seashells under her feet and tried to walk around them as she took a few more steps into the water.

Like the ten other beautiful young men and women gathered with her, Laia had just turned eighteen. The aged Hau stood upon the rocks, watching them from above. Laia sensed his gaze on her, but was no longer intimidated by it, for today was the last day of her strict training. She couldn't wait to engage in conversation and dance before everyone. Even stronger was her desire to be made love to by her elder sister's husband, Wimo. Laia straightened the tiare flower in her hair, its seven white petals the only things among the darkness of the sea that absorbed the fragile moonlight. The flower had a seductive fragrance. As it was the sole adornment to her nakedness, she could feel the currents of the tide on her skin.

Enveloped by the sea, Laia waited for the coming of dawn. Once the moon sank behind the volcano and the small twinkling of stars danced upon the waves, a faint white light began to waver on the horizon. Time seemed to quicken. Laia's chest trembled in anticipation. If, when the sun rose and she danced before Hau, the fruits of her training were approved, she would become an honored dancer among her people. There were no clouds along the open sea. Before long, a remarkably large sun showed its face in the distance. Tears fell suddenly from Laia's eyes, so joyous was she in her rite of passage. Something was changing inside her. The waters pulled back with the tide, lowering to her knees. The sun radiated above the water, burning like a jewel of fire.

Laia and the others ran back to the rocks. Hau bowed his head respectfully, after which they formed a circle around a large mound on the beach. At Hau's signal, they cleared away the sand from its surface and took out banana leaves from inside, filling the air with the appetizing aroma of the young pig they had pit-roasted in offering to the gods. Everyone took a leaf in their hands and placed a piece of meat reverently upon it, waiting for their elder. Hau gave a slight nod. Having fasted for an entire day, they indulged at once.

Too engaged in their meal to speak, the youths engorged themselves, raising their voices not in conversation, but in cheers of exaltation that echoed softly along the bay. The meat had been soaked in coconut milk and was slightly sweet. Eating pork was such a rarity for them that having it even three times a year was a luxury. Laia felt it was the best she'd ever tasted. It breathed new life into her flesh. She wasn't alone, as all eleven of them shared in equal rapture. Once they were satiated, they stood up and put on ceremonial skirts of pandanas leaves.

They first danced together in a leisurely rhythm, the only, natural beat that provided by the sound of the waves lapping onto shore. Laia found herself being swept away by her love of dance.

She shook her waist and stamped her feet on the ground. Hau waited for the moment when everyone was locked into a oneness of feeling before he began beating a large drum. Slowly at first...then with increasing speed. He understood their need for dance and the instincts behind it, guiding all eleven of them with great skill into a swirl of frenzy.

Laia was intoxicated. It was a dance of celebration, of joy, of sensuality, of conflict. She used every technique Hau had taught her and waited for the goddess of the dance to enter her completely. Extending her torso, she crossed her legs, threw up her hands, and shook her waist vigorously. The sacrificial meat she'd just eaten burned inside her. Overwhelmed with boundless joy, her vision blanked into white, and Laia fell to the sand. Just before she collapsed, her nipples had pointed proudly to the sky. At last she was one with the goddess of the dance. Henceforth, she would have the honor of sharing her dancing anytime and anywhere with a fanatic audience.

When she came to, she saw the others, lying on the sand too. Their chests were heaving, yet there was bliss upon every face. Kaheyo had fallen face up in front of her and Laia couldn't help but notice the erect member between his thighs. He, too, had transformed into something godly. Laia suddenly lifted her face, only to see a boat's silhouette edging its way into the cove. Even from this far, it clearly wasn't one of Talofa's double canoes. It was a rare spectacle; in fact, she'd never seen anything like it before. Laia shook Kaheyo awake. He sat up and she pointed to the open waters. Kaheyo remained still, eyeing the boat suspiciously. Laia quickly rose to her feet and threw off her skirt, the leftover excitement making her stagger as she ran into the water. She dove in and swam the great distance with ease, for to her, swimming was as natural as walking or running on land. As she made her way through the water, Laia thought of the legends of her people. Though many of the details were lost to her now, she wondered if any of them spoke of this event. She then recalled the earthquake a month before, for she had a feeling there was a legend about that, too. These awoke within Laia's heart vague memories of myths beyond her lifetime and aroused in her both curiosity and unease.

The boat was of a shape she'd never seen. The only vessels made on Talofa were the double canoe, made from two round trees with a slatted deck, and the outrigger canoe. This boat, however, had a deeply curved prow and was covered in some greasy substance that glittered banefully in the dawn.

Laia grasped the edge of the boat without hesitation and pulled herself lithely out of the water.

There were three men on board lying on top of one another. She didn't know if they were alive or dead until one of them opened his eyes feebly and seemed to look in her direction. Laia extended a timid hand and placed it on the man's body. Though not cold to the touch, his skin may only have been heated by the morning sun. Laia couldn't imagine how long they had been at sea. The man's skin was as dark as hers from the merciless sunlight. She didn't know his true color, but she did suspect that he was tan from the sunburn alone.

She heard splashing and turned to see the others swimming out toward her. When they reached the boat, they too pulled themselves out of the water and peered inside, letting out a unanimous gasp of surprise. Not because they feared these three tattered strangers, but because of the colored stains along the deck, which had congealed into a deep crimson and were sticky to the touch. It didn't take them long to realize what this color signified. These three men were sleeping in a pool of blood.

Meanwhile, one of the three men, Jones, was dreaming of a beautiful goddess dancing in the sky, watching over his fallen body bobbing among the waves. She placed her hand on his chest with a soft touch that comforted him beyond imagination. Her skin was not white, but her features resembled those of a white person. Her black hair extended infinitely behind her and Jones could no longer tell if he was dreaming or not. She leaned forward with concern in her eyes. He'd always imagined goddesses as radiant beings clad in white flowing robes, but she had nothing on. Her shapely brown breasts swayed above him in full view, and just the sight of them made Jones feel wonderful. Over the past twenty days adrift at sea, he'd dreamt of many things. In a reality no different than Hell itself, dozing off for even an hour was a welcome escape. Behind closed eyes, he ate and drank to his heart's content in the cool shade, surrounded by people he loved. A number of women appeared in these fantasies, but none so beautiful as the one before him now. Despite being a man of faith, for Jones this was the closest he'd ever come to experiencing God's presence in his dreams.

As for the other two men, Ed Channing was deathly ill with a fever, while the robust Tyler was just waking up from a sound sleep at the bottom of the boat. A bold smile came to his face as he looked around at this unusual group. Whether they were there to save him or to kill him, he received them with a grin as if they were angels...

The eleven men and women held on to the side of the boat, propelling it with their feet towards the rocks. All of them, Laia not least of all, regarded the three bloodied men as gods, and the thought of abandoning the boat never entered their minds. Had they simply entrusted the boat to the sea, it would likely have drifted to Talofa anyway to become a great influence on this civilization which had existed relatively unchanged since the Stone Age.

With the light of the rising sun at their backs, the island's luxuriant flora blossomed before them into a new day. The steep volcano sloped into the sea, lending a coercive force to everything on the island. The ravine at its base was steeped in shadow, imbued with an air of majesty and mystery. Thin palm trees combed the coast in all their elegance, leaves opened up like flowers, their insides hued yellow by the morning sun. Flowers bloomed in primary colors, blanketing the island with their fragrance. Everything here received the bounty of the sun. The beauty of the plants balanced the fierceness of nature, rolling down the foot of the volcano into a harmonious sea. Laia and the others pulled the boat along. Small waves lapped at the sides, while morning clouds drifted far into the distance. Laia had no reason to believe that her paradise, this island which had birthed and raised her all these eighteen years, would ever be altered. If only the boat had never come, Laia's dreams would never have been tainted. She knew nothing of the history behind the ominous boat, nor that this "history" encompassed the space of a mere twenty days. Had she witnessed even a fraction of the horrific events that had taken place upon it, her optimism would have faded instantly.

Laia released her right hand from the boat's edge and returned to the ocean to wash the blood from her fingertips. No matter how much she rubbed her hands together, it refused to come off. She was beset with some foreboding. She smelled her fingertips, only to find the stench of death upon them.

This boat had been marooned from its mother ship, a whaling vessel known as the *Philip Morgan*, and its arrival wasn't without connection to the earthquake Laia had experienced a month earlier. The boat was still rigged then to the *Philip Morgan*. On the day it was deployed, the sea was undergoing some rather unsettling changes.

3

Twenty days earlier, in the middle of the night...

The *Philip Morgan* was latched broadside onto a sperm whale. The sails were taken down and the helm turned westward. As the ship drifted in the night, all the men in its crew of thirty-one, minus the two on lookout, were sleeping in their hammocks below deck.

Ed Channing, one of the two men on guard duty, looked down upon the dark waters, watching carefully for any shark fins peeking out above the surface. This area of the ocean, just south of the equator, was known for its abundance of sharks, but tonight there were none to be seen. If he looked away even for a second, the whale they had gone through so much trouble to snag could fall prey to these predators of the sea, leaving nothing but a stripped carcass. Channing's duty as watchman was to harpoon any sharks that might approach, the idea being that its blood would divert the appetite of any others that might come swimming by. Blood was blood and sharks were hardly particular about where it came from. It was the only way to keep the whale from harm.

Spotting a shark fin on a moonless night, with only the bleary starlight and the lanterns hung on deck for illumination, was a demanding task. It was already well into the night, though the heat hadn't let up at all. Channing downed a cup of red wine to quench his thirst.

Meanwhile, the churning waters were already changing color all around the ship. Because this was night duty, however, Channing was entirely unaware of this. To him, the ocean was the color of night as always. He had to wait until the following morning to make the discovery.

Channing took an hour's rest while his partner relieved him, then started his last shift just as a transparent dawn was breaking from the long night. The *Philip Morgan* was barely drifting. Grabbing the bowsprit, Channing propped himself up on the beakhead and looked out to see where they were heading. He doubted his own eyes. He shuddered, and not because he'd discovered sharks. Something even more troubling was astir. There was a change in the bleak waters. He could literally smell it in the air. He stared at the ocean's surface; its color was changing. Various weather changes were known to cause such phenomena, but Channing had never seen *this*. The color became increasingly distinct as the sun overtook the sky. For a moment, Channing felt like the ship was quickly crumbling from beneath his feet. The ocean did not reflect the azure of the sky, but was steeped in a murky yellow churning from below. Channing rubbed his eyes a few times and, finally accepting that what he was seeing was real, went down on trembling legs into the ship's cabin to fetch the captain.

He knocked on Captain Violet's door and explained the situation, but was met with a violent outburst as the captain grabbed an empty wine bottle from his night stand and threw it against the door. After a few moments of silence came his reply: "I don't want to hear any more crappy reports, okay?"

Ed Channing next went to wake up Marty. The first mate,

Marty was more likely to take Channing seriously. As Channing relayed what he'd seen, Marty felt sick to his stomach just trying to get an image of it in his head, and his fears were profoundly realized the moment he climbed out onto the deck. The sun was nearly at its peak and the ocean's color deepened to orange, thick like the skin across boiling milk. And he began to wonder if the ocean actually *was* boiling. Bubbles popped on the surface, filling the air with putrid deep sea gases.

Marty shuddered. The two of them looked up at the deep blue sky, speechless.

When he was still a boy, Marty once accompanied his father on an expedition into the Bay of Mexico. While en route, they encountered one uninhabited islet after another and Marty had tried swimming the gaps between them. It was a little adventure that he began by diving from the anchored ship, but even an accomplished swimmer like the young Marty got so tired that he ended up walking back toward the ship through the shallows. The sand was deep brown, giving the shallows a yellowish tint, and seeing the ocean like this reminded him vividly of that scenery. The water was up to his knees and every time he raised and lowered his feet, it became clouded, marking a clear path behind him. The sands left a slimy sensation on his skin and were so deep, he felt they could pull him under at any given moment. It wasn't just the physical sensation of it, but the imagined wealth of unseen organisms he was stepping into that made him so uneasy. He feared that something might snap onto his feet at any moment. Unable to endure the horrible feeling, he tried to swim the shallows. But soon, his hands and feet grazed the bottom and he was unable to continue. Having no other option, he retraced his steps to return to the ship via a roundabout route. Though exhausted, he had no desire to take another step in the sand after the extreme unease it had stirred up in him. His father's eyes grew wide when Marty returned to the ship and told him what he'd done. "You mean to tell me you were swimming out there?" he said, pointing to the shallows with disbelief. He proceeded to tell his son that the area was a breeding ground for venomous sea snakes, and that just one step in the wrong place could have been potentially fatal. Marty's instincts were correct and had possibly even saved his life.

If that was true then... thought Marty as he stared at the yellow sea. He couldn't even imagine what dangers lay in store for him this time. Still, that was then and this was now.

This, now, was a much different feeling, as if the deck were sinking, as if creatures never before seen roved the waters in the thousands, eating away at the bottom of the ship, leaving them with no place to seek refuge...

Marty patted Channing weakly on the shoulder.

"Wake the captain again for me."

Channing shook his head.

"E-even if I tell him, h-he won't believe me. That guy doesn't g-g-give a damn about us. That's why it's come to this," replied Channing. He always stuttered when he was afraid.

Helplessly, Marty went down to round up the crew. He didn't give a reason. It would be obvious the moment they saw it for themselves. And he certainly didn't want to get yelled at the way Channing had.

4

The ocean was eerily calm. The thirty-one crewmen of the *Philip Morgan* added to the silence as they looked around them, unsure of what to say. Had this been a storm or other such crisis, they wouldn't have just stood there gazing out quietly at the water's surface. Commands would have been shouted from all directions as duties were allotted, their teamwork guided by years of experience. But in a situation like this that defied all logic, they had no choice but to be silent and still.

Once they agreed that what they were seeing wasn't some mass delusion, the dumbfounded sailors gazed at Captain Violet's face, waiting for his instructions. The captain shook his head in disbelief and called over his three mates: Marty, Claude, and Tyler.

"What should we do?" the captain asked in a low, threatening voice.

"There's nothing we *can* do. We'll just have to keep an eye on things," Tyler answered promptly.

Violet valued Tyler's fortitude as an officer, but disliked him as a person. Violet had worked hard to ascend the ranks from novice sailor to full-fledged captain. Tyler, a former British naval officer, seemed with his very manner to be mocking him. Worse, Violet's father had died, bravely, during the American War of Independence, in a bombardment by the British fleet.

"First, let's find out what's causing the ocean to change color. There has to be a logical reason behind it," offered Claude, a scholarly Frenchman who was so well versed in the living world that, had he not become a sailor, he would have made a perfect biologist. He explained to the captain that, in the same way abnormal outbreaks of plankton made the sea appear red, an ecological disruption in the population level of certain microorganisms could cause such a bizarre transformation.

"And, if that's the case?"

"Like Tyler said, we do nothing. I don't think it's anything to worry about."

"Marty, what do you think?"

Marty, who Violet had the most confidence in, was actually the most frightened of them all. His boyhood memories were still deeply imbedded in his mind and impossible to shake off. He was just happy to have made it back to the ship without getting bitten by sea snakes.

"We should get out of here as quickly as possible."

The ship was drifting languidly with sails down. A refreshing wind blew intermittently between the masts and crossbeams. Marty advised that they hoist the sails and leave.

Violet thought it over. Fine, they could take a few samples of the water as long as they were here. But what was the inconvenience of doing as Marty said? After all, they'd come to hunt and they couldn't return to their home port until the ship's hold was filled to capacity with whale oil. It was clear to Violet they weren't going to catch any whales in these yellow waters. Yet, he didn't know which direction they should go. The navigation charts said nothing about yellow patches of sea.

At the captain's command, a group of sailors swiftly scaled the topsail crossbeams. Pulleys clattered as the ropes were hoisted. Oncc thc sails were all in place, the *Philip Morgan* tilted to the right as they turned the prow. The ship cut through the waters with its stately hull, leaving haunting traces on the water in its wake.

About twenty minutes went by. The *Philip Morgan* was still in yellow waters. The color seemed to be deepening. Fearing they might be heading into even greater danger, the entire crew felt eclipsed by their anxiety. They climbed the masts for a better view but saw the same color spread in all directions and had no idea which direction they should go. Violet tried to convince himself that they were imagining the ocean getting darker, that in reality it hadn't changed at all.

"Captain!" shouted Claude from quarterdeck, running up before the captain could even react. "I think we should let down the sails," he said gravely, a cup of sea water in his hand.

"What is it?"

"It's not a plankton outbreak, that's for sure." The cup was swirling with suspended particles. Claude held it up to the captain's nose. "To tell you the truth, I don't really know what this is, but it appears that something is happening at the bottom of the sea."

Violet was doubtful about this.

"Shouldn't we just get out of here, then?"

"This color... Well, you see we don't really know what's going on below the surface. This place could be shallower than we think, so we need to act fast."

Violet shook his head to clear his mind of the words every captain feared.

"There's no reason why we would ever run aground in the middle of the Pacific with no land in sight."

"I realize that, captain, but I still think it would be wise to proceed slowly and check the water's depth along the way. That way, we'll sustain the least amount of damage if we *do* run into something."

Before the captain knew it, a crowd of sailors, beginning with Tyler and Marty, had gathered around him.

"Luz! Do a depth sounding!" barked Tyler, gesturing to a nearby harpooner.

"There's no need for that!" Violet shouted back, more than irritated at Tyler. What right did Tyler have to disregard protocol and give orders in his place? That Tyler had the sailors' trust didn't mean he could wear it on his sleeve. "What makes you think we're going to run aground in a place like this anyway?! Damned idiot!"

Violet scowled at Tyler, but he didn't even flinch and seemed to care little, if at all, for the captain's authority. The Briton was uncouth and no one ever knew what he was thinking.

"Call it a hunch," said Tyler as he probed the water, in total agreement with Claude. Marty kept his mouth shut and his eyes on the captain. His desire to get out of the area as soon as possible was written all over his face, and so, for the moment at least, he was on Violet's side.

"*I'm* the captain here!"

With these words, the bickering stopped. The chain of command was still intact and the captain's word was final as long as they were on his ship.

Meanwhile, Jones, one of the whale boat oarsmen who'd been keeping watch from the fore-topsail crossbeam, was holding on to the boom, ready to let up the sails at Violet's command. But wind filled the sails, pushing the ship ahead steadily, and it appeared the command wouldn't come. Jones glanced at the huddle around the captain below. From his vantage point, he could see better than anyone that the ocean's color was indeed growing darker.

Jones had yet to turn eighteen and still had much to learn. He'd worked various odd jobs so far, but it was his vague, yet constant yearning for the sea that had led him aboard. To know the sea was, for him, a doorway to changing his perceptions of the world, and the mysterious circumstances he now found himself in were doing just that. The orange waters changed into a yellowish-brown, and beyond that he began to see a large black shadow under the ocean surface directly in the ship's path. Jones swallowed and shouted at the top of his lungs.

"I see something ahead!"

At this, the captain and the others all ran to the prow. No sooner did they see the shadow than Tyler give orders to the helmsman, before Violet could even open his mouth.

"Turn starboard!"

Forgetting himself in a surge of fear, even the captain didn't argue back this time. He peered ahead, leaning forward to better make out the opaque shadow that was closing in on them. He knew exactly what it was. There wasn't enough time to steer clear of it. Strange as it may have seemed, the *Philip Morgan* was going to run aground. He knew all too well the implications of being shipwrecked in such a remote region of the Pacific. The captain had no choice but to pray, and he was sure most of the others were doing the same.

Jones held onto the crossbeam and prayed as well. He wrapped a rope around his body, tightened his grip, and braced himself for impact.

Everyone's eyes were glued to the water and a moment later the bottom of the *Philip Morgan* plunged into the shadow. The shock of it swept through the entire ship. The men on deck staggered into the masts, howling. In the blink of an eye, the boat was overcome with pandemonium—men shouting, cursing, some crying for their lives...voices dolefully accusing God.

It didn't end with the first impact. The ship made a terrible noise as it creaked loudly. After a second and a third jolt, the ship scraped to a halt. The sailors, crawling on all fours, stood up and saw that the ship was leaning severely to the right. A sailor at starboard saw bubbles rising and disappearing on the ocean's surface close by and nearly vomited. The current flowed quietly, pushing the incessantly bubbling foam past behind the ship.

5

The *Philip Morgan*, no longer worthy of its name, was leaning at a dangerous angle. The starboard side had lowered, hoisting the harnessed whale on port side high into the air. It would have appeared bizarre from a distance, like some giant flying fish. The whale's weight was the only thing that had kept the ship from capsizing.

Once the ship came to a standstill, everyone rose to their feet in a daze. Their confusion was evident from the looks on their faces as they leaned over the edge of the ship. Most could only stare at the ocean in disbelief, drained of the pride and confidence routine among whalers. They sighed in resignation and dropped their hands to their sides. They actually looked smaller. A whale they could fight, but this was more than they could bear. Out here, in the middle of the Pacific with no other islands within three hundred miles, they could do nothing but submit to the reality of the situation. They were stranded.

Among the speechless crew, Tyler remained the only one unfazed. He approached the captain and advised him on the first thing they should do. His plan was simple. They had to lighten the ship so that, once the winds changed, they could wait for the next high tide to push them southwest. Tyler made it sound easy. His voice was unhesitating and filled with confidence. Violet had no faith in him whatsoever, but nodded in agreement. The captain tried his best to mask his panic but was betrayed by the trembling in his voice.

"So the tide is ebbing now?"

If they decided on a fixed point and carefully observed the rise and fall of the ocean, they would know the tides. Violet didn't seem to understand this. Tyler ignored the question and laughed through his nose. At this point, whatever anger Violet felt was driven away by his fear. Even so, he wasn't about to allow such brazen behavior from a former British naval officer ten years his junior.

"I *asked* you whether or not the tide is ebbing now."

"You just don't get it, do you?" Tyler said flatly. He then ordered one of the other shipmates, a man known simply as "Spice," to keep an eye on the tides. Tyler couldn't have cared less about the captain's feelings. Violet was extremely irritated, wanting nothing more than to throw Tyler overboard. This man was just as insufferable as the absurd predicament of his ship. It was natural, of course, to feel as much irritation as fear, faced with the incomprehensible.

Violet glared at Tyler with utter hatred. He brought his ruddy face and disheveled beard closer to Tyler and clenched his fists in front of Tyler's eyes in an attempt to display his authority.

One of these days, I'll gut you like a whale, the captain thought.

Tyler shrugged off Violet's gaze, then turned to Luz coolly and shouted, "Go see if the bilge is flooding!"

Seeing that Tyler was in control, the more able sailors came to their senses. A moment later, they broke their silence and caused something of an uproar on the ship. Everyone's movements became faster, as if the constraints of time had snapped.

The crewmen ran around the deck. Some muttered under their breath and some made blatant threats, while others prayed quietly. Everyone had their own way of overcoming panic. Tyler and Violet exchanged silent glances as they returned to their respective posts, dragged into their mayhems.

In time, the tide receded. The ship's draft gradually lightened and the shadow beneath the water grew darker in proportion.

Everyone was gathered on deck. They would need to think fast about what to do next. The damage to the ship was so great, they were left with few options. Their first priority was to pump out the water flooding into the bilge and to get rid of as much as possible to lighten their load so that they might get the *Philip Morgan* out on one more voyage. The problem was deciding what to jettison and what to leave on board. The crew was divided on this matter. The whale they'd caught the night before was the first to go. Aside from that, many of the crewmen, including Tyler, insisted they get rid of the whale oil barrels as well, while the other group, spearheaded by Captain Violet, thought it best to wait for the next high tide to see if they might not leave without tossing any of these.

"No way in hell," was all Tyler had to say about it.

All the while, the water gushing through the hull breach was rising steadily. If they didn't lessen their draft soon, they would have no hopes of going anywhere, and Tyler didn't hesitate to stress this point to the captain.

Violet and his crew were well aware of the dangers involved in seafaring. They'd all signed on to this ship for different reasons.

While some were just trying to forget the lives they'd left behind, some of the younger men like Jones had answered a distant calling for the high seas in order to explore the world. Most, however, were in it for the money, which for them depended entirely on the number of barrels they had below deck. In the nearly three years since leaving the port of New Bedford, they'd extracted enough whale oil to fill the ship's hold completely. If and when they returned to port, their profits would make up for all their hard labor. Because their payment was contingent entirely on the amount of oil obtained, they would obviously get nothing if they returned with nothing.

Shattered at the prospect of losing three years of work in a single day, they were forced to seek out other means. This was to be Violet's last voyage and he was not about to miss his chance to retire.

In the end, a compromise was reached between both sides. It was wasteful to throw all of the barrels away, but the ship's weight was an undeniable factor. It was Marty who finally settled the dilemma. For once, his indecisiveness proved appropriate to the situation. He proposed that they simply divide their barrels among the six whale boats, then store them back on ship once they'd left safely. Everyone agreed this was an excellent idea and soon they set to work, but no one knew this was merely the beginning of the hell that was to follow.

As they loaded the barrels onto the boats and threw everything unneeded overboard, the ship grew considerably lighter. The six boats, hitched with rope, floated around the tilting ship. Once everything was in place, they waited for the next high tide. A few hours later, however, the sky darkened, plunging them into a violent storm. Wind came in from the southwest, blowing the rain diagonally. There was a crunching noise beneath the *Philip Morgan*, but the ship remained stationary. The flooding increased. They tried bailing as much as they could, but the water kept gushing in. The ship was doomed; everyone began thinking of how they were going to escape, how they were going to survive. They had no choice but to abandon ship and drift on the boats, but the boats were all stocked to the limit out on the stormy sea. If they sank, the crew would have nothing left.

Tyler stood on deck to assess the boat situation. Of the six, however, he could see only three. If he left them to the waves, they would be tossed about like toys, snapping out of sight from their ropes, assuming the weight of the barrels didn't capsize them first. The farthest boat he could see bobbed in and out of view. A large wave could have easily sunk it. Tyler took off his shirt and dove into the water. Jones, holding firmly onto the main mast, watched the brawny man dive headfirst into the sea. Though it was evening, the color of the sea by day had left such a strong impression in him that the waters still appeared yellow. The courage it took for Tyler to leap so calmly into the maelstrom on this wrathful night was something Jones would never know. Tyler swam out to the boat, threading skillfully through the waves. One after another, he threw the 250 pound barrels into the water. Jones, who could hardly hold on tight enough to keep himself from being blown away by the gales, watched with eyes opened wide, and felt ashamed at his inability to help. He began to feel dizzy and strangely ecstatic.

Never the most approachable man in the world, Tyler seemed his true self now. Jones had hardly ever talked to him.

The other sailors circulated rumors about him, most of which revolved around his reasons for abandoning the British Navy and ending up on the *Philip Morgan*. Jones found it all a bit hard to take in, so evil they made Tyler seem. But, as the saying went, there was no smoke without fire, and Jones was sure the incident had something to do with Tyler's reclusive nature. Assuming the rumors were true, Tyler was a ruthless killer, but this image clearly didn't fit with the man he saw now. Why was Tyler battling against the sea? Was it only to save himself? Jones saw no reason to think so.

In the end, Tyler rescued two of the boats. Having only two presented them with a big problem.

Just as the crewmen below were giving up on bailing water, Tyler returned and reported that he'd secured two of the boats. Normally, six people rode on a whale boat: four rowers, a harpooner at the prow, and a steersman at the stern. If the thirty-one men aboard the *Philip Morgan* were all going to escape at once, one boat would have to accommodate fifteen men, the other sixteen. This was next to impossible, considering they needed room to carry rations and water with them.

Everyone knew it was only a matter of time before the *Philip Morgan* went under.

Naturally, there were cliques among the sailors, companions who stuck together, friendships that arose from shared experiences. Even Weatherbee, a devil of a man who took refuge on the *Philip Morgan* after murdering a man in Hartford, had made a few friends. He called one of them over and whispered softly into his ear.

"I'm not gonna be beat to the draw, are ya?"

The friend stared back blankly. Weatherbee sighed and grabbed his ear.

"Let's get out while we still can. This's madness."

"Are you crazy? It's too risky," said the other man, appalled.

"What's risky is trying to fit all thirty-one of us on those two boats. We'll capsize in a second. I'm sure you know what that means. We either die or save ourselves, and I know God would want us to survive."

Weatherbee didn't trust Captain Violet, a man he knew would buckle under the pressure of any life or death situation. He refused to get the short end of the stick here.

Weatherbee rounded up five other men who were willing to sneak away with him, but they would also need a mate on their side. They could get by well enough on their own, but having an experienced navigator on board would improve their chances of getting to land. Asking Tyler was out of the question. Claude was smart and had a developed sense of justice, so they didn't think he would join them too quickly. This left the wishy-washy Marty. Weatherbee confided the plan to him and encouraged him to join them. This put Marty in a delicate position. Weatherbee's reasoning was certainly persuasive: sneaking out ahead of the rest would put them at an advantage. It was clear that death was the only possible outcome if everyone tried to cram themselves onto two boats. Marty nodded in agreement.

Weatherbee and his men made their way through the bilge and went up to the deck one at a time, so as to be less conspicuous. All the while, Marty was uncomfortable about how quickly he'd agreed to this. He felt a strong bond with the entire crew and couldn't bear the thought of leaving his mates behind to die. He began to regret his decision and blamed his own weakness for having been swayed so easily without protest. So he changed his mind. It wasn't too late. He would try to stop them, but what if he couldn't do it alone... He realized the gravity of the situation. Not thinking ahead as to how the captain might react to such news, Marty blurted out everything to him. Violet frowned with rage, gathered a few men together, and grabbed a harpoon. Weatherbee and the others were just about to scale a rope down into the boat as the captain came out on deck. Violet brandished the harpoon, shouted "Traitor!" and plunged the weapon deep into Weatherbee's chest. The latter spasmed, fell into the waves, and was swallowed a moment later into the depths below. His five accomplices were still on deck, but Violet showed them no mercy. With a wave of his hand, he had them all thrown into the ocean. While the captain and his faction's anger seemed motive enough to warrant such harsh measures, the true reason, lurking at the bottom of their hearts, was of a different nature: cutting down their numbers...a convenient rationale... Only Tyler became aware of the perverse force of reason that now besieged them all. With the battle, there were only twenty-three of them left. Six had been neatly labelled traitors and taken care of, while two others had somehow been tossed overboard, out of sight, into the rain. Twenty-three was a significant number. It was the maximum that could be fit onto two boats. A process of attrition had reduced their head count, uncannily, to a level that survival mandated.

Violet was determined to escape by any means necessary. He commanded Ed Channing, the ship carpenter, to prepare a raft with food and water. He then split everyone into two groups and assigned them to their boats. Captain Violet's group of eleven included Marty, while Tyler and Claude headed the other outfit of twelve. Jones, of course, wanted to be in Tyler's group. Remembering Tyler's bravery as he jumped into the rough sea to rescue the imperilled boats, Jones knew his strength would prove helpful.

Towing a single raft loaded with food, water, and wine, they formed an inverted triangle upon the water as they began rowing into the stormy sea. The boats were so crammed that there wasn't any room to sleep, and their less than sufficient provisions left them ill prepared for what was to come.

6

By morning, the storm had subsided and the twenty-three men awoke to find themselves surrounded by the deep bluish-green ocean they were used to. The change was so sudden, everyone thought they were dreaming. Some feared that, if they returned to the *Philip Morgan*, they would find only a ghost ship floating in the sea. In reality, their ship was still grounded in the abnormally colored waters. The *Philip Morgan* had been saved from sinking, though after twenty-four hours its starboard edge was leaning so much that it was being lashed by the waves. Though no longer functional, the ship's three masts slanted towards the sky at a rather intrepid angle. The keel of the ship was resting on something, but what... The *Philip Morgan* swayed back and forth, convulsing like some living thing, masts waving like an insect's antennae.

The twenty-three men, now divided between two boats, shared a common goal: to survive. Where there is a group, and where it toils after a single purpose, the instincts of each individual give rise to something different from them that is systematic—a "law" that governs their actions. Under severe circumstances, this law can have an extraordinary binding power. This isn't true just for the twenty-three men. Humanity as such, we might say, is a large collective drifting into the future with survival as its shared interest. This law differs from the "laws" that we have written down, and that have such an inorganic connotation. This law exists hardly to rein in outpourings of human instinct, but rather, is aligned with the inchoate impulses toward life ensconced in our hearts; it is an unspoken agreement among human beings where there are more than one. In short, this naked law, fundamental to survival, was altered and institutionalized over many thousands of years of history before our laws came to be.

The first thing these men did was to establish a fair distribution of rations. To do this, they had to decide first where they were going. If they could calculate the number of days it would take to arrive at an island where they could expect to find sufficient food and water, it would be easy to figure out how much of their rations could be consumed per day and dole them out accordingly. Because the currents south of the equator traveled westward, there was a strong possibility they would drift ashore onto the Tuamotu islands. Rowing against the currents was out of the question. Of course, if they happened to be picked up by a European or American ship along the way, all their problems would be solved. But the earth's roundness would hide small boats like theirs completely from view and the chances of being found were practically nil. They were about six hundred miles from the Tuamotu islands. Assuming they drifted at a speed of two knots, it would take them anywhere from eight to ten days to get there. Since they had four barrels of water with them, this meant everyone could have nearly two liters per day. Were it not for the unforgiving sun, this would have been plenty, but there was no guarantee they could get to Tuamotu as scheduled. If the wind changed direction, they might be blown completely off course. After careful consideration, it was decided that the water would be rationed out at one liter per day. In addition to the water, there were two barrels of wine. As regards to quenching their thirst, the situation was relatively luxurious.

All this was reminding Tyler of a report he'd read while still a naval officer. It detailed an insurrection on a British naval warship ten years ago, and its outcome. Twenty men were packed like sardines on a small boat and put out to sea with only thirty gallons of water and a negligible amount of rations. They endured drifting over a forty-five day period for a few thousand miles—without a single casualty... At least in their own case, they had the advantage of relatively sufficient provisions. Tyler thought hard about the report, hoping there might have been something in it that would be of use. However, the men in that case were well-trained British navy hands, and he doubted those lessons applied to the current whaling crew of murderers and ex-pirates. Yet, the desire to survive was just the same, and he was deeply curious as to how things would turn out.

Only when the current and wind were consistent enough did they raise the sails to gain some distance. When the wind blew in the opposite direction, they lowered the sails and rowed with oars, lowering their bodies to reduce drag. Everyone hated this part, because every moment spent rowing in the hot sun made them lose needed moisture, and they feared it might do more harm than good.

On the third day, Jones had turned eighteen. This was his first experience being lost at sea. He despised not only the erratic winds, but now the ocean as a whole. When, at the age of fifteen, he first came aboard the *Philip Morgan*, he used to romanticize situations like these. Faced with the possibility of being shipwrecked, he'd been able to imagine well enough the hardships, the hunger. His firm resolve had readied him for a death at sea should it come to that. He'd left behind an insipid life on land. As he rowed against the wind, muttering under his breath all the while, he realized the marked difference between what he'd imagined and the actual pain and hunger he was experiencing now. The captain was to blame for all of this. Wasn't it the captain who'd guided the ship through the yellow waters? Hadn't they lost the other boats because he wanted to protect his precious oil? Fearing these opinions might reach the captain's ears, Jones kept his mouth shut. But he could tell that the others shared his sentiment, with the possible exception of Tyler, who appeared seized by completely different concerns. Seemingly unaffected by the fatigue, hunger, and thirst that racked them all, Tyler exuded more and more strength each day. At times, he even looked happy, his face frozen in a trancelike grin. The eleven men on Tyler's boat eyed him with fear. Tyler himself remained neutral, accepting things as they came at every moment, and his unwavering composure instilled great trust in his group. Over on Captain Violet's boat, in marked contrast, Marty was deceiving both himself and the others with his blind optimism.

Here, there were two worlds, divided between the boats. Though they were connected via the rations raft behind them, they were far enough apart so that conversations didn't carry over. Indeed, Tyler and his men had no idea what schemes were being hatched on the other side.

Violet and Marty were met with silent reproach from the

rest and tasted the tension in the air. Marty hesitantly made eye contact with the men. Once he saw the hatred in their eyes, he turned fearfully to the captain for help. Violet paid no attention. He hated weak men. Not only because they were unreliable in a crunch, but because they were a real danger to themselves and to others.

Marty could only study the navigation map, fiddling with his quadrant and compass.

"If we continue in this direction, we should reach an island in two or three days!" he shouted hysterically.

"Not again..." the others groaned in unison, glaring at him with derision. Marty had boosted their hopes prematurely by blurting out these same words some three days before, after which time they'd seen not a speck of land. While they were forced to grit their teeth and bear it, Marty seemed blissfully unaware. In the off chance that land *had* appeared, he would probably have taken all the credit for it. They had been drifting for a total of eleven days now.

"You know, just because we find an island doesn't mean we'll be able to land on it, so what's the use?" a man sitting next to Marty muttered to no one in particular.

"What do you mean?" asked another.

"How do we know it won't be overrun with savages?"

"Enough! There'll be no more of that kind of talk."

Violet wasn't about to let his men give in to their fears so easily.

"No, go on," urged the men, ignoring the captain's words. Since leaving the *Philip Morgan* behind, they'd become increasingly indifferent to his authority.

"I once heard about these two men who were marooned with a boat just like this. They landed on an island. Just like that, they were captured by cannibals..."

The others swallowed their saliva and dropped the oars from their hands.

"I said, *Enough!* This is idiocy."

Violet shook the boat as he sprung to his feet. But the sailors paid no heed to him, their attentions focused sheerly on the face of the man telling his story.

"A-and then they tied the men up, gutted them alive and a-ate them."

The men's faces were filled with disgust. Their bodies went numb as the scene played out in their minds. Any hopes of being rescued upon reaching Tuamotu crumbled. If cannibals were lying in wait to inflict unimaginable agony upon them, they saw no point in rowing anymore. Most were too afraid even to ask why the man waited until now to tell them this.

Suddenly, Marty laughed.

"Hey, who did you hear that story from anyway?"

"From a guy who saw the whole thing, if you must know."

"If they got eaten, then who the hell was around to see it?"

The man was quick to answer.

"Someone else must've been there. He watched in horror as his friends got eaten, fled in panic, and lived to tell the tale."

Marty smiled in disbelief and looked around at the others.

"Of course, that makes perfect sense," he said sarcastically. "Don't let the foolish story get to you. We go west. Now keep rowing."

But no one moved a muscle. It didn't matter whether the

particular story was true or not. The fact was the man had a point. No one among them knew anything about the Tuamotu islands, or the Marquises for that matter. There was no way to predict what awaited them there. The more they thought about what strange customs might be practiced in such remote places, the more they became gripped by their fear of a brutal death. When they first settled on Tuamotu as their destination, they imagined even the most uncivilized land as a place where safety was assured. However, the closer they got, the more gaudily stained with blood grew the idea of "uncivilized lands." The fear of the unknown had birthed an even greater beast.

"I don't want to go to a place like that," someone said. He spoke for everyone. In an instant, the entire crew had let their imaginations get the best of them.

"You don't want to go there, huh? Then where *should* we go?" asked the captain. Seeing that the situation was getting touchy, Marty was on his guard. The skin on his cheek twitched and his eyes darted back and forth. He knew that nothing good could come from associating with these fools...

"Tahiti, we should go to Tahiti..." someone said.

"Tahiti, of course. The French are there and we're friends with them, so we shouldn't run into any trouble."

Tahiti was soon on everyone's lips and they were determined to change course before Captain Violet and Marty even agreed to it. The sailors knew something of Tahiti at least. The French navy often made stops there and American whaling ships used it as a restocking post for food and water supplies. Imagining an uncivilized land flying the flag of a civilized nation was enough to give them peace of mind.

Well aware that his position as captain had been forfeited, Violet tried his best to object.

"You really think that's a good idea? Tahiti is another five hundred miles west of Tuamotu. If we aim for Tuamotu, we can feed ourselves. It's too risky to try to go any farther."

"I think Tyler and the others would agree to it," said Marty.

"It's too soon to tell them anything," someone blurted out.

Violet and Marty looked at one another, knowing full well the meaning of those words. And then, it dawned on them. If they simply took the remaining water and rations and sailed for Tahiti by themselves, they had a real chance.

Violet didn't have his heart set on Tuamotu. Ultimately, all he wanted was to get back home in one piece. His original plan was to stop at Tuamotu first, stock up on food and water, and recover their strength before continuing on to Tahiti, where they would wait for an American ship to call at port. If they deserted Tyler and the others and took their rations, however, they could bypass the risk of going to Tuamotu altogether and head straight for Tahiti.

The men gazed at Captain Violet in silence, pressing him for a decision. One of them held a harpoon as if in silent threat. Violet weighed matters again in his mind.

He had to admit there was no way of knowing what dangers might befall them on unfamiliar islands. He, too, had heard rumors of cannibalism. It was clear now that going straight to Tahiti was their only option.

Violet wasn't a good man by any means, nor did he want to be. But he hated unmanly behavior. His impulsive killing of Weatherbee had certainly been fueled by an intolerance for treachery.

Violet admonished himself to stay calm.

Maybe we could ask Tyler to join us in going to Tahiti? But then, we wouldn't have enough food and water.

He was met with bitter faces in his silence. The anticipation was heavy and forced him to a hasty decision, though he was still hesitant to act the role of traitor.

Violet figured that, if he tried to swim over to Tyler's boat, he would just be harpooned like a whale by these men. They would take on Tyler next, but none of these rogues had the courage to face that formidable man, survivor of countless melee clashes who made friend and foe alike tremble in their boots.

Violet could see it now. The moment he jumped into the water, the two boats would come to arms, and the men on his boat would fall at Tyler's deft hands. They were about to fight over food and water, what stupidity... Violet was frustrated that his command was fading. The land had its law. A ship had its law. But whatever law had bound them on the *Philip Morgan* had deteriorated, and they had been forced to make their own. Strength had become their law and Tyler had it. Had Tyler been on Violet's boat, his crew would not have breathed a single word of betrayal, but Violet was getting on in years and lacked the requisite power to make anyone submit to him. Knowing this made him feel empty. He hated Tyler, but envied him and his boat even more.

Violet sought to compromise this dilemma. In order to avoid a futile conflict, he decided to conspire against Tyler. He felt justified in wanting to survive without losing face. Tuamotu was close, so he convinced himself that, even without sufficient rations, the others would make it just fine.

In any case, he never expected to see Tyler again.

Violet sat down and looked around at the faces of his crew. With that, the tense atmospherc lifted, filling everyone with relief.

"It's settled, then. We'll do it first thing tomorrow morning," Violet said, masking his lingering doubts with a bitter smile.

Billy, a young man with a tight grip on a harpoon, was standing right next to him. As far as Violet knew, Billy was responsible for the deaths of two men in some sort of altercation. One he'd killed by decapitating with a piece of broken glass, the other he'd knocked unconscious and drowned in the ocean. That such a brutal man should be afraid of facing cannibals was ludicrous. Violet didn't understand people. A fear hatched fairly innocuously had come to grip their very flesh. The process was almost humorous, from an objective point of view.

Morning came. Luz awoke and rubbed his eyes as he stood up and took a look around. The boat's draft was lighter. Again, he looked around slowly. The captain's boat was nowhere to be seen.

"Everybody wake up. They're gone."

Luz shook them all awake. Jones and Tyler opened their eyes. Not a trace was left of Violet's boat. As if that wasn't enough, the raft was gone, leaving only a flaccid rope in the sea. At first, they couldn't make sense of what had happened, but gradually the sick feeling encroached upon them that the others had left with all the food and water. For all they knew, the raft might have simply disappeared, taking their rations with it, but it was highly unlikely that it and the other boat would have gone under at the same time in such calm waters.

Tyler gazed westward, where Violet and the others had gone.

"Traitors!" he cried out. "Mark my words: *I'll kill you all!*"

But revenge was the least of their concerns right now. Tyler and the remaining men were stranded in the middle of the South Pacific, with only a little wine left with them. Before they wasted their energy on Violet, they had to figure out a way to get through this alive.

7

Ed Channing wasn't satisfied with the explanation of why Violet's boat had disappeared so unexpectedly. The Tuamotu islands weren't that far away, and they would have had plenty of supplies to get there. It was pointless for them to have reduced their numbers out here for that reason. Once on land, they could have gotten by easily. Having no way of knowing that the captain's decision had been forced on him by the deluded, Channing could only assume that the captain had done what he'd done to get more food and water. Just the possibility made his skin crawl.

"I-i-if I get my hands on those guys, I'll f-fight them to the death," he proclaimed repeatedly, his body shaking.

"Shut up, Channing. Are you really in any condition to kill a man?" said Spice.

Ed Channing had grown dangerously thin from malnutrition. As the ship's carpenter, his duties on the *Philip Morgan* had chiefly been the repair and manufacture of whale oil barrels. While not the strongest among the crew, he excelled in his craft, having expertly repaired many boats all but destroyed by less than willing whales. Channing always harbored a complex about his talents. His father was a skilled worker who built many ships on par with the *Philip Morgan*, but, try as he might, never received the recognition he deserved. His father was dead; his older brother, and not Ed Channing, now continued the family trade.

Channing's issues, however, were not with his older brother but with the fact that his father never got to show his true potential before his death. Channing had vowed he would someday build a ship that exceeded his father's, though he knew that would not be easy.

"If we have time to complain, why don't we make a fishing hook?" said Tyler calmly.

"W-we don't have any metal fittings."

"What if we used the tip of the harpoon?"

"I-I don't know, I've never tried it."

"Then try it."

Tyler broke off the sharp end of a harpoon and tossed it to Channing, who inspected the stinger-like point intently. Compared to the craftsmanship that went into his father's enormous ships, this was almost insulting. Even so, he rubbed the tip against the oar clutch to sharpen it.

Tyler grabbed the tipless harpoon and stood up, plunging it into the schools of fish revealed briefly among the waves. The expansive waters were teeming with life, but the fact that they couldn't drink the water or catch fish as they pleased made the circumstances that much more difficult to bear. A whale in the distance shot a spray of sea water from its blowhole as though to deride their past deeds against its kind. On this single boat, fully loaded with exhausted, hungry men, chasing a whale would have been an act of suicide. Everyone, from the harpooners to the mates, was equally powerless. Both the freedom and the order afforded by the *Philip Morgan* were a thing of the past. Tyler was the only one among them who had any confidence as he hunched over the edge of the boat jabbing the water tirelessly with his harpoon.

The law aboard the boat had to shift in accordance with the new reality. So far they'd been unsuccessful at catching anything, and though they had some wine with them, it was a paltry amount. Deprived of food and water, a new system of survival was only natural. Claude, being the most intelligent member of the group, proposed a few guidelines. Most important was limiting their intake of sea water. While it was common knowledge that drinking salt water only made one's thirst greater and could kill by dehydration, sailors knew this wasn't entirely true. They could actually quench their thirst by drinking a little at a time. Drinking salt water as if it were fresh water would have a fatal effect, of course, on internal organs, so Claude advised drinking it only in moderation. Everyone would be allowed three cups of sea water a day, supplemented with stored rain water and wine. They would keep an eye on one another to make sure no one drank too much, but they didn't go so far as to decide punishments for anyone who broke the rule. There was no need, for nature would provide anyone who drank too much her own penalty in the form of a painful death.

A related issue was how to manage the wine. There was no telling what men in a desperate state of mind might attempt. Perhaps there could be a fight to hoard the wine. Perhaps one of them, in a state of derangement, might throw it all overboard. In the end, Claude, Tyler, and Jones became the wine keepers. Claude and Tyler, who held high-ranking positions aboard the *Philip Morgan*, understood the value of protecting what little they had. This left the mystery of Jones' appointment, a move that was Tyler alone's decision. He was uncomfortable that only two people had control over the wine, and when he looked around at the others, his eyes fell on Jones.

"You, guard the wine," he said brusquely.

Jones was glad to be chosen, but the choice prompted disappointed looks from the other nine sailors. It seemed to mean that Jones could be trusted, but they could not, and the youth felt the crushing force of their envy. Despite the fact that it was Tyler's decision, it was Jones against whom they bore the new grudge. No one dared go up against Tyler, or so much as grumble openly.

Now a part of the leader group with Claude and Tyler, Jones was put in an ambiguous spot that segregated him from the others. In the event of an all-out mutiny, he would be among the first to go. Of course, as long as Tyler was alive and well, he didn't have to worry about any uprising...

Thus did it fall upon the three to ration the wine impartially. For the twelve on board, this became their basic system for survival. Claude's sense and virtue, Tyler's overwhelming force, and Jones' role as an errand-boy shielded by Tyler... The qualities of these three meshed marvelously to deflect the mutinous impulses of the other nine, but this of course wasn't a premeditated arrangement on anyone's part. It had instead emerged naturally from the time they'd spent together. Had the system been imperfect—if, in other words, anyone felt their lives endangered because of it—then a revolt was sure to occur. That none transpired meant that everyone felt the system was necessary. It had generated spontaneously out of a common consciousness.

When the chance arose, Jones caught everyone's attention by asking Tyler what he'd been wanting to ask all along.

"Say, Tyler. Why did you choose me to look after the wine anyway?"

Tyler drew close and whispered in his ear.

"Because you remind me of my friend's little brother."

Jones was disappointed by this answer. He knew Tyler wasn't one to joke, but there had to be more to it than that...

"That's it?"

Jones pressed him for more.

"That's it." A sudden smile rose to Tyler's face. "What, that's not enough for you?"

"No, not really..."

"Fine, if you must know, then I'll tell you. That friend was a very important person to me."

Jones had figured this already.

"Was it a woman?"

"Yes. I wouldn't speak this way about anyone else. For lack of a better word, she was my lover."

Tyler seemed embarrassed using the word "lover," and it piqued Jones' interest. The other sailors were hardly the type to speak of a lover as a "friend." For them, most women were merely objects of dcsire.

"And what was her little brother like?"

In keeping with his nature, Tyler seemed hesitant to provide details. Jones imagined the little brother as a masculine, strong, and reliable person. Seemingly without regard for Jones' pride, however, Tyler said calmly, "He was a crybaby, insanely jealous, a weakling."

Jones was confused. What was he trying to say? If Jones was such a weakling, why had he been given a crucial responsibility?

"Hey, why the long face? I'm talking about him, not you. I really don't know much about him. I only met the guy twice. Poor bastard died like a mongrel."

Tyler looked off in the distance, adding, "He was better off dead than alive, if you know what I mean... Just the type of guy he was."

Jones knew well enough not to take Tyler's story at face value and chose instead to see it as a metaphor.

At that moment, a voice came from the prow.

"I caught something!"

Everyone cheered at the sight of a glittering, silver fish. Ed Channing's craftsmanship had proven useful after all. Hands tangled together as the men scrambled for their prize, but the fish jumped around above their fingertips and fell back into the sea. More significantly, the fish escaped with the hook Ed Channing had worked so hard to make. Everyone was quick to blame each other for letting the fish go, and tensions mounted to dangerous levels.

"Stop!" Tyler barked. The men turned to him and froze. Some of them sat down in defeat and cried, wondering if they were ever going to get out of this. They'd nearly lost all hope, and their shame was overshadowed only by a concern over their own waning energy. Tyler and Claude both thought the same thing: if they did catch any more fish, they would have to be careful.

One of the men was clearly at the end of his tether. He quickly picked up one of the harpoons lying about on the boat and shouted with a crazed look in his eyes.

"That's it! I can't take any more of this. Just give me my share of the wine now. At least I can have one good drink before I die."

The man sobbed pitifully and begged for them to just divide the wine into twelve equal parts and drink up their share until they were drunk enough to jump into the sea.

"If I'm going to die anyway, I want my last moments to be happy ones!"

Very much tempted by the idea, two of the others agreed to it. They stood alongside the man with the harpoon and seemed willing to oppose Tyler at all costs, risking their lives in a desperate bid for a ration of wine.

"We'll do no such thing." Tyler's frame shook, his eyes locked on the weapon. "If you want to die, suit yourselves. You can drink all the sea water you like and die that way, but don't do it at the expense of the only amenity we have."

The other man stood there, a beast-like ferocity clouding his eyes. He was so delusional from hunger that he'd lost all will to live. Without warning, he made a jab at Tyler's face. Tyler dodged it effortlessly. He grabbed the harpoon's handle and pulled it towards him. The man lost his footing and fell forward, breaking his nose on Tyler's forehead. Tyler put his heavy arms around the man's neck and squeezed as hard as he could. Seconds later, the man went still and his head fell back limply. For a long time, Tyler didn't move. Everyone held their breaths. In the heavy silence, Tyler whispered something into the man's ear. So softly so that Jones, who was nearby, could hardly make out the words. Then, a moment later, he flung the corpse overboard, and it made a huge splash before sinking into the waves out of sight. Tyler gazed indifferently at the bubbles left behind. Thinking Tyler might have gone mad, Jones felt a cold shiver run along his spine. Tyler was only acting in self-defense. That wasn't what bothered

Jones. It was the strange way he'd embraced and whispered to the dead man that gave him the chills. Ironically, this episode of thirst-driven delusion and Tyler's own piece of madness quickly injected a temporary stability into their small world of uncertainty.

The other two men snapped back to reality and sat down in resignation, uttering not a single word for the rest of the day. However, it seemed that fear had gotten the best of them after all; the next morning they were gone. Everyone had mixed feelings about it. On the one hand, they were happy to know they would have a larger share of the wine, but they knew also that it was only a matter of time before death tempted each and every one of them...

"Haha! When morning comes...when morning comes..." said Spice, laughing giddily through a whirlwind of emotions. "When morning comes, the ocean turns yellow. When morning comes, the captain's boat disappears with our food and water. And when morning comes again, two of us disappear. Haha! Hey, I wonder what tomorrow morning has in store for us."

Spice looked deeply into Luz's face. "Hey Luz, when you wake up tomorrow, maybe your skin will be white."

Luz, a black man, laughed at this, as did everyone else, if only to distract themselves from whatever they were feeling.

What *would* tomorrow bring? It was a question that was on everyone's mind. And, while they knew the two missing sailors had chosen death of their own volition, at the same time the survivors worried there was a supernatural force at work that was beyond their understanding.

Five days had passed since they had been deserted by Captain Violet and the others, and seventeen since their narrow escape from the *Philip Morgan*. Hope was still nowhere in sight. The sky was perfectly clear—not a wisp of the cumulonimbus clouds that typically formed above islands. The ocean remained deep in color and didn't change to the light blue that would have indicated land was near. Had there been any birds around, they could have followed them to land, but they had yet to see a single one. They began to doubt if this was really the Pacific Ocean. Just then, three masts poked out from the waterline in the distance. The men shielded their eyes from the sun and quickly rose to their feet, shouting as loud as they could. They could only see the masts of what they assumed was a frigate just beyond the curve of the earth. They had only a one-in-a-million chance of being noticed, but they waved their hands and shouted anyway. It was a waste of energy. The masts eventually grew shorter and disappeared before they could even identify which country the ship was from. Unable to get over their despair, three of the men died soon after, two of them from drinking too much salt water. The once cramped boat was becoming emptier by the day.

The occasional fish they were able to catch provided hardly enough nutrition for the six remaining men and only served to whet their appetites. But it did provide them with a temporary boost of strength. Sometimes they even awoke to find that a few flying fish had landed in their boat, enticed from the waters by the light of the full moon. This madc everyone feel instantly optimistic. Perhaps God hadn't completely abandoned them.

Hope was an obvious necessity. If they were going to hold out to the brink of insanity, they needed to know that there were people waiting at home who would be sad over their deaths. Those who had no one waiting for them would just as soon throw themselves overboard.

"So, if we all make it back alive, what's the first thing you'd do?" said Claude, still holding on tenaciously to hope.

Everyone looked up at the sky. It wasn't their first time thinking about this. In fact, it was something they'd thought about often in the past weeks, and every time they did, their lives flashed before their eyes.

The men stretched themselves out along the bottom of the boat and talked about their lives.

Luz had a wife who'd given birth to a beautiful baby girl three years ago. It was just around that time that Luz was trying to get out of his whaling gig, but on the very day he resolved to do this, he caused the death of his child through his own carelessness. His baby, broken like a fragile vase, her head bent at an unnatural angle... His wife blamed him for it. The tragedy drove a wedge between them and tore their relationship apart. Luz had no choice but to return once again to the whaling business. He hoped that three years out at sea would be ample time for his emotional scars to heal. Returning home therefore meant little to him. If he did manage to survive, his only wish was to have another child. Luz placed himself at God's mercy and was hopeful that his redemption would come.

Jones was the next to speak. Still only eighteen, he didn't have much to say. He was still unclear about where he'd come from, where he was going, and who he was. He was too busy trying to make sense of his life so far. His father was missing. There were rumors he'd been killed in a drunken brawl, though there was no proof to support this. His mother took these rumors at face value, however, and eloped with another man, abandoning

Jones at fifteen. His hometown of Providence was a hot spot for whalers and so he joined the crew of the *Philip Morgan* to make a life for himself. Aside from an attraction to the ocean, he didn't have any real reason for signing on. At the very least, a life of whale hunting on the high seas meant he would never feel alone.

"So what will you do? If you make it back to Providence..."

"No idea," Jones answered promptly. He'd never really thought about the future. All he knew was that, right now, he wanted to keep his mind clear of wicked thoughts. The others felt the same way. Were they not in such a dire situation, they would have laughed and shared their typical lewd banter, but now, even when they thought of women, their dreams were purely platonic and cloaked in nostalgia. They even forgot about the enemies they'd made. If they could only make it back, they would start their lives anew. In the face of death, their sexual desire had dwindled into a fear that God saw clearly into their heads. There was no use in hiding any deviant urges from the Creator, lest they be forced to endure the wrath of Hell when their time came. They tried to think only of virtuous things, hoping for nothing more than a respectable future.

Channing told them his dream of building a large ship in homage to his father, and Claude spoke in greater detail of his knowledge of the world of living things.

Spice's conscience weighed heavily on him and he seemed unwilling to share. The others wanted to know what was in his head, even if only to keep the conversation going, but they failed to get a word out of him.

Claude turned his gaze timidly towards Tyler.

"I guess it's all on you now, Tyler. Tell us what you'd do."

"Fight."

"Fight? With whom?"

"No one. I'd fight everything that surrounds me."

Having lost his faith three years before, Tyler was the only one unafraid of God. It was almost as if he wanted to fight God Himself.

There was once a woman he loved more than any other, the very same woman whose little brother he'd compared to Jones. Not long after conceiving Tyler's child, she died in great pain. Tyler cursed the child for killing her and, in some ways, that was not far from the truth. An autopsy wasn't warranted, so there was no way to know for sure, but it was concluded that the egg had developed not in the uterus, but in the fallopian tube. As the fetus grew larger, it tore through the tube lining and hemorrhaged into the abdominal cavity. She lapsed into acute anemia and died. In his grief, Tyler denounced God and detested himself even more. Her younger brother chased away the sorrow of his sister's death with alcohol. This led to a drunken altercation with Tyler, who killed him and left the navy. Tyler was the type who had difficulty being stable without some sort of conflict in his life. He'd chosen to fight whales instead of enemy nations, hoping to drown his sorrows in the process.

Hearing this story, Jones finally caught a glimpse into one aspect of Tyler's character. In a way, Tyler was enjoying these extreme circumstances, because he was fighting now. The sun beat down upon their skin mercilessly, intensifying their hunger and thirst. Mother Nature was the only thing that stood in the way of Tyler. He got up and slashed at the ocean with a harpoon, the wound upon the water sealing up with a small curl before fading away. Tyler couldn't have asked for a more unrelenting opponent.

Spice eventually stopped breathing. The five remaining men gathered around his body in silent prayer. Normally, Tyler would have dumped the body into the sea, but this time he made no effort to get up. He merely fixed his eyes on the body, deep in thought. Almost at once, the others realized what he intended. They were sailors, and they had heard numerous tales of shipwrecks, many of which ended with a certain odious ritual. It wasn't even rare, actually. Under such circumstances, it was almost a natural solution, and the possibility had underlied everyone's thoughts for some time.

Tyler looked from face to face. Claude turned away. Luz glanced skyward and began to pray. Ed Channing's face twitched as he averted his eyes. Jones looked back and forth between Tyler and Spice's corpse, his eyes growing larger by the moment. Only he, in his innocence, was unsure. How were they going to give him his rites? He could only assume from the mood what they were about to do. But would they really resort to...?

"If you're going to eat him, he's all yours. I just can't do it," Claude declared. These words confirmed Jones' suspicion.

Tyler plans to eat Spice.

Luz's prayers grew louder. He would have none of it.

Tyler sprung into action. Without hesitation, as if merely doing his job, Tyler stuck a harpoon into Spice's body. After cutting out the innards, he lined them up beneath the glimmering sun, and placed one into his mouth.

"If only Spice had more flavor..."

The obvious pun did nothing to break the tension. Claude

and Luz both looked away at the calm sea, trying not to vomit. Jones was in tears, unsure of how to deal with this. He never hated Tyler more than at that moment.

"Here, try some."

Tyler held out some flesh in front of Jones, who merely shut his eyes and mouth tightly to repress the disgust surging slowly up his system.

"It's okay," Tyler said. "Death is all around us. Luz's daughter broke like a toy, your father was killed in a fight. And the woman I loved...she died because of my child, and I killed her little brother. So what? Terrible? There's nothing to be done about it. Death comes no matter how much we fight it. But we're still alive here, in spite of it all. There's something to be said for that, huh?"

Jones didn't understand what Tyler was getting at. Sure, death was all around them. *But to what end? Why should they have to eat one of their own because of that?*

"You're still young. How old are you now? Nineteen? Twenty?"

Jones shook his head.

"Eighteen?"

He nodded.

"Eighteen, huh? Well, Claude and Luz are past thirty. They're old enough to make their own decisions. But you're not. So, here, eat."

Jones refused. He was afraid to even look at the unidentifiable piece of meat and its dangling blood vessels. He closed his eyes tightly until tears came out. Instinct was battling against instinct in his heart. Human beings have an instinct for self-preservation, but also an instinct for preserving the species. The refusal to eat human flesh is not an ethical impulse so much as a manifestation of the latter instinct; if we could delight in each other's flesh, we would eat ourselves into extinction. From the time we were monkeys, a taboo has been in place against preying on each other for food. The conflict inside Jones was fierce. He knew that he would never survive if he didn't do this horrible thing.

Tyler grabbed Jones' nose and pried his mouth open. He pushed his fingers between his teeth and yanked them apart, jamming a piece of Spice's thigh between them. Jones gagged in revulsion. Tyler grabbed him by the head and moved the youth's jaws in a chewing motion. The natural reflex forced the meat down his throat, making him want to throw up. Jones cried. Tyler merely laughed at his tears.

Tyler then poured some of the blood-colored wine down his throat to help settle his stomach.

Jones felt distinctly filled with energy. His entire abdomen grew hot. At the same time, the world around him began to change color as Tyler tightened his grip. Not that the sea was undergoing another transformation. Caught between Tyler's knees, Jones was looking up at the sky, which had turned slightly yellow. Intense sunlight branched off into long sinews stretching from the heavens, filling the sky with boundless warmth. Tyler put another piece of flesh into Jones' mouth, while Channing timidly stretched a hand out towards the gutted body.

Perhaps it was an illusion, but Jones swore he saw the faint silhouette of an island bridging sky and waterline. As his body absorbed the flesh of his fellow man, the lush scent of soil came wafting upon the air and the waves grew more animated. Just when he thought it was real, the island disappeared, but he was certain he smelled land. Assuming he wasn't going crazy, this was the promised land they'd be searching for these past twenty days.

Three days later, their boat drifted ashore on Talofa, an island rich in ancient myths. Jones, Tyler, and Ed Channing were the only three survivors.

8

Jones heard the buzzing of an insect and was awakened by small wing beats tickling his nose. He opened his eyes slowly, shielding them from the sun with his right hand. This action had become habitual over the past twenty days, but there was no longer any need for it. Just ten feet above him, a thatched roof of long hemp palm leaves gave him shade from the harsh sunlight. As he opened his eyes, the face of the goddess from his dream appeared before him. Jones thought he was in paradise. The goddess smiled at him and opened her mouth.

Jones couldn't understand a single word she was saying. He listened hard as she repeated herself over and over, pointing at the ocean. Jones lifted his head, but even that small movement sent a splitting pain through his skull. Maybe he wasn't dead... Jones tried to remember, and shuddered as the hellish scenes suddenly came flooding back. He watched as the dark boat was lifted onto the luminous beach. The stage of a twenty-day-long tragedy, it defiled the beautiful sands with its unsightly form. The ominous color of the ocean that had started it all floated vividly before his eyes. Spice's flesh was now living on as part of his own. When he thought of this, he felt no guilt. Luz and Claude both perished for their pride, but Jones owed his life to Tyler.

The woman held out a hollowed coconut shell that was filled to the brim with water. Jones propped himself up and grabbed the bowl ravenously. He tried to gulp it down, but his weakened body wouldn't accept such a large amount of fluid all at once. Spilling water all over his face, he did empty the bowl. The woman held out another one, which Jones took more time to savor. It was sweet; coconut milk, no doubt. He thought how wonderful it was to be alive.

The young woman smiled and touched her chest, saying, "Laia, Laia." Jones told her his name in return. Laia's perpetual smile was all he needed to see. At last, he knew they were saved. Knowing their boat had washed ashore on an island in the South Pacific, Jones felt his faith restored and thanked God deeply. God indeed worked in mysterious ways and was the only one who knew their fate.

He guessed that Tyler and Ed Channing were receiving the same hospitality under the nearby canopies. Indeed, a large group of the island's natives were gathered around Tyler, while Laia in all her loveliness was the only one tending to Jones. There was a man next to Tyler who stood out noticeably from the rest of the natives. Jones could see only his back and the magnificent tattoo upon it. A single white line ran the length of his spine from his neck to his buttocks, crossed by three horizontal lines. Geometric patterns were rendered in between them, but what they represented was unclear from where he lay. Jones was relieved because, even though he didn't know who had made the tattoo, it was done with great artistry. In other words, it wasn't the product of a culture that believed in conflict and bloodshed, but one that upheld peace and beauty. He saw no reason to think of the island's people as barbarians. Channing looked to be on the other side of Tyler, but Jones wasn't sure.

The structure Jones found himself in consisted of only a roof. The lack of walls allowed the pleasant breezes to blow through the supporting tree trunks undeterred. But their function as domiciles remained intact, as they kept out the sunlight. Jones and the others knew just how important this was after experiencing the intense effects of prolonged exposure out on the high seas.

The group huddled around Tyler came over to Jones. The tattooed man sat next to him and Laia withdrew. The ten men made a circle around Jones, looking down at him with the same unmasked curiosity. Every face appeared the same. They whispered to each other in words he couldn't decipher. There was a pause and the men watched the tattooed man in anticipation, marking him as the leader.

Jones was afraid. Welcomed by Laia's beautiful smile, he knew he was saved, but for a moment before that he'd had no idea what ill fate might be in store for him. Barbarian behavior was unpredictable; yet, Jones still saw no reason to think of them as such. As long as they believed in some semblance of God, they weren't to be feared as enemies.

Fear is born where there is no conscience. Put your trust in God. Do this, and all the fears of this world will disappear.

He'd heard the words in a sermon, and they'd stuck with him ever since. And now that his faith was being put to the test, he tried his best to hold onto it. What did he need to do to strengthen his faith? Should he simply keep crying out to God inside?

The tattooed man placed his right hand on Jones' chest. Jones' heartbeat quickened. The man didn't smile. He kept silent, pressing down his hand with the utmost seriousness. His shoulders and chest were well defined and he exuded a sense of authority not found in the others. The tattooed man pulled his hand away and turned to everyone. After offering a few words, he got up and left. For reasons that escaped him, this put Jones at ease. Laia came immediately to his side again and held his hand. She was still smiling.

Ten days went by. Jones and Tyler were both recovering smoothly. They were being shown nothing but total kindness. Every day, Jones ate his fill of the local fruits: bananas, coconuts, mangos, baked taro root and breadfruit, most of it delicious. Jones was unsure of how they cooked anything, but the breadfruit was smashed and fermented, which gave it a certain pungency that was a little too much for his palette. Once he got used to it, he was able to eat it. The smell wasn't something he ever would have found back home and he found its sticky taste disgusting. The people of the island made it a staple of their diet.

Jones, Tyler, and Channing lived in separate houses and didn't sleep or wake up together. The natives understandably seemed to have misgivings about what terrible things the three strangers might conspire were they allowed to live together.

Tyler rebounded most quickly and only Channing was still at death's door. After a spell of cold sweats and incoherent mumbling, a healer was summoned to administer tree oils and incantations, but to no effect. People began to wonder whether he was really sick and thought that perhaps he was feigning his illness. In fact, Channing first began showing these signs right after he'd eaten Spice's flesh. It was as though he was making a subconscious plea to exempt himself from consideration should they go through all of Spice. *Don't eat me next unless you want to get this terrible sickness...* He was therefore left to recover on his own. The island seemed replete with curative power, and it was this which ultimately healed him.

Jones was the first to explore the landscape of this South Pacific paradise. Ocean blue and deep green filled his vision. The rocky shores and grass back in his hometown of Providence were beautiful enough, but Talofa was an incomparable realm unto itself. Everything that grew here was infused with the sun and even tasted of the sun. Bright green palm leaves sprouted distinctly along the coastline. The view was impeccable. Not one thing was obscured. The volcano stood proudly, striking a magnificent harmony with the cool river flowing at its base. The spectacular scenery was matched only by the beautiful women who inhabited it. There were no words to describe them in a Providence boy's vocabulary. Without exception, the women were genuinely kind and honest and embodied a carefree existence. Their system of kinship was nothing like what Jones was used to, however. Men and women weren't exclusively bound and could love one another as they wished. Of course, Jones could be granted this favor, too, if it was his pleasure. Paradise. After traveling through an inferno, he'd reached paradise. Like Laia, Jones believed this was a place that would never change...

9

For dozens, hundreds of days, the sun rose and set. Jones and his companions forgot about the calendar of the civilized world. They had no idea what the date was. They had an inkling that the eighteenth century had ended, but had no way of knowing for surc. And yet, none of the world's rampant corruption reached Talofa. On what should they base the end of one century and the beginning of the next? The island enchanted with its amazingly leisurely sense of time. Far removed from the everyday crimes of civilization, nothing existed here that even bordered on the hateful. There was no murder, no theft, and, in fact, no concept of personal property at all. Even adultery was impossible to commit.

Jones had been shown the peaceful world painted for him by his pastor. He wondered if thc picture hadn't been modeled on Talofa. His pastor's paradise was populated by a seemingly uncivilized people; it was a place where lions sprawled in the grass while people yawned at their side, not a particle of brutality between them. Wives and husbands ate wild fruits and children frolicked at their feet. Long-bearded elders waved as they climbed hills. They lived in perfect health, appreciative of everything they had. Dogs and cats played together. The gentle slopes of the hills were bathed in sunlight, with no indications of rain or storm. Because of this, the grass was always verdant. Everything from the smallest living organisms to the fiercest predators were granted equal life and infinite blessing. The only drawback was what to do with all that time.

"That is the utopia that all humans must strive to reach," his pastor had said. "This is how we will thrive in God's kingdom. Hard as it may be to imagine, it is a world without death."

The pastor's eyes had brimmed with joy at the thought. However, Jones wasn't so taken with it. Only fifteen at the time, his imagination was, however, quite precise. Living in a world without sickness or strife...he could think of nothing more boring and frowned at the idea. His pastor was concerned; he did not understand why Jones didn't view such a paradise with twinkling eyes.

Jones now found himself confronting that very problem which had made him doubt the pastor back then. It wasn't anywhere near as boring as he'd originally thought, and he began to suspect that perhaps his pastor had been right all along, so content was Jones with his life here, if only because of Laia's constant presence. Jones versed Laia in English, while she taught him the speech of the island. Talofa had no need for an extensive vocabulary, so Jones had a much easier time understanding Talofa's language than she did his. In the Talofan tongue, there were no ways in which to express complex emotions, as most words revolved around everyday objects, and its many homophones were easily distinguished by context. The two of them sat on the beach exchanging words, food, and keepsake shells gleaned from the sands. Laia touched his blond hair and Jones pointed to the flower in her hair. He taught her the meaning of the words *I love you* until she understood it and repeated the words back to him.

It had now been nearly a year since Jones arrived on Talofa.

Paradise

He was almost nineteen. Having lived exclusively in a man's world ever since he joined the crew of the *Philip Morgan*, this was the first time he'd ever felt anything akin to romantic love. But Laia and Jones saw love differently. The night before, Jones had witnessed something he never would have dreamed of and felt the many words shared between them turn to dust. He awoke with the pain of it fresh in his mind and went to look for Laia in the trees.

The women were sitting in a circle, beating tapa cloth in the shade. The clear rhythm of the mallets mingled with their familiar laughter, echoing melodically over the hills and the beaches.

Jones didn't have the confidence to tell Laia everything that was in his heart. Not only because of the language barrier, but because by doing so he would be opposing some of the island's customs. At the same time, however, he was too jealous to just stand by and let this happen. Yet "jealousy" was something Talofa had never known until the night before, when Jones tasted it for the first time.

Though only a half-moon hung in the sky, the night had seemed much brighter than usual. Jones lived on the outskirts of the Talofa village with two others of the same age. He'd been lured out onto the beach by the moonlight and walked along the rocks to where Laia lived. Her house was shaped like a large birdcage but the trunks propping up the roof made it difficult to see inside. Jones searched for Laia among the people sleeping peacefully on their mats; though there was no wind, the tapa cloths hanging from the rafters swayed enough for him to see that she wasn't there. Just then, he clearly heard voices behind him. Descending the stone steps, he went around the barn-like structure in the rear of the house and came out onto the shore where the mangroves grew thick. He spotted Laia on the sands beyond the overgrowth. Bathed in the moonlight, her body looked whiter than if he'd seen her at midday. She was face down, both hands on the sand, and beneath her was Wimo, her sister's husband. His face was obscured by the shade of the mangroves, but Jones knew it was him. His usual tunic was gone, and the smooth lines of Laia's waist were undulating as an elegant extension of his own. Jones just stood there with his back to the moon. And, just when he was having trouble breathing from the jealousy welling up in him, he lifted his head and met her eyes. Her cheeks flushed red as she faced the moonlight, her body moving beautifully according to the rhythm of carnal desire. Her large eyes were unfocused at first, but discerning Jones, opened wide as she smiled at him. When that charming, alluring look fixed itself on him, the passion left her face and her healthy girlishness returned. She actually seemed happy to see Jones there, as if there was nothing wrong in the act of being seen. Jones couldn't take any more of it. He stepped back, keeping his eyes upon her, before running back the way he came. Laia continued with Wimo as if nothing had happened.

For the rest of the night, Jones was haunted by the image of Laia's body in the arms of another man. It was strange to him. She was practically nude around him all the time, save for the tunic around her waist. Nevertheless, he could not forget the hue of her skin at that moment. The bright moonlit night had made her all the more alluring. Jones tried putting himself in Wimo's place as he recalled what he'd seen, but the image soon crumbled away. Jones had, of course, never touched her inside.

Paradise

As he expected, Laia was among the circle of women beating tapa cloth. Jones placed a hand on her shoulder. When she turned around, he signaled for her to come with him. She got up and followed.

There was a waterfall halfway up the volcano that grew into a small river and poured into the cove. He brought her through the river and the two of them sat on the bedrock, looking at each other in silence. Jones' face was stern, but Laia tickled his chest and forced a smile out of him. He grasped her hand and, speaking mostly through gestures, asked her who she loved most. She raised her right index finger and pointed it directly at his heart.

"Then you'll stop doing that with Wimo."

"Wimo?"

Though Jones brought up Wimo, she still didn't understand the reasons for his displeasure.

"I can't...with Wimo?" she asked again. Jones nodded.

"Why...?"

"Why? Because it hurts me. Look at me, I can't take it."

"Understand. In place you not see, I do."

Laia couldn't fathom jealously, and so she had no way of knowing his pain.

Jones shook his head in frustration.

"No! That's not it. I don't want you to do that with anyone. Whether I see it or not..."

"Why...?"

Her eyes grew round.

"Because...my heart can't take it."

"Why? Why?" Laia's surprise was endless. "So, who I do with?"

Jones wanted to point to himself. However, in his faith, sex just for pleasure was strictly forbidden. Seeing the dilemma he was experiencing, Laia said, "You, with me, not do."

"It's forbidden by God."

"God? What is God?"

Jones wondered if a people who had no word for jealousy could be made to understand the concept of God. He tried anyway. *God was...God was...* But nothing came to mind. Was there no word for God on Talofa? No, he *had* heard one. Upstream from the river, above and deep beyond the waterfall, there slumbered a myth from ancient times... If anything, it was equal to what he called God. Jones pointed towards the backwoods of the dense jungle above the waterfall.

"God...God is there."

Laia looked back and forth a few times before she was at last enlightened as to what God meant. It was something that no human power could ever approach—the same unpredictable force that made the land tremble and fire spew from the mountain's summit. It had also given birth to countless legends and myths and had guided Laia's people to Talofa. God slept in some guise in the far reaches of the jungle.

At that moment, Laia understood: God was not a definite idea, but a special sensation. It was beyond smell, beyond music, the realm of a sixth sense. Though only vaguely, Laia could sense what Jones spoke of.

"You, see?" said Laia as she gazed beyond the waterfall.

"See what?"

"God."

Jones laughed.

"No, you can't see God."

But Laia shook her head, a most serious expression on her face. She turned to the side.

"God, there, always, above."

But Laia had never actually seen it. Much of the island's folklore touched upon a mysterious force deep in the jungle, and she thought perhaps some object there corresponded to Jones' God. At first she was just speculating, but soon, images etched deep in her subconscious began flowing into her mind.

...God is there, God is there. Nestled in the jungle, where the sunlight didn't reach... An aged megalith shaded by intertwined ivy... Something was there. Laia had yet to see it with her own two eyes, but she knew God was there.

"You can't see God with your eyes," Jones repeated.

"We go, there," Laia pointed. "If go, you understand."

Laia was driven by an impulse to go to that place. It was barely visible from where they lived and the Talofans avoided it completely. It wasn't necessarily forbidden to climb up the volcano, but there was an unspoken agreement which kept anyone from even trying. Because it was far from the shoreline, where food grew in abundance, no one had reason to risk the dangers of exploring too far inland. It was a different world on the mountain, and no one had any desire to search uncharted territory.

"You, go?" Laia beckoned him.

"Is it far?"

"Not know, never go."

"You know the place?"

"I think I know."

Clouds flowed above the island, blanketing the mountainside in shade down to the ocean. Unseen birds twittered deep in the woods; the leaves shook but the bird calls seemed almost wholly contained by them and served to deepen the overall silence. Under the sun, such quiet had a dignity and mystery that was altogether different from the silence of nighttime. Jones was moved. More so than Laia's innocence in wanting to go see "God," it was the profound quietude of that slice of time in the valley that moved Jones to make the trip.

"Okay, let's go."

When they reached a steep cliff, Jones wondered how they were ever going to scale it. The only plausible way was to climb the rocks on either side of the waterfall, but Jones surmised there were paths that only the people of the island knew about. He felt uneasy, but he had to trust Laia.

In addition to her usual skirt, she was wearing a tapa cloak draped loosely about her shoulders. Whenever Laia and the other women worked tapa cloth in the woods, where the palm leaves provided only some relief from the sunlight, the cloaks were worn for extra protection. Laia was still wearing hers and she lifted its hem as they waded through the water. When they entered the shade, a cool breeze brushed past them. This, along with the cool water at their feet, made them feel like they were in another world entirely.

The sound of the waterfall grew louder. The basin was quite deep, the spray from the rocks below adorned by a rainbow. As they approached the cliff, Jones was hoping Laia would end their expedition there.

But she took him by the hand, saying, "This way, this way," and led him into the overgrowth at the basin's edge. They hoisted themselves up using the tree trunks for support. However, climbing the nearly three hundred foot cliff was backbreaking work. Laia was calm and collected, going up effortlessly as if she'd done it since birth. When they soon came upon bare rocks with no footholds in sight, Jones had no idea how Laia could go any further. A moment later, she disappeared. Jones immediately looked down, fearing she'd fallen. His head swam from the height and he turned back to see Laia's hand beckoning him from a crevice in the rocks above. Jones went up to her and slipped into the hollow where she'd hidden, only to find that it extended into a cave. Cool air brushed past him from deep inside.

"This way."

Laia grabbed Jones by the hand and led him in.

"But it's dark. I can't see a thing."

"It okay, if go, understand."

In the darkness, Jones had only the rustling of Laia's cloak and the occasional touch of her warm hand to guide him. From these sounds, he projected an image of her in his mind, weaving her way skillfully through the rocky passageway. It was less the narrow space and more Laia's closeness that nearly suffocated him. Her scent, her breathing, and the contact of their skin made him feel her all the more intensely. The cave sloped upward and Laia's waist brushed his nose. He could smell her in the darkness, and she radiated womanhood more strongly than ever before. When he reached out a hand to touch her, he could see her as vividly as the dawn. And just when he was dizzy with the sensual images in his mind, the sun peeked through a gaping hole high above his head. The opening looked like a distorted crescent moon. Jones looked up at it for a long time. The sunlight increased steadily and shone upon their feet.

When they got above ground, the soil was damp, which told them the source of the current lay close by. The water flowed in smaller streams below ground before joining to become the waterfall below. Jones was amazed that something so majestic and powerful emanated from such humble beginnings. Where was that vast energy hidden?

As they took in the beautiful view, Jones narrowed his eyes. The shoreline was obscured by the slope of the mountain, but the ocean was clear and infinite. From this, he knew just how far they had climbed. He could just see the whitecaps frothing on the waves. He turned around and looked up at the summit. The mouth of the volcano was farther up and he couldn't even guess how much longer they would have to go to reach it. In that direction, there was much less vegetation, and towards the top it was sheer rock. Of course, Laia wasn't aiming for the top and guided him into the dense overgrowth of the slopes.

Jones was worried.

"Do you know where we're going?" he asked.

Without answering, Laia gazed into the jungle with a gravity he'd never seen in her before. She was completely fixed on it. Every sense in her body had been awakened and heightened in search of something. If she did have the ability to sense the presence of "God," then she would find it.

Having chosen her path, she started walking. Jones followed close behind. Laia then stopped, turned around slowly, and chose a more precise direction. The large tree leaves blanketed them in dark shade. They spotted a heavily shaded arch, its base covered in ferns. Their feet squished in the soil as they walked. A fog rolled in and enveloped them. There were no sounds of flying birds, no calls of animals. Jones was nervous but wasn't sure why. He simply walked behind Laia. When the mist cleared, a large silhouette loomed before them. Jones became dizzy just looking at it. He felt like he was going to fall, but somehow endured it. Laia placed her hands to her face and looked up at the shadow. She walked over to it, determined, and touched it, then turned around and called to Jones.

"Here, come."

He extended his right hand. His fingertips touched cold, moss-covered stone. The statue was fifteen-feet tall and ten-feet wide. The top of it divided the trees, revealing a face above them.

......This is God?

Jones tried to laugh, but nothing came out. He didn't feel like laughing. Jones had been taught by his pastor that idolatry in any form was meaningless, but now that he was faced with this thing, he was suddenly at a loss for words.

Laia broke off the small branches, pulling away grass and moss from the stone's surface. Jones helped her by using long fallen branches and even climbing some trees. Together, they managed to remove a veil of excess from most of the south-facing surface. How long, they wondered, had it taken to create such a thick layer? Certainly more than generations. More than centuries. They noticed that something was carved into the rock. The surface was dark and the design still unclear. Laia removed her cloak and wiped the stone. Jones leaned a rotted tree trunk against the statue and climbed it to clean the area above her. Gradually, a vivid red began to peek through here and there. In order to see the entire image, they had to look at it from a distance.

When they were finished, Jones climbed down, pulled the log away and took a few steps back. As the image grew smaller and smaller, it became clear. He felt dizzy again. Why was there an image like this in such a place? A crimson deer was rendered clearly in the stone. Its fine lines appeared to have been modeled after a constellation. The front legs were bent with great power as the deer prepared to leap into the sky. It was an image of conviction, infused with a strength of will that went into its creation. Was this the heart of Talofa mythology? Had this guided the Talofans to their island? Jones was tempted to kneel before it. Not knowing why...

"Are there deer on this island?" he asked, unable to keep his mind clear.

"Deer? What is 'deer'?" Laia replied simply. She made no efforts of her own to name the animal painted in the stone.

"This is called a deer."

Jones pointed to the red deer. However, from the way Laia asked her question, his own was answered. They had no word for deer. The only animals he'd seen on this island were boars, dogs, chicken and wild fowl. He was certain there were no deer at all.

If that's the case, then what is this? There was no mistaking the design for anything else. How was such a thing possible? Who painted it and what was it modeled after, then? When was it made?

Jones didn't notice yet that the statue was facing due south, which meant the deer was jumping into the east...

"You, with me, do?"

Laia pulled him close. This was a most unlikely time to be seduced and Jones was bewildered. The upper half of her body was bare. She exuded nothing but confidence. It said: *You can't refuse me any longer*. He wrapped his arms around her. Scattered light slipped through the leaves and illuminated the clods of dirt they'd just stripped from the stone. The sun rays were lean but blinding. Jones bit Laia's bottom lip gently. Suddenly, he remembered the taste of Spice's flesh and his mouth watered. Spice had no odor or taste to him, but Laia's lips were sweet. There was no feeling of disgust and his heart was uplifted. It made him feel alive. A doctor could have taken his pulse off his capillaries, so vigorously was his blood coursing through him. Why hadn't he ever thought of it before? There was a way to make love to Laia without turning his back on his faith. It involved a certain decision on Jones' part. And the stone statue that embodied, in the form of a people's myth, a dream which a man had failed to see come true in his lifetime, yet which had spanned generations and accumulated as the memories of their very cells, loomed before the two now, urging another man to a decision.

The fern leaves were cold to the touch, Laia's body warm.

10

Jones and Laia were bound body and soul. Ed Channing could not watch them without thinking bilious thoughts.

......Just when the three of us are supposed to stick together, he falls for a woman!

His eyes twitched. He spat onto the beach. Now that Jones was in love with a Talofan woman, he would probably never want to leave the island. Ed Channing didn't like it one bit. Jones was completely enchanted by Talofa and made no effort to hide his affection for Laia.

As if that wasn't enough... Tyler is our only hope and I have no idea what's going on in his head. Well, he's been crazy from the start.

Channing tacitly set to work doing what he did best. He would just build his own boat and return home alone. However, he had no tools and there was no iron on Talofa. They did use axes in their festivals, but these were made of stone. The only iron he had was in the two harpoons he had from the *Philip Morgan*, but these too were useless. Besides, he didn't have to make anything too elaborate to cross the Pacific by himself. He therefore decided to construct a large raft in secret. As one who was always bragging about his skills, he was ashamed to be building a makeshift raft. Yet the first thing he ever built had been a raft. With this in mind, he sighed as he went about the island gathering whatever raw materials he could find.

As Jones devoted all of his attentions to Laia and Channing absorbed himself in his lone endeavor, Tyler searched the island for a "fight." He soon found, however, that fighting was not only nonexistent here, but unnecessary. They never even had disputes over food. If they were hungry, all they had to do was climb a tree. There was no need for manual labor or agriculture, as the continual sunlight made for ripe fruits all year round. Tyler felt there was nothing he could contend with.

One day, as he was gazing sternly out into the ocean, Tyler suddenly called Jones over for a haircut. All Jones had to work with was the harpoon tip, and he used it awkwardly to scrape Tyler's coarse blond hair. But when he was done, Tyler placed a hand on his head and told him to cut it shorter. Jones moved the tip unskillfully and accidentally cut his scalp. Blood mixed with Tyler's sweat and rolled down his forehead. Tyler kept telling him to cut it shorter, shorter, until he was one step away from being completely bald. Once he touched his scalp and felt no hair, he finally released Jones. Tyler then grabbed him by the head, which Jones took to mean he wanted to return the favor, but Jones shook him off. Having long hair was in accordance with the customs of this island, and Laia had braided it for him. The trust he'd shared with her, laying his head in her lap as she braided his locks, wasn't something he was going to throw away just to humor a fellow shipmate.

"You really love it here, don't you?" asked Tyler.

"I do."

Jones was being completely honest. Seeing as he had not a

single relative, going back home held little meaning for him. While he did miss the sights of Providence, he wouldn't give up his life with Laia for anything in the world.

"I'm about to die from boredom myself."

"What if you fall in love? There are plenty of beautiful girls on this island."

Tyler laughed. It had been a long time since Jones saw him smile.

"I'm not like you."

He said this insultingly, but Jones was used to Tyler's gruff attitude and took it without offense.

"Why's that?"

"Because, if I did fall in love here, I'd never have to fight for it. It doesn't do much for me without the challenge."

He wondered if this meant Tyler had only had women after fighting for them literally, but knew better than to ask. Tyler wasn't one to talk about women. Jones changed the subject.

"So what will you do, Tyler?"

As always, Tyler's answer was clear and concise.

"Finish off Violet."

Jones was surprised that Tyler's hatred for Captain Violet was so strong. But maybe that wasn't the case. Maybe Tyler was just looking for a nemesis, and Violet was the only one he had right now.

"You really hate the captain that much?"

"If he hadn't betrayed us, we wouldn't have been reduced to cannibals. Claude and Luz would still be with us. I'm going to find Violet and end that bastard's life once and for all."

Jones found it hard to sympathize. Captain Violet's betrayal was certainly upsetting, yet without it Jones might never have met Laia.

"But how will you ever find him? Seems like a lost cause to me."

Tyler was silent. He wasn't one to admit defeat. The only possibility was to go back to Violet's hometown and wait for him there. This was assuming that Violet was still alive. He and his men had stolen plenty of food and water, but that didn't mean they'd reached land safely. It was more likely, in fact, that they'd disappeared into the ocean long ago. Either way, Jones and Tyler had fate on their side in reaching Talofa.

"So I guess I can't change your mind, then?" Jones asked.

"It'll weigh on my conscience no matter where I go."

"But you'll never get Violet if you stay."

"And what about you? You're content to die here?"

"I'm fine with that...because, actually...Laia's pregnant." Saying this, Jones cast a sideways glance at Tyler and searched his face. Tyler broke into a smile and looked into the sky.

"Good work, boy!" he shouted.

Then, he quickly grew serious and, with his large hand, grasped Jones' neck firmly.

"But how do you know it's your child...?"

Talofa was a matriarchal society. Women didn't devote their fidelity to just one man, which made the father of any child virtually impossible to determine, so Tyler had a point. Jones couldn't be completely certain. Ever since he'd ventured upstream through the waterfall and made love for the first time with Laia in front of the red deer statue, she had made her vow to Jones quite clear: she would not love anyone other than him. Jones wanted to believe her, but he couldn't trust a promise provoked by his own jealousy. Such narrow-minded emotions threatened the very social fabric of this island.

"I'll know once it's born. If it has blue eyes and blond hair, that'll be all the proof I need."

Jones then looked at Tyler strangely.

"What is it? Why are you looking at me like that?"

"Come to think of it, you've got blue eyes and blond hair just like me..."

For a moment, silence reigned between them. Tyler then started to laugh so hard he eventually had trouble breathing. He grabbed a handful of sand, threw it up into the air, and rolled on the beach.

"So what if I did? If I slept with Laia and her child was mine, what would you do about it?"

"Fight."

"Are you actually challenging *me* to a fight?"

Tyler was simultaneously shocked and amused.

"I learned from you."

"I'm surprised."

"Why?"

"There never used to be such a thing as jealousy on this island. You're the one who brought it here. When in Rome, do as the Romans. Don't get too serious."

"And what about you? You're trying to bring conflict to a place that hasn't seen a single fight," said Jones reproachfully. It was the first time he'd ever verbally opposed Tyler.

"That's *my* problem, you fool. You're the one who's destroying this society by trying to impose your feelings on others."

"Destroying? How could I possibly be destroying it? What could be more natural than a man and woman making a child together?"

"We're upsetting the natural order just by being here. There's no labor on Talofa and no need for strong family ties. Talofa is really like one extended family. Who would ever devise such a system? Certainly not us. Not even God. It's the nature of the place itself."

Remembering how naturally they'd created a little society of their own in twenty days of drifting out at sea, Jones quickly realized his error in trying to apply the standards of the civilized world to Talofa. The unforgiving sun, the hunger, the thirst, and the despair that they induced... Factors beyond the control of human volition coming together to form a system slowly but surely. They could never have imposed, on that boat, the norms of a halcyon island.

Back in that hell, thought Jones, Tyler was truly intense. Though Jones would never forget the sensation of eating another human being, it was Tyler's forcing him to it that left the stronger impression. Tyler had a twang.

"Tyler, why do you enjoy fighting?" Jones asked abruptly.

"You like peace don't you?"

"Of course I do. Death doesn't appeal to me."

"When I was in the navy, there were a lot of guys just like you. Actually, there were *only* guys like you. They hated fighting, feared death, and took every opportunity to wax about the virtues of peace. But when they became marines and faced the harsh realities of war, they turned into ruthless killers who would do anything to survive—and still kept their peaceful ideals intact. It was amazing. After all, they were surrounded by ocean with no place to run. Peace meant simply the absence of enemies, so it was only natural that they eliminated anything and anyone that stood in their path. But I'm different. I always try to live as a warrior."

A warrior? Jones didn't quite understand the distinction. How was it any different from being a soldier? Tyler saw the confusion on Jones' face and answered for him.

"A warrior dies dancing."

But the word *warrior* stuck in Jones' head. Afterwards, when he was asked by Laia, "That person, what is he?" he remembered the word. Laia was, of course, referring to Tyler, and she was asking what made him tick.

The Talofan festival was drawing near. Laia explained to Jones her role as honorary dancer, and he realized for the first time that the island did have something of a profession after all. He explained to Laia that, in the same way she was a dancer, he was a sailor. Even as he said this, however, his life as a sailor didn't seem real anymore, as if his actions had been those of another person.

"So, your friend, strong man, what is he?"

Jones wanted to say he was a soldier, but he had to respect Tyler's self-definition.

"A warrior."

He explained it to her in the simplest terms. Of course, he couldn't tell Laia that a warrior was someone who died dancing, as it might have disturbed her as a dancer. But there was no need for too many words. For some reason, she understood him readily.

"Understand, him, warrior," she said, her eyes filled with yearning.

Knowing he would never live a warrior's life like Tyler, Jones was envious.

"Also on Talofa, warrior, Niku."

She pointed towards the center of the village. Jones knew who Niku was. He was Talofa's chief, the imposing tattooed man. The same man who, with a single touch of the hand, had inspired great fear in him. Tyler inspired that same sense of unquiet awe, so it only made sense that Niku was worthy of the title as well.

"Other man, what is he?" she asked.

As far as he knew, Ed Channing had stayed in his own little shell ever since he got to the island, and the natives eyed him warily. Jones found him exasperating, and the man's getting a bad reputation wasn't exactly good news for Jones or Tyler either.

"A shipwright."

Jones spoke of Channing's masterful abilities.

"Make boat?" Laia asked, pointing to one of Talofa's typical double canoes on the beach. "That kind?"

Jones shook his head. He'd never actually seen any of Channing's ships. If all the boasting was to be believed, he was capable of building something ten times better than a canoe. Jones drew a long line in the sand with his foot about the length of a keel and spread his arms.

"A boat this big."

Laia's eyes went wide with surprise.

"Amazing."

She visualized the large ship above the sand. The size of it made such an impression on her that, later that day, she told

Niku about it. Channing could make an enormous boat... Niku took Laia's vision a step further when he made a decision that was to alter thousands of years of history.

When the deer statue had been polished and the red hue of its emblem seemed to pulse again, as though the will painted into it had been reawakened, a kind of mindset softly descended on the island and began to exert control over its inhabitants. This, coupled with rumors of gigantic boats, revived an ancient myth. Not one person on the island was aware that a myth was coming back to life.

The people of the island focused their efforts on the upcoming celebration, which was meant to bind all their wills into one.

11

All Talofa was bustling with activity. Laia especially was looking forward to this day when she could demonstrate her talents fully. Yet, by now she was nearing the end of her pregnancy, and three days before the festival, it was clear she was in no condition to dance. Laia would have to be a spectator.

The festival began at sunset, filling the night with music and dancing. Shark skin drums resounded with a steady rhythm, accompanied by tritonic singing bows strung with hemp fibers. The melodies were simple, but because of the intensity of the rhythm, they echoed beyond the waterfall and shook the red deer statue to its foundation in the gloomy darkness, until the deer itself was dancing.

The elders joined in as well, slapping wood and clacking stones together, while Laia's chosen replacement joined in freely and swayed her hips at the center of the circle. Everyone but Laia, who was deep into her pregancy, and Jones, who stayed with her outside the circle, seemed caught up in the rhythm. Even Tyler was dancing.

The music, song, and dance had a unity. Some invisible force of attraction pulled the people together, and the seeming disorder flowed in one direction. Though there was no evident drama, time seemed to flow in reverse toward a primordial chaos when life and death were one, as at the beginning of the universe. Unnoticed, a legend was coming back to life. Roused by the tides of their ardor, an ancient myth had awakened. Formless wishes and dreams from an ancient time, when mankind was still young, were etched as afterimages into the consciousness of everyone participating in the festival; while they would soon forget the sights and sounds of their celebration, the memory of these afterimages would remain, deep within their being.

Laia went into labor. She fell face up onto the sand and felt the vibrations of dancing feet behind her. And, in the instant when she felt at one with the land beneath her, she gave birth to a healthy baby boy. Its cry was erased by the din of the festivities, but Jones was right by Laia's side and heard his son's voice clearly. Illuminated vividly in the torch light, the newborn's hair glistened with amniotic fluid. Jones looked closely and saw that his eyes were blue. He then severed the umbilical cord with a stone knife, forgetting all about his conversation with Tyler.

The festival continued all through the night.

Two days later, Niku appeared before Jones, accompanied by two younger men. He said something to Laia. Jones was holding his son in a swaddle of cloth.

"Shipwright, where?" asked Niku. Neither Jones nor Tyler knew what Channing was up to.

"I don't know." Jones tilted his head.

"Something ask, have, we."

"Ask Ed Channing?"

"Yes."

"What?"

"Big boat make. He do. Laia say yes."

Jones turned to Laia and remembered how he'd exaggerated Channing's talents.

"Why?"

Niku looked out towards the rising sun.

"We go east."

"Where in the east?"

"I not know. Go east. Not know where."

The Talofan people had come to the island thousands of years ago after a long voyage at sea, so it was no surprise if their yearning for the ocean returned. But what had evoked such a collective desire now? Was it the festival or simply the rumors surrounding Channing? Whatever the cause, Channing's intention to build a large raft overlapped with the Talofan people's intentions perfectly. Though his project had proceeded at a snail's pace, Channing had mixed feelings upon learning that the whole island wanted to help him out. Building a raft together with the islanders was not a problem. His worry was that he and they might not have the same destination in mind. Channing made sure about this.

"Are you really going east? Really? East?"

He tried explaining to them that if they sailed north and caught the equatorial current, there was a strong chance they would land on American soil. Niku nodded firmly to Channing's question.

"East, we go."

"Understood. Suits me!"

Channing nodded, satisfied.

12

Meanwhile, the object of Tyler's hatred was alive and well. Violet and his crew had reached Tahiti even before Jones and the others drifted ashore on Talofa. All eleven of them suffered some skin inflammations from the constant sun, but Violet's bravado paid off, as there were no casualties. They stayed for a little over a year in Tahiti, waiting for a ship that might bring them back. A French or English warship wasn't likely to have enough room for all of them, so they decided to wait for an American whaling rig in need of sailors or some kind of privateer to call at port. No matter what the ship, the captain was sure to be concerned about two things: money, and making sure there were enough people on his ship at any given time. Just enough sailors were kept on board that could be sustained by whatever food and water they had. But many lost their lives at sea and ships often docked with a shortage of hands. Violet was looking for just such a ship and planned to propose a contract should the opportunity arise.

His waiting paid off. One year and some months later, an American privateer dubbed the *Rattlesnake* dropped anchor in Tahiti. The *Rattlesnake* was a pirate ship involved mainly in contraband trade. Since leaving its home port of New Bedford, the *Rattlesnake* had been in continuous pursuit of another privateer called the *Florence*, known to be harvesting a spice newly discovered in the South Pacific islands. Two years before, the captain of the *Florence* had brought back a large cache of spices with a fragrance finer than anything being gathered in Sumatra and Borneo at the time. One in particular, touted as an aphrodisiac, garnered a high price on the black market, from which the captain made himself a tidy sum. Once his rivals became aware of this new commodity, they wanted to know the origin of the exotic spice, but the captain of the *Florence* guarded his secret well. These unique spices were worth their weight in gold. If he were to divulge his secret, the treasure would be gone in a heartbeat.

Victor, captain of the *Rattlesnake*, refused to let it end there. He decided to follow the *Florence* on its next voyage once he was sure they were headed for the South Pacific. The *Florence* pulled quietly out of the harbor during the early morning hours when the waters were calm. Victor anticipated this move and was ready to follow.

After trailing the *Florence* for a year, the *Rattlesnake* followed her into Tahiti's harbor. It was there that Victor happened to run into Violet. When they were younger, they'd sailed together on a three-year voyage, during which Violet had actually saved Victor's life. So, after meeting again in such an unlikely place, Victor accepted Violet and his men without question and they were welcomed aboard the *Rattlesnake* as members of the crew. With this, the ship's crew surpassed fifty. The ranks of ruffians from pirate and slave ships reinforced thus, they wouldn't be outnumbered. Once they found out where the spices grew, Victor would be more than ready to wage battle with the *Florence*.

After a ten-day sojourn in Tahiti, the *Florence* set sail again. Victor and his newly fortified crew waited until its masts sunk just out of view before they followed them anew. As long as they maintained the distance, the *Florence* would never suspect a thing. Their rivals were probably on to them already, but after coming all this way, they would never abandon their voyage and return without collecting what they'd come for.

However, three days after setting out from Tahiti, the *Florence* disappeared unexpectedly among the silhouettes of islands that dotted the horizon. The *Rattlesnake* hoisted its sails and slalomed through the islands, but the ship was nowhere to be seen. It seemed the *Florence* had been waiting for this opportunity to pull off some navigational sleight of hand. Victor stamped his feet and cursed himself. After all their efforts, their year-long voyage now amounted to nothing.

It wasn't an easy task to find a ship once they lost sight of it and Victor sailed far and wide to spot it again. He took out his anger on the crew, who fought back with equal dissatisfaction. They were in a tight spot. If finding the *Florence* was a lost hope, they at least wanted something for their trouble. Tensions were sure to mount to destructive levels if they didn't do what they'd come to do. They were used to a little danger now and then, but what was the point if they couldn't get compensated for it? With greed in their hearts, these men had endured tight quarters without women for over a year. No matter what wicked thoughts they withheld, it was no mystery that the crewmen were all hungry, not only for food, but for something to calm their shattered nerves. Blood, flesh, anything. What they wanted went beyond money. What they wanted was an outlet for their rage.

And just when they were reaching the end of the food and water supply stocked in Tahiti, a dark volcanic island loomed ahead of them. Once they were close enough, they saw the waterfall as a thin glittering line in the distance. At the very least, they would have plenty of water.

That island was Talofa.

The *Rattlesnake* prepared to drop anchor. It was still early morning, and the final vestiges of night lingered in the crisp air.

13

Where did they find such an amazing amount of energy? Jones was in awe, admiring the Talofan people all over again. For an island that had no physical labor to speak of, they showed great industriousness in banding together for the project. Their efforts were bound by something even greater than for the festival. The trees felled in the jungle were carried to the site, where they were notched with stone axes, then piled and assembled. With each passing day, the raft grew one step closer to Channing's vision. Under Niku's guidance, labor was divided fairly and the work progressed without a hitch. It was Tyler's unspoken duty to ensure that the finished product was seaworthy. His masterful navigational skills would see to it that the raft went where it was supposed to. The South Pacific currents, and especially those near the equator, all flowed from east to west. Sailing against the current was therefore easier said than done. Then why did they have to go east? No one on Talofa would have been able to answer such a question. Just as it was meaningless to ask why people fell in love, it was pointless to ask for a reason. At any rate, they had to go east, to where the sun rose. Perhaps this had a special meaning, but in the same way that most human acts were quite meaningless, there was nothing to do but to accept that some impulse of unknown provenance had worked its way into them long ago.

Laia's child was growing well. When Jones was thinking of

what to call him, names such as Eddy, Ralph, and Andy came to mind. But when he realized that the boy would not be growing up in civilization, he thought it was only appropriate that he have a name indigenous to the island. He asked Laia for her opinion, and decided on the name Aida. It was not a very masculine sounding name, but its similarity to the English word "idea" gave it a ring of intelligence. Jones ultimately chose to stay behind on the island. He could have joined the others if he wanted to. He spoke with Laia on the matter numerous times. Laia's thought was the same all along: *I will follow you wherever you wish to go*. Jones chose paradise. It would be difficult saying goodbye to Tyler. But otherwise, he would have no regrets. He'd become disenchanted with what he once knew as "civilization."

The raft was nearing completion. A select twenty of Talofa's young men and women would join Tyler and Channing. With the prospect of this new voyage, Tyler's typical eagerness returned full force, because, for him, purposeless adventure was the norm for a warrior. A string of futile deeds upon each of which he might stake his life was the only kind of existence that made him feel alive.

"I'll be praying for your safety, Tyler," Jones said.

How foolish he'd been to think that Tyler may have been Aida's father. Tyler wasn't the kind to fall in love like most people or get mixed up in some love triangle. He was in a class all his own, and Jones now realized that whatever doubts he harbored had been born out of envy. Perhaps it was a silly thought, but were Jones a woman, he probably would have fallen in love with Tyler. No matter how much he tried, he knew that he would never even approach Tyler. Though Jones would feel a little lonely without his shipmate around, he knew Tyler had to escape if he was going to find some equilibrium. A reckless soul like his was out of place in paradise, and whatever his presence provided was no match for a woman's love and comfort.

"You know, you're even starting to look like them," Tyler said brusquely.

"Is that a compliment or an insult?"

"Neither, really. All I mean is that you've managed to rid yourself of the stench of civilization."

"The stench of civilization"? Can't you put it better than that? Jones thought as he clicked his tongue. *Why do I even bother fishing for compliments from this man?*

"So, you plan on going home?" he asked.

"I don't know, we'll go as far as we can. I need to repay these people for their kindness and my life here. I'd like to see Violet dead, but for the time being these people are my top priority."

Tyler and Jones were sitting on the deck of the nearly finished raft as they talked. The morning work had yet to begin, so Channing was the only other one there, giving everything a final check from all angles. The raft was being assembled on the south side of a hill opposite the village, a high place that overlooked the bay. Because Channing had originally chosen this inconvenient location to operate in secrecy, it was far from an ideal spot to continue in, but too much had been done to move it elsewhere.

Jones and Tyler were unexpectedly interrupted as Laia came bounding through the overgrowth with Aida in her arms, breathing heavily and with a seriousness that was uncharacteristic of her. The aged tattoo artist appeared behind her.

"Come this way," Laia said, taking Jones to the hill where

they could see the bay. "Look!"

She pointed to a ship anchored out at sea. A wriggling snake was painted broadside, and next to it the word "Rattlesnake," though the name was illegible from this distance. A stench of evil wafted from the ship, and they could smell it.

Laia had foreseen the ship's arrival, having dreamt the night before of something that had lost its way coming to the island. Laia, who rarely woke up in the middle of the night, was startled from her sleep, knowing that the ground would shake. Then, not ten seconds later, the earth trembled violently beneath her. The wildlife of Talofa cried out and the sky echoed with birds flocking away. The earthquake soon abated, yet her premonition grew stronger. Something would come. Soon. It was then that a sudden flash of intuition told her what she needed to do to prepare. She would have to get a tattoo, as did Jones and Aida. She even knew the design: the red deer. All three of them needed to have this image on their bodies...

When Laia awoke that morning, she searched among the elders for the tattooist Tokuma. The shadow of something long foreseen had at last caught up with them. They had to hurry. Holding her son, she took Tokuma's hand and ran for the hill to find Jones.

Laia and Jones looked down at the *Rattlesnake* as it floated in the mouth of the inlet. Certain that this ship was her premonition come to life, Laia knew it meant nothing but trouble. What frightened her was not the ship's presence itself, but the unshakable feeling that something even greater was to follow.

Before they knew it, Tyler and Channing had come up behind them, looking down onto the open waters. Channing shouted for joy, knowing they would no longer need to finish the raft or risk the dangers of their planned voyage. If the ship would have them, they could get back home in no time. Regardless of who their captain was, Channing was sure he would find a use for his skills. He called out from the hill, waving his hand, and made to run down to the shoreline. But a moment later, Tyler grabbed him by the scruff of his neck.

"Don't even think about it," he said firmly, pressing down on Channing until the latter felt like he might sink into the dirt.

Channing managed to speak: "Wh-wh-what the hell do you think you're doing? Are you mad?"

"You're going to run away just like that and leave things unfinished here?"

"I-I know what I'm doing."

Though Tyler rarely asked for anyone's opinion, he said, "Jones, what do you think?"

Jones felt Channing was being insecure and cowardly and his gut reaction was to just let him go.

"It's fine. If he wants to go, let him go. The raft is as close to finished as it'll ever be. You'll manage just fine without him, anyway," Jones spat out.

Despite having been advised to release him, Tyler simply stood there staring at the ship. He was hesitant to let go after seeing the genuine fear in Laia's face. Her legs trembling, she clutched the baby to her chest and grasped Jones by the hand. Tyler believed that Laia had a sixth sense, never forgetting that she'd been the first to discover them and offer help when they came to the island. The fact that she treated these newcomers with the opposite reaction told him this was serious, a harbinger of things to come. It was obvious the ship wasn't a whaling vessel, nor a legitimate trading ship. Was it a pirate ship? And if so, what did they expect to find here? Tyler's misgivings weren't unfounded. He'd heard of the atrocities committed by pirates on small islands in the South Pacific, many of which had been decimated as a result.

That very danger was becoming a reality. Two boats were launched from the *Rattlesnake* with twenty men on each, and just as many muskets, their black-lustered barrels glittering in the morning sun. The men seemed to be itching for blood. A bunch of wooden containers were also loaded onto the boats, presumably to stock up on food and water. If that was the case, Tyler didn't care. There was more than enough water to go around, and Chief Niku would gladly offer whatever they needed. But if they demanded more than that...

As they rowed deep into the inlet, the men's faces were still hard to see, so there was no way Tyler could have recognized Violet astride the helm of one of the boats. The men variously shouldered their guns or rowed their boats toward shore.

Tyler couldn't take his eyes away. If he let Channing go, there was no telling what kind of disadvantage it would cause for Talofa. Tyler loosened his grip a little, but not enough for him to escape. They would have to scope things out until they knew for sure where the men were headed. Two dozen muskets, while all he had were harpoons... And yet, Tyler made a new resolution. He realized that he would have to protect this paradise at all costs, even if it was the last thing he ever did. It was his duty as a warrior.

Laia fixed her eyes upon the approaching boats, then turned to Jones.

"My wish, listen."

"What is it?"

"Our bond, want strong."

Laia called over Tokuma the tattooist, introduced him to Jones, and instructed him to give them each the same design.

"Okay?" Laia asked.

"What will he make?"

"Red deer."

Jones remembered the statue Laia had shown him above the waterfall.

"Why the deer?"

"I not know. If not same, bad!"

"It's fine with me, but won't it hurt for Aida?"

"Is okay, this child, strong child."

As Laia carefully explained the design to Tokuma, she laid on her side and stuck out her left arm. She wanted him to tattoo a deer running across the sky on her arm just below her shoulder. Tokuma first mixed some ground candle nut seeds with coconut milk to make the dark pigment. Then, applying it to the tip of a sharpened stick, he burrowed it into her skin by tapping from above. The moderate pain was actually comfortable for her if only because of what it represented.

While Laia, Aida, and Jones each got their tattoos, Tyler kept watch over the situation unfolding below. Once the boats reached shore, a man who looked to be their leader stepped onto the sands. Tyler watched as Niku, accompanied by a few men armed with spears, greeted and exchanged words with the man from the *Rattlesnake*. They were all just specks in the distance, so there was no way to hear what they were saying. It was like watching a silent play, but there didn't seem to be any tension in the air. After conveying their intentions through body language and gestures, the men seemed to reach an agreement. At this, the rest of the ship's crew grabbed their storage barrels and went downstream of the waterfall to fetch water. When they appeared again, the barrels were noticeably heavier and it seemed their request had been well met. The men piled the barrels onto the boats and rowed back to the *Rattlesnake*. Seeing that everything had gone off without incident, Tyler was relieved. The *Rattlesnake* quickly pulled up its anchor. Tyler waited eagerly for them to leave. Channing was raging in his grasp.

"A-are you a complete idiot? You're just going to let them leave? What the hell is wrong with you?"

After his furious spout, Channing broke down with a final appeal.

"Tyler, I beg of you, let me go," he said pitifully. "I want to go home. If I miss this chance, I'll never be able to go back again. I can build as large a raft as I want, but I don't think it'll ever get across the Pacific."

Tyler would have had no problem letting Channing go had the *Rattlesnake* not given him such an eerie feeling, but those last words offended him.

"Channing, you're not capable of making anything bad and you know it. The people of this island are depending on you. Your fate is sealed. You won't be getting on that ship. Stay here and finish what you started. That is your mission."

Ed Channing was close to tears as the two boats were hauled up the sides of the ship. Tyler hoped they would make a quick departure, while Ed Channing wanted the exact opposite. It seemed

God was on Channing's side, however, for the boats stopped and, after a moment, were let back down into the waters. Two more boats were then launched, making a fleet of four that carried the entire brigade of fifty armed men to the Talofa shore. As they approached the rocks, they broke formation to either side of the inlet. There were no barrels aboard, which could only mean one thing. Tyler let go of Channing's neck and stood up.

14

To explain this turn of events, we must go back in time a little.

While the young sailors went inland and filled their water barrels, Violet had stayed behind on the beach, taking in Talofa's scenery at his leisure. Through the gaps in the palms, he caught glimpses of a village in the distance and, more importantly, the beautiful women who populated them. Beyond the line of Niku's guards, the women were going about their daily activities, beating tapa cloth and playing their ukekes. Violet was captivated as one woman after another caught his eye, each more beautiful than the last. It then dawned on him that there might be hundreds of them on the island. He knew this would help to calm the frustrations that had befallen the *Rattlesnake* and appease any lingering resistance among Captain Victor's crewmen. In fact, this was an even better discovery, a new treasure far more valuable than any spices the *Florence* might have led them to.

Once the water had been loaded on board, Violet and Captain Victor discussed their options. At first, Victor was unconvinced.

"Are you sure there's that kind of money to be had?"

He turned to Violet with doubt written all over his face.

"You wouldn't be saying that if you saw these women, Victor. They're the most beautiful creatures you'll ever set eyes upon."

Victor compared the money he would obtain from the spices with that from these women.

"I'm not really familiar with that whole business, you see."

"Don't worry about it, just leave it to me." Violet laughed. "Women are sold into slavery all the time. I guarantee these brown beauties will fetch a high price."

Violet had plenty of experience in the slave trade from his younger days and possessed a detailed knowledge of it. Victor weighed the dangers of pillaging Talofa against the possibility of finding the *Florence*. The latter was pretty much a lost cause, but the women of Talofa were right here.

"Okay, it's settled then. Let's do it."

Once the decision had been made, Victor ordered that the boats be readied while he assembled his entire crew on deck. He explained the details to everyone, exaggerating the finer economic points to garner their support. The men cheered in unanimous approval of this proposition, ready to cross the waters and pillage their newfound treasure. Their eyes sparkled with the prospect of the fortune they would make from their catch. Just the idea of having captive women with them for the entire voyage home made them ache with a desire to touch their flesh.

"What about the men?" someone asked.

There was a long silence before Victor's answer.

"Kill them."

Talofa's warriors had only stone weapons and posed little threat to the sailors with their muskets. Killing these men and taking their women would be extremely easy. They soon forgot all about having lost the *Florence*.

Several navigational officers were left to tend the ship, while the rest boarded the boats eagerly and loaded their firearms. Their hearts throbbed with the thrill of the hunt, as if they enjoyed nothing more. What they never guessed, however, was that Tyler was lurking in the bushes overlooking the cape, watching their every move. Had they known he was there, Violet would likely never have spoken of attacking Talofa. Even with the protection of fifty gunners, Violet was smart enough to avoid a showdown with Tyler. As long as they were both alive, he knew Tyler would never forgive or forget the treacherous incident at sea, and that if they ever bumped into one another somewhere, Tyler would kill him. Violet had no desire to meet him again, as though Tyler had the strength of a hundred marines.

The boats rowed in two separate groups into the shallows. Once they were on land, they commenced an immediate pincer attack on the village. After a while, the sky pealed with fifty guns going off at once, their sound threaded by long screams and battle cries that blended into the beautiful serenity of the island. For the first time ever in Talofa's history, guns were sending metal flying through the air. With that, heaven became hell.

15

When Jones heard gunshots ringing in the morning air, the deer on his upper arm was only half finished. He sat up in surprise.

"Don't move!"

Laia pressed him down and bade Tokuma to continue. She looked down at the shore, only to see people running in all directions amid gun smoke and shouting. She watched as figures the size of a fingernail fell to the sand in scattered heaps. She knew that a tragedy far from ordinary was unfolding. As someone who knew nothing of fighting, however, the meaning of this scene was difficult for her to comprehend. Still, she said to Tyler:

"Please, do something."

"I'm planning on it."

Tyler was actually closer to giving up. He hardly stood a chance against fifty pirates armed with muskets when he only had two harpoons. Yet he made the decision to accomplish his mission as a warrior. As he'd said to Jones, a warrior was one who died dancing. He knew what these men wanted simply by observing how they fought. Women. They were here to kidnap the beautiful women of Talofa. In light of things he'd heard, such a heartless act wasn't hard to surmise. While normally, both the men and the women would have been taken and sold into slavery, the crew of the *Rattlesnake* were only concerned with high profits, and knew the women would fetch the best price. Tyler was fuming with hatred, so much so that he was in tears. He was, in fact, sad. This meaningless slaughter was upsetting enough, but even more, among these fifty outlaws, there wasn't a single warrior. Not one of them upheld the same standards that he did. They weren't true fighters and this made Tyler feel utterly alone. What were they fighting for? Money? Women? What they were doing, of course, was not true fighting. Try as he might, he couldn't understand the nerve it took to do what they did without shame. For him to feel this way was nothing new. That was why he'd had to become a warrior in the first place. The only way for an odd-man-out like him to live was to throw himself onto battlefields. He reveled in conflict, mind, body, and soul. It was a part of every human being's instinct, and Tyler was one of its most devoted servants. He couldn't live without fighting. But the pursuit of it inevitably led to death. It was a conundrum and now was the time to crack it. Tyler prepared for battle. He would ambush these men who killed merely for money and deal them the surprise, the empty deaths that they deserved.

As he watched the battle unfold before his eyes, he asked himself: *Why is it that, when the civilized and uncivilized wage battle, it's always the uncivilized whose bodies pile up in countless numbers? Has the opposite ever occurred?* There was some tapa cloth on the ground set aside for making sails on Channing's raft. Tyler cut a number of strips from this and wrapped them around his torso. *Why is it that when civilization pits itself against the past, the past always loses?* The tapa cloth, made from the bark of the mulberry tree, was incredibly resilient and perhaps could protect him from musket shots, except of course at close range. And in Tyler's case, any bullet that made it through would still have to get past his thick muscles to reach any vital organs beyond them. Though he was one man acting alone, Tyler vowed to kill many. The makeshift armor was merely a precaution to ensure he didn't fall to the first shot. Perhaps this was a contradiction. Filled with hatred, he readied himself to run into the massacre, his blood close to boiling.

"Tyler, I'm coming with you," said Jones as he shook off Laia's hand.

"No, you still need to finish your tattoo. What is that, a deer?"

The indigo-colored deer on his arm was nearly complete. It was impossible to make the deer red as Laia wanted. It would have to do.

"I'm fighting with you, Tyler."

Tyler held Jones' face in his hands.

"Do you like me?" he said with a strange intonation.

Tyler's hands burned. Jones was at a loss for words.

"I..."

"You what?"

"I worship you."

"Oh, is that so? Then shut up and listen to what I have to say. You're going to help Channing and take the survivors on their voyage east. You should have no trouble navigating the map. You'll get that big contraption off the ground just fine without me. Give it a shot. You're an excellent sailor."

Jones made to say something, but Tyler cut him off.

"Enough! I don't want to hear another word from you."

Tyler put a finger on Jones' arm and traced the nearly finished tattoo.

"It's an amazing tattoo. I'd get one myself if I had the time."

With this, Tyler turned around and, a harpoon in each hand and a stone ax hanging at his waist, disappeared down the hill. Jones did as he was commanded, and just silently watched him go.

Tyler knew he couldn't save Talofa on his own. All he could do was commit a meaningless slaughter himself. It would be much more meaningful, in fact, if he went on that voyage with the survivors and Jones. For a moment he wondered if he shouldn't actually head back, but his elated body refused to do so. Perhaps because he was going downhill, inertia drove forward his 250-pound frame. Another inertia worked on his will, and it wasn't possible to change course now. It all had to end sooner or later. Delaying his moment of truth was against his nature.

Tylcr soon ran into Ed Channing crouching in the bushes at the edge of the shoreline. Watching the appalling slaughter unfold before his eyes had dispelled any illusions he'd had of escaping. At first, he'd planned on appealing for safe passage on their ship, but now the thought of returning home with fifty murderers who'd wiped out the men who saved his life made his hair stand on end. He would much rather rot away on this beautiful island. Piles of corpses littered the beach, the white sands stained with blood. No more gunshots were heard. Victor had the women chained and lined up on the beach.

Channing's heart stopped as Tyler grabbed him from behind.

"You lunk, it's just me."

"Oh...y-y-you..."

With just one look at his expression, Tyler knew what Channing was thinking.

"Given up your plan, haven't you? Sure, their ship surpasses the raft you built, but that's not the problem. Go back. Jones and Laia are waiting. I think you'll be needed."

He made no answer.

"Be proud of what you've built."

Channing then spoke, his eyes still fixed ahead of him.

"Tyler, can I just look on from here?"

"At what?"

"At what you're going to do."

"Do whatever you want. But when you're done watching, go back to Jones and the others."

"U-understood."

As Tyler made to leave, Channing held him back.

"W-wait a minute, Tyler. What's that design on your ax?"

"Oh this? Tokuma carved it."

Tyler wrapped his fingers around the ornate handle, tested its weight, and swung it in the air a few times with a hum. It was as if the weapon had been made for him.

"Well, I'm off."

Tyler ran for the shoreline.

Tyler hung the ax at his waist and, brandishing the two harpoons, rushed out onto the beach at full sprint. Before him were nearly one hundred of Talofa's women, chained and frightened by the muskets pointed at their heads. The men surrounding them were too overcome with curiosity to be worrying about defending themselves. One of the sailors lazily pointed a finger at Tyler and said, "Hey, what's he up to?" At that moment, Tyler threw both harpoons and pulled out the ax from his belt, jumping into the enemy ranks as if trying to reach them before the harpoons did. One of the harpoons pierced the chest of the man who saw Tyler coming, while the other tore through the neck of another and lodged into the sand behind him. Watching the two men fall in succession, Victor was finally aware of what was happening. By then, Tyler was already finishing off a man with his ax, after which he broke the neck of a second. A third man drew out a dagger, but Tyler dodged his parry and dropped to the sand, hitting the man's knee with so much force that it bent backwards. The man died from shock. When Tyler got up, he broke the spine of a fourth man who was fleeing in terror, then turned around and brought the ax down on the forehead of a fifth. This last one was Violet. In that brief moment before the ax crushed his skull, Violet realized that the muscular man he thought was just a native had blue eyes and blond hair...and was in fact none other than Tyler in the flesh. Memories of the *Philip Morgan* flashed across his mind, and he was overcome with a strange feeling of both nostalgia and hatred. There was no mistaking it. Tyler was his executioner.

How? The thought repeated endlessly in his consciousness as his skull caved in and pressed into his brain. *Tyler, how?... Tyler, how?...* A chill fear swept through him. *What a strange place the world is!* And with that, nothingness engulfed him.

Using the cutlass he snatched from a sixth kill, Tyler lopped off the arm of a seventh. He was laughing, because he was asking the same question of Violet.

That couldn't possibly have been Violet I just killed! Why would he ever turn up in a place like this? What the hell is going on?

Tyler laughed boisterously, bathed in blood as he threw his enemies to the ground and crushed their bones like some warring demon.

"Run!" shouted Tyler in the Talofan tongue to the frightened, cowering women.

"Get out of here! Run into the jungle!"

The women ran. Many of them had chains on their feet, but managed to get themselves quickly into the backwoods. However, it was not only the women who fled. "It's Tyler!" came a cry, at which a number of Violet's men threw down their muskets and blades, scattering into the jungle in the women's wake.

Victor gathered ten of his crew and ordered them to load their muskets. Tyler noted this in the corner of his eye while he fought. As the ten men were packing in gunpowder, he knew they planned to fire at once. After they'd finished loading, they pointed their muzzles at Tyler. He held two corpses in front of him to stop the barrage of shots that came flying towards him. He was well protected, and the bullets merely met dead flesh. Tyler threw the bodies down and rushed his attackers. With no time to reload, the men threw down their guns as well and made a run for it. What they'd done to the Talofa natives a short while ago was now coming full circle.

Tyler let out a battle cry. His cutlass dripped with blood and his cheeks, indeed his whole body was colored a faint crimson. He exchanged his blood-dulled blade for a new one. He was ecstatic. His spirit was beginning to wander in a strange world, and he thought, *Now, this moment—I would gladly die.* This was the end. He could feel it. He'd been in many battles during his lifetime, but this was the first time he was feeling tickled by it.

Suddenly, he recalled making love to the only woman he had ever truly loved. Her tender skin, which he'd forgotten for the last few years, came back to him right now in the midst of reality's stench.

Outside the ring of the battle, Victor organized a second wave of gunners. He rounded up fifteen men this time and broke them into three groups for a rapid-fire attack. Tyler was on to their strategy now and wanted to catch them off guard before they were finished loading, but there were too many in his way. His tapa cloth was dripping with sweat and blood.

With the preparations in place, Victor shouted, "Fall back!" At this, a number of the men fell to the ground, while others hid themselves behind trees. Immediately after, five shots rang out, three of which hit Tyler square in the chest. They were slowed by his armor, which he'd soaked with water, and lodged themselves halfway into his thick layer of muscle. Tyler fell, but only to his knees. He gathered up two daggers and belted them at the waist. Victor watched him carefully. They mustn't waste their shots. He tried to figure out just how much the man could take. When Tyler jumped to his feet and started running towards them again, Victor hastily ordered his men to fire, but the target was still too far away to suffer any real damage.

As Tyler ran, he threw the daggers into the air. Two gunners in the third squad fell, but the other three held their aim and fired. One of the rounds grazed Tyler's temple and tore off an ear-lobe. He collapsed at last onto the sand. Salt water stung his wounds as the waves came in, but his silence concealed the pain. He heard the sounds of the ocea, and could see only the sky above him. His insides felt like they were on fire. When he managed to lift his head, the thirteen remaining gunners had lined up double file and were just finishing reloading. If he stood up, he was going to be rained by rounds of bullets. It was obvious. Still, he got up anyway. Then, raising the cutlass above his head, he charged. Seven guns went off at once, tearing through the now ragged tapa armor and collapsing Tyler's lungs. His throat gurgled with blood in rhythm with his heartbeat. Six more rounds exploded into his body. His short blond hair turned red with blood and Tyler reeled back onto the ground. He was still alive, but every breath was increasingly difficult. The morning sun burned brightly above, while the damp sand beneath him was cold. No regrets. He was satisfied with everything. He felt calm. Vision narrowed, voices grew distant. The golden sunlight clouded into a deep orange, then a red, then a black—and stayed black. John Glen Tyler was meeting his end.

Jones and Laia witnessed from afar every moment of Tyler's fighting. Laia was grateful to him. Many of their men were slain, but thanks to him the women had managed to escape safely into the jungle. Jones was in tears. Laia held his hand. Ed Channing walked back up the hill to join in their mourning.

With muskets and cutlasses in hand, the seventeen remaining men on the shores below timidly approached Tyler's body in the waves as if he were more than human, a monster they could never be quite sure was dead.

Just then, Laia started. For a moment, the colors she'd seen in her dream, the earthquake, and the terrible sense of foreboding made her forget about Tyler's death. She ran to the other side of the hill and looked out onto the open waters. The ocean was changing color. Though the sky was a magnificent blue, the ocean was heavily laden with gray. She'd known that something unthinkable would come from the open waters...

But it wasn't the *Rattlesnake* she'd foreseen. It was this.

The earthquake that morning resulted from a major tectonic shift a couple hundred miles off the coast. This sudden slip of the earth's crust had produced an enormous tidal wave. The color change was the first indication that the wave was coming their way, followed by a deep rumbling.

As the men on the beach were about to finish off Tyler once and for all, they stopped dead in their tracks, watching in awe as the tide pulled back suddenly. The gray waters quickly darkened and left a black film along the ocean floor. The *Rattlesnake*, still anchored, fell to the sediment and heeled to one side as the water receded around it. Victor and his men were struck dumb with fear.

Jones and Laia, watching from above, could see the edge of the water clearly as it pulled back. The ocean floor was much darker and uglier than they'd ever imagined. Stranded fish jumped around on the exposed gravel. Dogs and chickens were making frightened noises and the birds all flocked into the sky.

The water's recession halted a few hundred yards from the shore and the ocean's surface elevated as energy gathered from below. Waves then pushed forward, tumbling over one another with overwhelming force back towards Talofa like a mountain crashing in on itself. They came down upon the *Rattlesnake*, snapping its masts like twigs, reducing the ship to kindling. By the time Victor and the others saw the tidal wave heading for them, it was too late to run. They cried out and made a dash for the trees, climbing as high as they could go, but were immediately overtaken from behind by the raging tsunami.

When Jones and Laia saw the waters pull back into the sea, they'd immediately run for the raft. Whether they liked it or not, the time had come for them to leave. Ed Channing, who'd joined them along the way, and Jones grabbed onto the masts and waited for the sea to rise. Channing's decision to work on the raft on this small hill overlooking the cape had proven to be most fortunate. Had it been on the beach, it would have been destroyed just like the *Rattlesnake*. Though they didn't have enough food or water, Jones didn't care. As long as his beloved Laia and Aida were at his side, he could endure drifting at sea again for twenty days. It would be possible to replenish their supplies along the way. Jones caught a glimpse of Tyler's corpse as it was tossed about by the turbulent sea, but he didn't cry this time. He had gained much from the man; it wouldn't do to wallow in sorrow. He could still hear Tyler's voice loud and clear: *Fight! Fight whatever stands in your way!* The world was a strange place. It was a rough place. But Jones resolved anew to see it out. One step at a time, he'd try to approach Tyler. He'd journey into the unknown and peel away the world's veils one by one. *Tyler, watch me do it!* As though the plea had registered, Tyler's corpse sank into a surging wave and disappeared into the bottom of the sea.

The destruction of the island paradise that Jones had known for a year and a half was breathtaking. The time it had taken for the culture to mature and the time it was taking to bring about its extinction were beyond incomparable. What was truly breathtaking was that the same sun that had nurtured Talofa from its beginnings shone so indifferently upon its instant obliteration.

Paradise

The water level climbed past the hill. Jones, Laia, and Aida were clutching the same mast, while Channing held on to the other. The violent tsunami shook the raft and lifted them in a sheet of spray. When he felt the raft leave the earth, Jones looked up to the sky in relief. They were carried further and further upward, higher than any mountain—it felt like the sheer power of the water was carrying them closer and closer to the sun. Jones held Laia and Aida tightly, looking up into the blinding glare. The tattooed deer on his arm also turned towards the sun, animating itself as if to leap across the sky.

Part Three

The Desert

1

1990s, New York City

Looking out at the seats from the stage of the enormous concert hall, he felt like he was inside a large snail shell. No one has ever been in one, but Leslie knew at least three others who had the exact same impression: Ferard, the regular conductor, the double-bassist Kaschenbach, and Gilbert, the only one of the three who wasn't a musician. He would be sitting in on today's rehearsal and was scheduled to see Leslie afterwards.

Leslie Mardoff had been grateful to Ferard, who'd agreed to conduct his new composition, a symphony entitled *Beringia*. Because of irreconcilable differences over interpretation, however, Leslie finally told Ferard with great tact that he would conduct the piece himself. If the composer took the podium himself, the intention of the piece, at least, would be conveyed accurately. With arms outstretched, Ferard nodded repeatedly and said, "Sure, sure!" What he really thought went something like: "Have a go at it, hot shot. Let's see how you do trying to manage an orchestra." Leslie could never fathom the true intent behind words. Actually, he could, but he felt it was too much work.

A luminary among his generation of composers, Leslie Mardoff was thirty-four. At sixty, Ferard was nearly twice his age and knew firsthand the complexities involved in handling a large group of musicians. Though he had to admit that Leslie had conducting techniques down pat, he was certain that the orchestra members would greet his lack of experience with a mean-spirited recalcitrance and make him flounder. Ferard knew quite a few conductors who'd been forced to resign in the face of subtle boycotts. A conductor was only one man, who had to direct a band of more than a hundred. It was far from easy.

The recording date was coming up soon and the New York Philharmonic was about to begin its last rehearsal under the baton of a first-timer. Leslie stood out—passionate eyes, curly black hair, a stiff jaw that spoke volumes of firm resolve, and muscular shoulders, unbefitting a composer, that were noticeable under his shirt. He looked vaguely Asian. Most of the musicians knew all about his career and exploits from the magazines and had discussed the man with no little mirth. The fact that he was a quarter Native American served to make him more intriguing. He was also a playboy famous for a long string of affairs with various actresses and singers, one of whom was reportedly driven to a suicide attempt, an incident that compelled the media to portray him as a beast. How could a Casanova with Indian blood who looked like a heavyweight boxer create music of such refinement? Yet his music was indeed exceptional enough to make up for any flaws in his character, a fact that all but a handful of composers admitted.

Leslie's presence at the podium caused a peculiar disharmony on stage. When, with the snail-like curves of the walls of the upper seats behind him, Leslie's conspicious figure raised the baton, the air became thick with an oppressive imbalance. None of the players of the New York Philharmonic liked this man who didn't come across as an artist. Composers and conductors had to have a certain image; the ones that didn't fit the mould were not to be accepted too soon.

Alan Autry, cellist, felt this way as well. He thought he'd play a little prank again today. He had no intention of trying to understand Leslie's music. Alan was the sort of musician whose joy was partaking in tonal music that sounded beautiful chords, and who could not stand having to lend a hand to atonal chaos. In actuality, Leslie's new piece wasn't a concatenation of chaos. Compared to some modern composers, whose music couldn't be expressed fully in notation, Leslie was in fact relatively orthodox in his approach. The first movement began rife with dissonance but soon crossed over into premonitions of an emerging unity, and indeed the final movement was an overwhelming flood of perfect, rapturous chords; the audience would have to sit up straight to keep their heads above the deluge of sound. The three-movement symphony *Beringia* attempted to express the states of the cosmos from its origins to, over time, completion, unity, and order. The irony was that in expressing the passage of time from past to present, the symphony started out atonal and ended tonal, in effect tracing the history of music in reverse chronological order. Contemporary classical music had gotten to the point of incorporating sounds unrelated to music and substituting charts and diagrams for scores.

The use of chance to express chaos—a fascinating enough method. Indeed, it was thanks to a series of chance reactions that stars and planets emerged out of the free-floating hydrogen that drifted the infant universe. In that case, the symphony *Beringia* could actually use some chance noises—or so went Alan's unauthorized interpretation. For instance, you could throw a ball at a piano and see what kind of discordant sound it made; if the ball hit the lid and it shut with a slam, that was good, too... But Leslie himself was opposed to incorporating chance. Other composers had tried to use everyday noises in their music, having pots beaten and glasses broken onstage. As far as Leslie was concerned, such methods had gone extinct. They had failed to attain immortality as art. Not that the experimentation was useless. The only way to interrogate the audience about whether or not something passed muster as art was, after all, to perform it onstage.

Beringia... Not a single member of the orchestra knew the meaning behind this title. Leslie had elected to leave it unexplained because, even if he did tell them, it wouldn't have meant much to anyone without Indian blood. It was said that more than ten thousand years ago, during the final epoch of the Diluvial Ice Age, the ancestors of the Native Americans crossed over the Bering Strait from Asia into a new land in several migratory waves. This glacial road of the far north was called "Beringia." Leslie wanted to link the genesis and transformation of the cosmos with the dreams of Asians who had crossed the glacial corridor when they were still an infant people. Leslie wondered if a "chaos" that was slouching toward a "becoming" had in it any will to shape the future. Likewise, he was interested in whatever it was that had stirred the hearts of those ancients ten thousand years ago to traverse such a forbidding path. Did they dream of fertile lands that lay beyond the glaciers? The genesis and becoming of a people, and of the cosmos—the two were organically intertwined in his symphony. Even if the performers didn't understand it, the concept was there complete in the fibers of his being.

Leslie stood at the conductor's podium, peering at the members' faces one by one. Some overtly avoided making eye contact, while the gazes he did meet showed only faint flickers of light. His impression was that he didn't have these people. No respect for his work, no faith, no confidence. Disdain, more like. It wasn't possible to see this sort of thing if you just observed from the seats. You had to take the podium.

Leslie raised his baton. A four-piece woodwind section sounded a grave but discordant strain that filled the hall, while the strings, each playing their own distinct parts, hinted at the formation of stars and the birth of life in different locales of the universe. Melody quarrelled against melody, ignoring the rules of counterpoint and creating dissonance. Leslie's perceptions were heightened. His entire body served as ears, every cell in him responding and vibrating to sound. It was as though he had lost his skin and his raw membranes were painfully exposed to the barrage. In such a state, it was only natural that Leslie should pick up on even the slightest anomaly.

As Alan's individual part approached, he decided he would play *The Swan* by Saint-Saëns. In Ferard's rehearsal the day before, Alan had chosen Prokofiev, and before that, Mozart. Ferard hadn't noticed in either instance. When they'd finished playing, he'd said, "That would do" and even beamed with satisfaction. From this, Alan felt he'd done the right thing. There was a particular bar in his part that he couldn't begin to stomach, that he found physiologically repulsive, that gave off a foul stench. So he'd gone ahead and played a different melody. Given the chaos of winds and strings performing wildly discordant strains, there was absolutely no point—Alan thought—in sticking to the melody that the composer had relegated to him in the score. Ferard hadn't even noticed, had he? It proved Alan was right on the mark! Inserting whimsy and chance into this piece didn't alter it one bit. Maybe it even improved the damn thing.

Suddenly, Leslie's senses registered acute pain and his thoughts grew confused. He stopped his baton in midair, trying to figure out what it was. Seeing their conductor's lack of direction, the musicians gradually stopped playing. As the chaos marked down in the score receded, the sound of a single cello remained stuck in the folds of Leslie's mind, having stumbled there as it were, an echo foreign to the melodies he'd composed. Leslie glared at the faces of the six cellists on the front right side. The sound lingering in his mind turned into a melody he knew and then faded away.

Idiot!

Leslie was outraged and felt the blood rush to his head.

Five of the cellists just sat there, looking up at him with mouths agape. Alan, sitting on the far right, was the only one who averted his eyes. Leslie snapped the baton in half and threw it at him in disgust.

"You! Did I just hear you play Saint-Saëns?"

Alan started. His eyes grew round as he looked up at the conductor's stand, at the man who seemed poised to pounce on him, and he instinctively slid backwards, his chair with him. He couldn't believe it. The man had not only noticed the discrepancy but had ferreted out the melody, the instrument, and the performer. Alan took this in slowly. Ferard hadn't even noticed! Alan's imagination failed him. He was terrified. Against his will, Alan was beholding Leslie with awe. In this composer's head was no amorphous chaos, then. Was he to believe that each of the motifs actually had a proper significance? And, what, this guy's ears differentiated amongst the hodge-podge of a hundred different lines played all at once?

Alan's shock turned into respect. Where did this barbarian of a man hide such a fine sensibility?

He closed his eyes for a moment. A wave of heat, not exactly anger, blasted from Leslie's direction. *What's this energy*, he thought. *Where does he get it?*

Alan had no way of knowing. When he opened his eyes, Leslie's gaze was still upon him. Alan swallowed audibly and said in a near whisper:

"I'm sorry. I'll play it as it says."

Since everyone was holding their breaths in silence, Alan's voice reached Leslie's ears loud and clear. The confrontation hadn't lasted ten seconds. This brief exchange instilled in the others, too, the same awe that Alan now felt toward Leslie; they felt ashamed, even foolish, for not having made an effort to comprehend the music. The seemingly senseless, inchoate mixture of successive sounds actually had *meaning*! As soon as they awakened to this, they were able to feel confidence and pride in the piece they were to perform.

Leslie had no need for a new baton. Once he was aware that his outburst actually had drawn them to him, his anger was replaced by a surge of excitement. This was where Ferard had failed.

Leslie raised his hands. This time, the response was overwhelming.

......Maybe this time I'll find it.

He was full of energy. What was it that he wanted to find? He didn't know. A passionate desire to find it was the source of his music. But he didn't know yet. He didn't know what it was that he wanted to find.

When he brought down his arms, a solemn chaos filled the hall.

2

Two months after the recording, the *Beringia* CD hit record stores nationwide. It was lauded by the critics and Leslie Mardoff himself was quite pleased with the product.

I'm glad Ferard ended up not conducting it, he thought time and again. *That old fogey would've made a mess of my masterpiece.*

Since Leslie was the sort of man who spoke his mind, he said as much in interviews with the media: "Had I not taken away the baton from that old fogey, *Beringia* wouldn't have been such a success..."

Leslie no longer felt all that angry towards Alan Autry. If anyone was to blame, he thought, it was Ferard, who'd waved on his baton without even noticing the prank. Leslie despised incompetents who'd acquired authority. In spite of being the New York Philharmonic's permanent conductor, Ferard merely swung his arms like an automaton, making no effort to understand a composer's intentions. Just thinking about it irritated Leslie even now. He was indifferent to the doings of incompetents as long as their paths didn't cross, but once he suffered any damage, attacking the fool became an obsession. He heaped abuse on Ferard through the media, asserting, with deliberate exaggeration, that the masterpiece of the century had nearly been spoiled. It was Leslie's habit to refer to every new work of his as "the masterpiece of the century" before the critics' verdicts were in.

As a result, some people couldn't stand Leslie. At the same time, strangely enough, some women fell for him. While most women tended to find him coarse and stayed away from him, a few declared him to be cute. He was like a child in a man's body, and perhaps this played on their maternal side...

It was Labor Day afternoon. Summer was nearly over, but Manhattan was still sweltering, and Leslie was fast asleep on the damp sheets of his bed. His apartment was a remodeled loft, and one would have been hard pressed to find a better place in the Village. It was simple and fitted with two spacious rooms: a bedroom and a work space that housed his grand piano.

As Gilbert ascended the steps for his two o'clock appointment, he wiped the sweat from his brow.

Gilbert had only seen Leslie twice so far. The first time was when Leslie was still a student at Julliard. The future composer was working part-time at a jazz club to pay for school, and Gilbert just happened to be there for one of his shows.

Once the piano trio had finished its set, Leslie tried his hand at improvisation for the first time. Striking the keys, he let monotones roll into the hushed silence of the small crowd. The smooth balls of music bounced merrily in the audience, brushed Gilbert's ear and disappeared behind him. Leslie began producing more and more particles of sound. For Gilbert, the performance was beautiful just to watch. The particles of sound absorbed the stage lighting and came rolling towards him in primary colors. The trickle became a torrent, and then a flood. The moment had nearly made his eyes water. A hope was kindled in him: perhaps this man had the power to revive the music that had been lost in those desert wanderings.

Then, a few years later, Leslie made his brilliant debut as a star of the music world. Gilbert bought the CD and all the others that followed. He bided his time, waited for his opportunity. At last, two months ago, he got the chance to have a few words with the young composer before and after a rehearsal of *Beringia*. And now, this would be his third encounter... In most cases, Gilbert would have had a spokesman from his sect handle the negotiations, but this was different. It wasn't a matter of his sect's mystical teachings, but rather, a purely personal matter.

Though already over fifty, Gilbert still had a spring in his step and walked wherever he could despite the slight limp in his left leg. He'd recently stopped using elevators. With the subterranean journey only a few days away, he had to make sure his legs were in optimal condition.

"Don't get ahead of yourself. Leslie hasn't even agreed to it yet," he muttered. Gilbert had been talking to himself more than usual lately.

He stood in front of the door and rang the doorbell. After a long pause with no response, he tried again. He was sure he'd made the appointment for two o'clock. Gilbert put his ear to the door and heard snoring. With such a regular rhythm, this was no midday nap.

"Don't tell me he's sleeping?"

Gilbert pulled away from the door. It seemed Leslie was fast asleep. Gilbert figured the composer must have worn himself out working late into the night. He thought of trying later, but the appointment *was* for two.

He rang the doorbell again. If this didn't work, he would just call him.

"Good morning, Christine!"

The door opened suddenly, and there he was, Leslie, standing in the nude. Meeting Gilbert's eyes just as the older man was about to avert them, Leslie cried out in surprise. Clearly, he'd mistaken Gilbert's arrival for a girlfriend's. Ignoring the awkwardness of the situation, Gilbert extended a hand and said, "Hi, we met a couple of months ago in the concert hall lobby. The name's Gilbert, Gilbert Griffith."

Leslie was covered in sweat and his hair was a mess. He managed a flustered hello before shaking Gilbert's hand. Leslie obviously didn't remember him at all.

His hand was hot and sweaty. To judge by his appearance, he'd just gotten out of the shower, but once Gilbert stepped inside, the room reeked of body odor. That ruled out the shower.

"Why don't you wash up first?" Gilbert suggested.

"Oh, you must be the reverend..." Leslie pointed, his mouth opened wide.

"So you *do* remember. I was watching from the seats when you chewed out that cellist during the rehearsal. It was intense to say the least. I'll never forget it. In fact..." He wanted to tell Leslie that he'd actually first seen him ten years ago in a jazz club, but stopped himself.

"We had an appointment for today?"

"Yes, at two this afternoon."

Leslie looked at the clock. It was exactly two.

"Sorry about that. You go through all the trouble to come here, and here I am snoring away in my pig sty of an apartment."

"Don't worry about it. Just take a shower and put some clothes on first, okay?" Gilbert spread his arms and added, "Is there any reason why the windows are closed?"

The room was hot and stuffy and Gilbert didn't know how much longer he could handle it. Leslie actually thought it quite rude for someone he hardly knew to be ordering him around like his mother, but he drew the shades and opened a window anyway, letting in the muggy breezes of early September. The room cooled off a little nonetheless and the fresh air put Gilbert at ease.

While Leslie was in the shower, Gilbert waited for him on the sofa near the open window. Either the bathroom was too small for Leslie or he was moving about too frantically; Gilbert heard, in addition to the noise of the shower, loud bumps accompanied by bizarre howls. He laughed to himself.

A strong man. The man had more power in him than he knew what to do with—no wonder he made such sounds.

The curtains fluttered as the draft blew in, though this did little to lessen the stench in the room.

Leslie was a completely different person than Gilbert remembered. When they'd met two months earlier in the concert hall lobby, Leslie seemed nervous and reticent. He stared into space the whole time Gilbert was talking to him, so fixated was he, apparently, on making *Beringia* perfect. Leslie definitely exuded the air of the artist then. The all-too-brief conversation left Gilbert dissatisfied and he knew he had to see him again. It was no use talking to him while he was still obsessed with his piece, and so it was that he'd arranged to meet with Leslie several weeks later.

But here at home, he didn't act anything like an artist. This was not to say he gave a bad impression. In fact, Gilbert wasn't one for the so-called sensitivities and sophistications of civilization and was pleased by men like Leslie who were free of such constraints. There was a wildness about him, a sincerity that spoke straight to Gilbert's core.

"Ah, sorry to keep you waiting."

Leslie emerged from the bathroom, looking rugged in his T-shirt and sweatpants. A pendant hung beneath his shirt, only the chain visible around his neck.

"Would you like a beer, Gilbert?" he asked, drying his coarse, curly black hair.

"Yes, a beer would be great. Oh, and please call me Gil from now on."

"Sure thing, Gil."

They drank straight from the can, and Gilbert lavished praise on the newly released *Beringia* CD. Not one for modesty, Leslie seemed genuinely glad. It was almost refreshing, the way he beamed with pride.

Gilbert then told Leslie a little about himself. He was the guru of a new religious sect based in California and enjoyed nationwide influence as a thinker. He had already told him this two months before, but Leslie reacted as if he were hearing it all for the first time. It seemed he hadn't remembered anything.

"So you must be like the new Nikolai Petrovich."

"That's what people say. Actually, he and I were friends..."

Leslie whistled.

"Really? I'm a huge fan of Petrovich."

Leslie stared at Gilbert and was somewhat skeptical that this short, well-dressed gentleman had the charisma to succeed the greatest mystic of the twentieth century. Gilbert was just your average middle-aged man, without any aura to speak of. Leslie, in fact, fit the part better than Gilbert.

After a pause, Leslie cut to the point.

"So, what is it you wanted to talk to me about?"

"I want to commission a new piece," Gilbert stated simply.

"Well, you came to the right place..."

"There's one condition."

Leslie paused for a moment. "Huh, what is it?"

"Well, exactly six months ago, an enormous limestone cave was discovered on the border of New Mexico and Arizona. I've been down there only once, but there's an enormous underground lake there. Quite a sight. It's impossible for me to put it into words. Anyway, I want you to see the world of that subterranean lake."

Leslie frowned.

"What does that have to do with my music?"

"I wish for you to stand there by the lake and take in whatever inspiration you can from it."

Leslie was silent.

"Then, I would like you to create a motif out of this to be used in some visionary concerto or symphony."

"Sounds interesting."

Leslie had a fascination for the subterranean world. Extracting music from the darkness lurking within the Earth was perhaps a natural extension of themes he'd treated in *Beringia*—the genesis and becoming of a people and the universe.

"So you'll do it?"

"Sure, Gil."

Gilbert could hardly believe he'd convinced Leslie so easily. People like Leslie, who were willing to say yes without even hearing the whole story, were a dying breed.

"I want you to know that this whole idea has nothing to do with our sect's teachings. It's not some ruse to advance missionary work. All I want is to confirm my own individual experience—and also, to contribute to the arts. I'm giving you total creative license in this project."

"This 'individual experience' of yours...what is it exactly?"

"You really want to know?"

"Why not."

"When I was about your age, I fell into a drain on the roof of an old, run-down building on the West Side. It must have been at least ten feet deep. I broke my left ankle and had no way of climbing out. I was trapped there for a week without food or water."

Leslie wasn't sure how he should respond to this and wondered how it played in to Gilbert's commission.

"There's one more thing..." Gilbert continued, ignoring Leslie's confusion. "I have wandered the desert, guided by music."

This, of course, did not help. Leslie decided not to pursue the matter too deeply and said, "Yes, well, to each his own, I guess. These experiences are obviously important to you."

Gilbert nodded. "By the way, would you be willing to leave in three days?"

"To the cave you mean?"

"Yes."

"Sure, I'd be comfortable with that. I just took care of a few things."

"We'll be flying out to L.A. first, in the morning. The sect is providing us with a pickup to get to the desert. Sound okay?"

"Just the two of us?"

"Yes. Just you and me. The whole trip shouldn't take more than a week. In that time, I can hopefully clear up your doubts about my individual experience."

"Don't trouble yourself. Doesn't matter to me either way."

"Well, I guess that's it for today then."

After a firm handshake, Leslie showed him to the door. A head shorter than him, Gilbert's eyes lined up with the top of the younger man's chest. The pendant in Leslie's white T-shirt glittered red through the cloth. Gilbert was intrigued.

"What's the design on that pendant, if I may ask?"

Leslie removed the chain from his neck and pulled it out to reveal a flat stone pendant. It had a red deer carved on it. The deer's front feet were flexed and it seemed poised to jump into the sky.

"It's a deer. According to Native American legend, the deer carries a strong spirit."

"I see."

Gilbert took the thin stone in his fingers. It was warm from Leslie's body heat. Gilbert felt a faint dizziness, his perception of time having been dealt a mysterious blow.

3

It was past nine in the evening. People were jogging along Park Avenue; as they passed by Flora Aideen, the scent of their sweat blew past her. It was a September night, the air so damp and uncomfortable that walking was enough to break a sweat. Even so, Flora hurried along. In her purse was her newly purchased copy of *Beringia*.

Flora had just finished work at her office on the East Side. She was an editor for Log Books, a publishing company that put out paperbacks and three lines of magazines. It was only a ten-minute walk from her apartment, also on the East Side, which wasn't a place she could have afforded on an editor's salary. Whenever those who knew nothing of her current situation came to visit, they were surprised at its size.

Flora began her stint at Log Books three years ago but had been making her living as an editor for ten. During a yearlong maternity leave, she'd quit her previous job. After that it was Log Books. Few of Flora's friends supported her move from a first-rate publisher.

"Are you out of your mind?" they told her. "You should get *him* to leave."

The words may have been rough, but they had a point. She couldn't stay on at her former husband's workplace. She'd asked herself, too, why *she* had to be the one to leave, when the divorce had been his fault. Why shouldn't she drive him out of the workplace the way she'd driven him out of her home life? She understood the logic. Yet, Flora didn't have it in her to continue on there even if he were to leave. His influence was everywhere in the office and she couldn't stand it. Because of his high position, her husband's inner circle was large, and working among them was more than she could handle.

Flora took the elevator up to the fifth floor, her keys jangling as she walked down the hallway. The sound never failed to make her feel lonely. She opened the door into an empty, spacious apartment, a desolate place with little sign of life. She'd considered moving into a smaller place, but didn't have the willpower to go through with it. Her friend Jennifer had once urged her to change her living environment.

"Look, in a way, wasn't it this room that caused your divorce? I don't get it. You gave up your dream job in a flash, but you can't seem to leave this place. Doesn't make any sense."

Flora turned on the living room lights and drew the curtains from the bay window overlooking Central Park. In her teens, when she was poor and went to high school in Port Phillip, she always dreamed of someday having a fancy place on the East Side. Her dream was now a reality, but she never imagined her life would be so wretched. All the unnecessary space was like a manifestation of the emptiness in her heart. It was unbearable. Not that she needed a man around to be happy. It wasn't like that at all.

Flora let herself sink into the comfortable leather sofa and unfastened the hooks of her blouse. Almost everything in the apartment belonged to Richard. He'd left behind the furniture, dining room table, grand piano, even the Chagall pastel... But these were all eclipsed by the best thing he'd ever given her, which was of course her darling son. Gone now—but her son's voice was fresh in her mind—helplessly calling out, "Mama, mama."

Wasn't it this room that caused your divorce?

No wonder Jennifer thought so. Three and a half years ago... Flora had given birth to a boy, and the luxury items in her apartment were gathering dust—and being dirtied.

During her recovery period, Richard was always "too busy" to make time for her. Leaving him in the apartment, she'd spent three months at her mother's in Port Phillip. Then, during her second month away from New York, Flora received an anonymous phone call. The woman on the phone informed her, rather matter-of-factly, that Richard wasn't living alone in his apartment, that the woman was an NYU student, and that they'd been an item for nearly a month. When Flora hung up, she realized that she was calm. *I guess I don't really love him, then,* the curious conviction came to her. *Come to think of it, did I ever love him?* She certainly respected him. Perhaps Richard, for his part, did love her. But she, Flora—she wasn't sure. If she hadn't believed every word of the phone call and returned to New York right away, the marriage might have lasted. His infidelity didn't make her jealous. Of course she didn't love him. But a marriage could survive that.

She had given her son into her mother's care and driven back home. Though no one was home, it was obvious from the looks of things that another woman had been living there. Flora rubbed her eyes. The apartment was such a mess that it didn't feel like her own. The piano lid was left open and the dust cover had fallen onto the floor. To make matters worse, what looked like corn chowder had spilled onto the keyboard, its yellow crust caked along the D, E, and F keys. There was a mountain of soiled underwear on the living room carpet, scattered magazines, popcorn in between the sofa cushions, and a foul stench coming from the kitchen. And when she held her nose and went into the kitchen, it was just as bad as she thought. A pile of dirty dishes, leftovers scattered on the floor, a trickling faucet, and all of it clearly illuminated by the open refrigerator.

Discolored sheets were thrown onto the bedroom floor. When she tried picking them up, they smelled of semen. Pajamas, briefs, and shirts all reeked of festering body fluids. The alarm clock near the pillow had stopped at 6:10.

She had then gone into the bathroom to find a stained toilet and a bathtub stopped up with tangled clumps of long hair. And then, under the sink near the toilet bowl cleaner, was a used tampon. Flora felt nauseous when she saw this. She buried her face in the toilet bowl and threw up, her eyes watering from the fumes. This had nothing to do with jealousy. It was fear. A fear that, for three years, she'd been married to a man who lived in a world she could never understand. No matter how she put it together in her mind, it made no sense to her. Where had her Richard gone? She wasn't exactly head over heels for him, but Richard's charming gentility and air of refinement had won her over. It was he who had pushed for the marriage.

Richard had just turned forty at the time of their divorce. His career was soaring and he was on his way to making director at his publishing company. He had a sharp eye for anything literary and was equally shrewd about marketing. He wasn't a bad writer himself. Flora had never met a more talented man. With his receding hairline, he wasn't particularly handsome, but he'd inherited a vast sum from his parents and had attended the best schools. All of Flora's friends were envious of her married life. But then this betrayal... How could someone who displayed such discretion and attention to detail in his work be so insensitive in his personal life? Was that chivalrous Richard she remembered from their courting period a total sham?

Flora asked herself over and over if it was his infidelity that she couldn't tolerate. Each time her answer was a no. She thought she wouldn't be in so much pain if he'd had a clean and discreet affair with some stylish woman. She questioned herself repeatedly on this point.

It's true. I'd be able to put up with that.

That was her conclusion. While this...the insensitivity of it! Port Phillip was only a short drive from the city, and she could have come back unannounced at any moment. Yet this...flagrant...as if the affair were being put on display. Did her husband think even once of the pain she might experience if she saw this? She felt as if she'd caught a glimpse of the deep hollows of the heart, an endless subterranean world.

I'm not the one who's trying to annul our marriage. He is...

She realized this, and their marriage indeed came to a close.

Flora shook her head now to free herself of those memories. The apartment looked different from the way it did then. The carpeting and wallpaper had been changed, and the kitchen and bathroom had been remodeled. Even so, the scene and the odors sometimes came back to her vividly.

Maybe Jennifer is right. Maybe I should move out.

The Desert

Were the place rented, she would have moved out right away. But she'd considered the place ideal for raising her son. Just thinking of all the trouble she'd have to go through with some real estate agent was enough to zap her will to up and leave.

The only thing of her own she'd brought to this apartment was the JBL stereo system. She turned it on. Leslie's third album was still inside, a concerto called *Rainbow* featuring jazz vibraphonist Stephen Daniel. She'd listened to it hundreds of times in the last six months. From spring to summer, when her will to live was flagging, it was *Rainbow* that kept her going, she thought now. She exchanged the concerto for *Beringia*.

I have this, at least.

No matter what state she was in, immersing herself in Leslie's work was a reliable way of regaining emotional stability.

Beringia began so quietly that Flora wondered if she'd forgotten to turn up the volume, but before long, she was blanketed in delicate sounds, a music that evoked dripping water. That was her impression: droplets falling. Soon, a noticeable dissonance swelled from beneath. She expected an all-encompassing maelstrom to ensue, but instead it manifested itself as small pockets of chaos which rose and faded.

On a flood of sound, the chaos began to take shape, before overflowing into tranquility. It was a contradiction: How could a flood express silence? But Leslie Mardoff's music was a treasure trove of contradictions. His monotones stimulated color perceptions and made flowers blossom in primary hues in the listener's mind. His simple melodies spoke of countless dramas that would unfold. And then, in the end, an overwhelming confession. Was it an illusion? Flora knew that there was no way Leslie composed his music for a single listener. Especially when he'd never even met that woman. But she couldn't help thinking that the music was being performed just for her, that creator and listener were linked through this music.

The piece finished playing. Flora rested her head on the back of the sofa and looked up at the ceiling. She closed her eyes and thought of Leslie's face as it appeared on the CD jacket. The powerful message of the piece had an immovable presence that induced a sort of vertigo. Had Leslie been standing right there when she opened her eyes, it would have felt like the most natural thing in the world. She didn't move from the sofa for what seemed like forever.

Though she'd planned on taking a quick shower, Flora decided to run a bath instead. The flood-like imagery in *Beringia* made her want to immerse herself. She stood naked in front of the mirror and tied up her hair. Flora had the type of skin that most of her friends spent hours at tanning salons or beaches to attain. She had no need for any of that; she was born with her beautiful brown skin. Her eyes were passionate, her hair pure black. Flora herself had always felt there was something "ethnic" about her body. Even so, she never believed her grandfather's stories. Before she started school, she used to live with her parents and grandfather in a house overlooking the sea in San Diego. It was there that her grandfather often told her: "You know, our ancestors crossed this huge ocean on a large raft." He would say this with pride, gazing out at the water at dusk.

Until she was ten, Flora accepted this as the truth. Even after her father's job brought them to Port Phillip, she remembered the color of that water. As she looked out across the Pacific as a little girl, just thinking of the great perils her distant ancestors must have suffered in crossing that great expanse made her heart pound with excitement. However, as she got older, Flora knew that such a feat was impossible and downright pointless, and came to see her grandfather's stories as nothing more than tall tales. But she missed her childhood. A house by the sea, blue skies all year round...it was a time when her world was filled with dreams, not hardships—a world where all her wishes came true, no matter how impossible they seemed.

Why did my great-great-great-great-grandfather come here on a raft? If I tried to do that, they'd scold me and wouldn't let me. But they did it. Why? Was it for "romance"? Or did they want something else?

Many tales had found their way into her young mind, but now, there wasn't a single childhood dream left in her, all gone with her faith in her grandfather's stories. Her passion for life had begun to dissipate steadily since she'd stopped believing in them.

Nothing good came out of her relocation to Port Phillip. Her father's business went under and her parents fought constantly. Eventually, her father grew destitute and passed away far too young, leaving behind nothing for a mother and her daughter. Flora made up for it by studying as hard as she could. She climbed to the top of her class, met a man most women would have killed to get their hands on, and found herself in a high-end apartment on the Upper East Side. All the while, her only objective had been to escape a life of poverty.

She laughed at herself in the mirror, thinking her life to be totally textbook: a scholarship to Columbia, a marriage to a rich

Yale alumnus, divorced after three years but still in the trendy apartment. Why did she feel so empty then? It was years since she'd experienced anything like the happiness she knew when she'd still believed her grandfather's stories. Flora braced herself on the sink.

Oh, if only I had my darling boy, how that would save me!

Please forgive me, mama was upset, so I didn't... No, I did hear you calling, but I never turned around.

There was no use in regretting it. She wanted to blame it all on Richard...

It was the beginning of spring, at a shopping plaza parking lot. She'd just opened the passenger door to put her heavy shopping bag onto the front seat and was lifting up her son in her arms when the car phone rang. The phone was only for emergencies, so Flora sat down on the unoccupied half of the seat and answered it. It was only Richard, calling for the usual reason: "I was wondering if I might take the boy for a week in May." His passive-aggressive way of asserting his rights over their child always upset her to no end.

"Didn't we already discuss this?"

Meanwhile, the voice of her son, who had just turned three, was fading. He had gone looking for his toy car; it had fallen out of the bag and rolled away in its round plastic case across the asphalt surface of the parking lot.

"Mama, mama, where did my toy go?" the boy wondered out loud, crawling around on the asphalt.

A car had pulled out of the neighboring parking space a short while ago, and a pickup truck quickly backed into it before anyone else could get it. The truck's high cabin blocked the midday sun and cast a shade over Flora. Suddenly her spine tingled with fear.

I don't hear my darling. He was here just a minute ago... and...what was that sound? that thud?

Flora dropped the phone and stepped out onto the asphalt. Right by her feet—she saw it. She let out a scream and fell to her knees. Then she collapsed.

During these past six months, the shock of that moment never left her. She'd seen a psychiatrist for a month after the accident. She took it out on everybody; she hated everything. She wanted to curse God. Richard, of course, was the real culprit.

It's his fault. He shouldn't have called me on my car phone. If he hadn't upset me...

Flora knew she was being irrational but couldn't get beyond her anger or her tears. She began to suffer from neurosis, and to take sleeping pills for her insomnia. Once, she seriously considered ending it all by downing a lethal dose. She'd poured a tall glass of water and stared at it for a long time, a small mountain of capsules on her hand. The capsules felt pleasant against her palm. It was Leslie Mardoff's music that saved her from going any further. Yes, just when she tried to pop the pills, Leslie's music came charging at her. The blow of sound made her flinch and spill the capsules. His music had come and gone branding her heart with hope for life. She felt it clearly. And how strongly she still felt it. She felt needed somehow, and that repelled all morbid thoughts.

As hot water filled the tub, she tested it with her left hand. It was still lukewarm, so she turned the hot valve higher. When she removed her hand, she noticed the bluish-purple birthmark just below her left shoulder reflected in the cloudy mirror. The mark had been with her for as long as she could remember, and it grew bigger with every passing year. She'd had a doctor look at it, but he didn't know the cause. Recently, it hadn't shown any signs of getting any bigger. Instead, it was changing color and settling into some sort of design. Flora was suddenly concerned about it and wiped the fog off the mirror. She brought her shoulder closer. The mark's shape was more detailed than it had ever been. It was only the size of a silver dollar, but it kept Flora from wearing tank tops. It had been a while since she'd taken a long, hard look at it. The design could have been many things, but for some reason it looked like a constellation to her. A constellation of an animal. Depending on the angle it looked like it could be anything. She felt there had to be an interpretation that was dead-on. As a teen and as a twentysomething, she'd hated her birthmark and wanted very badly to get rid of it. She didn't feel that way anymore. She found herself feeling quite attached to it.

Flora shut off the faucet and slipped into the tub. Another day was about to end. Remembering the past brought her so much pain—and what would tomorrow bring? the day after tomorrow? Not much, she feared. This was how she was going to age. If God asked her if she wanted to redo her life, she would promptly have said no. Not because she was satisfied with the way things had turned out, of course, but because it was pointless to do it all over again. The myth of Sisyphus.

The bathroom was quiet. Flora lifted her face, keeping the rest of her body still. Steam condensed and dripped down from the ceiling. When a droplet hit the surface, the imagery of *Beringia* spread across her mind. Sound precipitated landscapes for her. *Leslie Mardoff, Leslie Mardoff.* Thinking of him, she at last regained some calm.

4

Flora sat by the phone wondering if she should really call him. She'd never been so nervous about requesting an interview. She had already submitted a proposal for a feature article on Leslie Mardoff to one of the magazines published by Log Books. After listening to *Beringia*, her desire to meet him had burgeoned beyond control.

An outline for a photo-essay publicizing the well-received *Beringia* had already been sent to Leslie; the article would also cover the composer's upbringing and his motivations for becoming a composer. Flora had to call Leslie to see if he was interested. Had it been anyone else, she would have made the call without a second thought, but she was uneasy. She'd be hearing Leslie's voice, coming into contact with him over the line. Her relationship to him might advance from that of a mere listener to something new. She hadn't been nearly so nervous when she'd confessed her love to her first boyfriend in high school. Maybe it was fear. Her conviction that she owned his music would crumble, and with it her reason for living, if he just brushed her off and declined. If the music that had pulled her from the brink of death turned suddenly into some distant thing, what else in life was she to rely on? Flora was frightened. She had to make up her mind and pick up that phone, and, in fact, somewhere in that anxiety was also a grain of confidence. *Pick up that phone!*

PARADISE

Leslie's been waiting for you...

It was nighttime. Leslie was exercising alone in his room with all his windows shut. He wasn't working on his muscles. The exercise, developed by Nikolai Petrovich, greatest mystic of the twentieth century, was intended to foster self-discovery. Leslie stretched his fingers as high as they would go. Next, he lowered his arms slowly and bent them at right angles, and, resting on his side in a V-shape, extended his arms alternately and in succession. This routine, repeated at a leisurely pace and accompanied by deep breathing, helped its practitioner discover where he was, what he thought, and what he wanted.

The room was silent. The tightly shut storm window had liberated him from the bustle of the streets below, and the air in the room was perfectly still. Leslie was trying not to think—an inexorable paradox that he confronted head-on. To think not to think. Emptying your mind. He'd never once pulled it off.

According to Nikolai Petrovich, there was no such thing as free will. The power of one's volition originated in the vast energy that existed outside the individual. Though human beings tried to live by their own will, they were always swept up in the flow of a "something"—genes and environment and what-not. Swept up in a flow whose source, naturally, they could not locate.

Leslie had just learned that Nikolai Petrovich's thinking had a sole inheritor, namely Gilbert. Through his own individual experience, Gilbert, too, had come to doubt human free will and had sought out and befriended Nikolai Petrovich, whose mystical ideas agreed with his own. When Petrovich died, his followers united around Gilbert, perfecting the meditative exercise and mounting a unique movement. The fledgling sect wasn't based on an idea of God derived from Christianity. Its attempt—rooted in mystical thought—to gain absolute freedom through an encounter with core cosmic principles was, in short, pantheistic. The sect's operations consisted of grassroots missionary activity and putting out books that presented its teachings. There were fewer than a hundred adherents who made their living as actual members of the sect, but more than 400,000 people across the country were estimated to have come under its direct or indirect influence. Leslie was in fact one of them.

Why was there no free will? One had to go back in time to the very moment life was created to see why... In sum, Petrovich and Gilbert believed that free will was denied to humans because humans were born whether or not they wanted to be born. People never *chose* to be born; they always, passively, got born. Human beings were chained to the endless cycle of life, and, whether they were conscious of it or not, their cells retained memories of the primordial past and acted in complex ways to ensnare them.

Leslie was almost overwhelmed by the strength of his own energy but had no idea to where it radiated. Precisely because he didn't, he was attracted to Petrovich's teachings.

The phone rang. He was wearing only his black exercise clothes. The ringing invaded a gap between his thoughts. Normally, he wouldn't have bothered answering the phone during meditation. But tonight, the ringing interrupted his thoughts and a voice seemed to tell him to take the call. The trilling assumed the guise of words, addressing him plaintively. Leslie broke off his meditation and lifted the receiver.

"Yes, this is Leslie."

"Hello, um, my name is Flora Aideen. I'm an editor at Log Books..."

His ears perked up at hearing the name. "Flora..." he said strangely, interrupting her. Leslie had sensitive ears. Flora's voice seeped into every one of his cells through his eardrums, and rocked him gently from within. Something was coming to life in him. A distant passion—an intense longing—the sound of ice, sliding, and of the wind, the life of that wind... Leslie closed his eyes and spoke her name again. He let Flora's voice roll in his heart and relished its echo. It was a pleasant feeling he'd never experienced before.

"Are you all right?"

Flora was feeling tense. Not only was she hearing her idol's voice for the first time, but it had uttered her name passionately—twice. She wondered what this meant and suspected, for a moment, that he was taking her for someone else.

"Oh, ah—sorry. I blanked for a moment there," he said, then fell silent again. Finally he continued, "Would I have heard your voice somewhere?"

"I doubt it... We've never met."

"Are you sure?"

"Positive..."

"Your voice sounds like home to me."

Leslie was a notorious womanizer.

God, is he hitting on me? Flora suspected for a moment. But the man's face, which she'd seen in the magazines, wore a sincere expression as it gazed at her, full of feeling, from the other end of the line. Flora was completely forgetting something. The first time she'd heard Leslie's music, she'd felt the same way, too—

that somehow she'd heard it before.

"How strange," Leslie muttered; Flora was silent. "I wonder why I feel that way..." Leslie lost himself in thought, oblivious to the fact that he was on the line. Your self was something you never really understood.

"Um," Flora tried, but couldn't continue.

For a moment, both of them clutched their phones in silence. They each felt like they were holding the other's hand—they felt warm.

It was Leslie who broke the modest silence: "So, your magazine wants to do a write-up about me? Is that what you're calling about?"

"Yes, exactly. Did you have a chance to read over the propsal we sent you?"

"Well, I did read it."

Leslie recalled the letter he'd received from Log Books. Flora's request began with praise for *Beringia*. Always eager to bask in praise, Leslie had been tickled by the letter and was ready to accept the request. But he never expected that hearing the voice of the woman who wrote it would give him such a shock. Now, he felt he had to meet her. And soon.

"*Beringia*'s been doing so well, and personally, I was really moved by the piece, too. I thought our readers should know about your new work and what you are up to—"

"Boring," Leslie interrupted. Flora swallowed her words, afraid he was about to turn down her request. But, without so much as a pause, and in a jaunty tone, the composer said, "How 'bout I give you an exclusive?"

Flora nearly sighed with relief. She was used to refusals, but it was never easy to take, and a refusal from Leslie would have been more than just a disappointment.

Leslie told her about Gilbert and having accepted his strange request to visit a newly discovered limestone cave with a huge underground lake on the Arizona-New Mexico border.

"So, I'll stand on the shore of this underground lake, become all inspired, and compose a new piece. What do you think? Awesome, right? You'll join us as our special guest reporter, take notes, take pictures. How do you like that for a proposal?"

The moment he stopped speaking, Leslie wondered if he was supposed to be babbling to the media about this. Gilbert might not like it. In fact—Leslie couldn't quite recall—Gilbert might have asked him not to tell anyone that he was taking this trip. But it was no big deal. At any rate, Leslie couldn't resist the temptation to summon Flora to his side.

"Wow. I love it."

Come to think of it, introducing *Beringia* to a wider audience in the context of a photo-essay on Leslie Mardoff, composer, was exactly the kind of feature any old magazine would run. If, on the other hand, Leslie went underground with a New Age guru and found inspiration for a new piece, that was nothing other than a real scoop. The very idea of Leslie and Gilbert together—the latter was famously media-shy—more than sufficed. For Flora it was irresistible, in fact. Added to that, shots of a newly discovered underground lake...

"We'd fly out to L.A. tomorrow afternoon. From there, we'd be driving out into the desert in a pickup truck."

Flora froze when she heard the words. Six months after the fact, the image of a weapon that had taken her son's life still hadn't left her—it possibly never would. She remembered the loud rock music blasting from the stereo, the young driver's face as he chewed gum and swayed to the beat, his yellow sunglasses, the crimson spreading across the asphalt.

"Hey, you still there?"

Flora fought back the surge of memories and came to her senses when she heard Leslie's voice.

"What?"

"I said, you ought to book a ticket for L.A. asap."

Flora collected herself and said, "Sure, but how do you know Gilbert will agree to this? He hates publicity."

She'd tried to get an interview with Gilbert once. He had declined, and some colleagues of hers shared the experience. It wasn't just from hearsay that she judged him to be media-averse.

"Oh, really?"

"You didn't know?"

"Well, I do now. I'll ask Gil. I guess I can't just invite you all on my own. But if Gilbert agrees, you're okay with it?"

"Yes, by all means. Thank you."

"It's settled then. I'll be calling you."

Flora gave him her number and hung up.

Before calling Gilbert at his hotel, Leslie had to stop and think how best to break this to him. If he told Gilbert flat out that he'd already spoken with someone from the media, that might actually scotch their plans. Even Leslie could sense that Gilbert, while a gentle and sensible man, heeded something like a divine voice and was fully capable of saying, with perfect calm, something like: "It's over, Leslie. So long." Leslie liked Gilbert's idea. If such an subterranean world did exist, he wanted to see it with his own eyes. He was also interested in Gilbert. Gilbert knew something that other people didn't. Though humans were probably destined never to understand the structure of the world, Gilbert certainly understood it better than other people. Leslie was looking forward to visiting this place with him. He didn't want the trip to get cancelled.

"Don't tell me you told someone," Gilbert quizzed in a solemn voice after Leslie had spoken a few sentences.

"No, I didn't tell anyone," Leslie lied. "I'm just asking, *if* I got such a request from a reporter, what should I—"

Gilbert immediately cut in. "A reporter? Absolutely not. No one else can come with us to the world underground. Am I clear?"

That was all there was to it. Leslie's fears proved to be on target. Taking Flora along was out of the question.

Leslie confirmed the time they were supposed to meet at the airport and ended the call.

But he wasn't about to give up so easily. Having heard Flora's voice over the phone, he was helplessly in thrall to a wish. It was his wish to stand by that underground lake with her. He didn't care why he had to do this; he just hoped to be true to his overwhelming desire. He had no idea exactly how or where the will originated, but to what his body demanded he wanted to be true, because it was the senses that were in contact with the phenomena of the universe and that worked upon one's awareness.

Leslie came up with a plan. He and Gilbert were both celebrities in a way. What if a nosy journalist hungry for a story just happened to bump into them in L.A. and started to tail them?

He spread open a map and made a cross on the Arizona-New Mexico border where Gilbert had said the caves were. It was several hundred miles from L.A., much too far for a woman to drive alone. Flying to El Paso or Phoenix and driving a rental car from there would be easier. Leslie himself had to go into L.A. and get on that truck, so there needed to be a rendezvous point. He traced a route from L.A. toward the limestone caves. He and Gilbert would most likely head east on I-40 and take Route 66 south to Springerville. That was where he'd link up with her, Springerville. From there, it was less than twenty miles to the caves, though that was the desert and wouldn't be an easy drive.

"...So we'll meet up in Springerville," Leslie offered.

"You make it sound like you've been there," Flora teased. She was much less nervous this time around. Talking to Leslie was in fact relaxing.

"Been there? I'd never even heard of the place."

"Then who knows. Maybe it's big and bustling."

"Let's see, then. What does every town have?"

"Well, there's the post office, and..."

"Perfect! Wait for me at the Springerville Post Office at noon sharp, day after tomorrow."

"Wait?"

"Hey, I'll be heading there via L.A. You'll get there first."

"What happens then?"

"I'll stop the car in front for a minute and pretend to mail out a postcard. That'll be your cue. Just follow us as we drive out into the desert. Don't worry about losing sight of us, we'll probably be kicking up a dust cloud. Gilbert couldn't possibly turn away a woman who's come down after us into the cave."

"If I don't see you at the post office?"

"In that case, wait for me at a motel in Springerville. After a few hours of subterranean composing, I'll say goodbye to Gilbert and link up with you."

"What if there's more than one motel in Springerville?"

"Then stay at the southernmost one. I would gladly spend all my life looking for you if I knew you were waiting for me. Even if it meant going through every single motel in L.A. So trust me."

This overdramatic assurance raised some doubts in Flora's mind as to the man's intentions.

"Uhh, and then?"

"And then what?"

"What happens after we meet up?"

"To the cave, of course. You want to get some photos of me composing by the lake, right?"

She did want those photos. This would be an unprecedented way of making music; if, in addition to her own prose, full-color photos captured the no doubt phantasmal scene down there, it would make for a top-notch feature piece.

"Then why shouldn't we just do that?" Flora said. "We don't need to risk offending Gilbert. If you can spare me some time afterwards, we could just meet afterwards."

Leslie thought this over. She was right. There was no need for childish spygames; they could simply visit the caves the next day. But Leslie wanted the woman whose voice he was hearing to be there when he did the actual composing. It contradicted the wish of his host Gilbert, who wanted him to be inspired by the lake only, free of unnecessary intruders. Yet Leslie was utterly captivated by Flora's voice; his keen ears had gained inspiration from her already.

"No. You have to be there. Please wait for me at the post office."

"Got it."

"Until then."

"Hold on. Just to be safe, can you tell me roughly where the cave is?" Flora asked.

"You have a map handy?"

"I do."

"All right, going south on Route 66 from I-40, you get to Springerville. Ten miles south of the town, you have to turn into the desert and proceed compass east until you reach where the border's supposed to be. The caves will be right below you."

Flora followed Leslie's directions on her map.

"Got it. Okay, see you then."

"Take care, Flora."

Leslie kissed her voice and hung up.

5

On the night of Friday, September 8th, Flora flew in to El Paso. Leslie and Gilbert had arrived in L.A. on schedule and were now going east on I-40. Because of the mileage they had to cover, they'd had no time to rest in L.A. If they drove through the dark, the next day would be that much easier.

It was approximately 300 miles to Springerville from El Paso. If Flora averaged 60 mph, it would take her exactly five hours to get there. What was great about country roads was that as long as you kept your speed and knew the distance, you didn't need to be on a freeway to be perfectly punctual.

If I leave at seven in the morning, I'll make it by noon, Flora concluded. No need to rush... Her thinking was based partly on a facile presumption that Leslie wouldn't really mind if she got there late, that he'd let her photograph him in the caves anyway.

Clothed in a T-shirt and jeans and hoisting a traveling bag with her two Nikons in it, Flora looked tough enough, but her arms really weren't that strong. Her brown skin might have led one to believe she was the outdoors type, but it was simply the color she was born with, and in all her nearly thirty-five years, she'd always preferred reading books to playing sports. The bag felt too heavy for her, and she got into a cab and gave the name of her hotel. It wasn't that she was tired. She was just aloof and distracted as she vacantly gazed at the scenery outside and mused about meeting Leslie the next day.

She'd already reserved a room at a motel that was part of a nationwide chain, a little ways down Montana Avenue. When she checked in, she instructed the front desk to have a rental car ready for her by seven the following morning.

A car she could take into the desert, she thought she told them.

After taking a shower, she gazed out from her room. Though it was dark, on that side across Montana Avenue, she could almost feel the dry expanse. Beyond what the neon lights illuminated lay the vast desert.

The desert.

There was something undeniably familiar about it. In her life, she'd called three places home: San Diego, where she was born and raised, downtown Port Phillip on the East Coast, and her current apartment on New York's Upper East Side with a commanding vista of skyscrapers. She'd known only the oceanfront and the urban life. The desert shouldn't have been familiar to her at all. Yet, she felt at home. Its air, its smell put her at ease. And Leslie was just about to guide her into a cave under the desert.

You're a strange one, Leslie.

From their conversations on the phone the evening before, she'd sensed that he was a different sort of character. Different from Richard, certainly.

Flora wasn't a conceited person by any means, but after talking with Leslie, she'd become confident. She was smiling to herself.

......Maybe I was right. Leslie was making music just for me, sending me messages.

It was like the story about her ancestors crossing the ocean on a raft—an absurd, baseless conviction. But absurd was fine. Because thinking such thoughts made her happy and the dreams she once knew as a child seemed to be reawakening at long last.

Their pickup truck had just passed through the town of Needles on I-40. Leslie was at the wheel with Gilbert in the passenger seat. Just as Flora was thinking of Leslie, he was consumed with thoughts of her.

"Say, Gil. You have a family?" he asked, Flora's voice still ringing in his head.

"No."

"You've never been married?"

"No."

Leslie hesitated to ask why, but Gilbert told him without his asking.

"Never met the right woman."

The highway was beginning to veer north, but where it met Route 93 at Kingman it resumed its eastward stretch. The oncoming traffic was sparse, and whcnever town lights became visible in the distance ahead, Leslie caught himself feeling happy. Yet he, too, liked the desert.

"Plan on getting married?" asked Gilbert. Perhaps it was only the monotony of the drive that prompted him to say anything, as a precaution against the driver falling asleep.

"Yup."

"Huh. Who's the lady?"

"Flora."

"Flora?"

"Yup, Flora. It's Flora or no one."

"You're engaged to her?"

Leslie had uttered the woman's name with such conviction that Gilbert made the natural misunderstanding.

Leslie burst out laughing.

"I'm only joking, I haven't even met the woman yet."

Leslie checked the clock. It was just before nine. Still an hour to go before they could take a nice hot shower at a motel.

He stepped a little deeper on the gas. He couldn't afford to miss his appointment with her at noon the next day. He wanted very badly to compose a new work in that subterranean world, inspired by both the lake and Flora.

"Say, Gil. What's the significance of composing by that lake?" Suddenly, Leslie had recalled that Gilbert was supposed to enlighten him about his intentions on the way to the cave.

"As I said before, I've wandered the desert with music as my guide."

Leslie's silence urged him for more.

"Do you like the desert?" Gilbert asked.

"I do, as a matter of fact."

The vast, dry expanses of the West. It was to these parts that Leslie's grandmother's tribe had been driven against their will.

Ten thousand years earlier, tribes from the cold Mongolian barrens crossed the Bering Strait lured by dreams of a better life on more fertile land. When they crossed Beringia, they encountered not a lush paradise, but a bitter landscape enclosed by ice. They were forced to search for a yet narrower corridor that would take them south. Modern geological findings suggested that the only iceless path existed in the eastern reaches of the Rocky

Mountains. The number of people who actually traveled this corridor must have been miniscule. When they finally found the land they sought, they spread further east and south to extend their territory. Their life in paradise continued for thousands of years before European explorers came in and destroyed it. The Indians who lived in the fertile lands to the southeast were driven back by the westward expansion of the Frontier and were ultimately relegated to the arid deserts. Leslie never had the chance to hear any of this firsthand from her grandmother, who'd left this world by the time he was born. His parents had raised him in Richmond, Virginia, where his half-Indian father proved to be a rather astute businessman. Thanks to him, Leslie's upbringing had been above average by that city's standards. His father never talked too much about their roots. Instead, Leslie spent hours on end reading books about his ancestors and imagining their lives. With a dream in their hearts, they'd left the deserts of Asia and suffered a terrible journey, but they had found a new world, and happiness with it, only to be driven, in the end, back into the desert...

Like Leslie, Gilbert had a special regard for the desert.

Peering into the darkness off to the right, Gilbert saw that the headlights did not reflect off anything like water. No water out there. Yet there had been, one June evening twenty years ago.

People carry with them unforgettable sights. Though meaningless to others, they can be life-changing for the one who retains them. As a thinker, Gilbert was quite conscious of this. His life as a bum in New York—the seven days and nights that he looked into himself, pelted by rain, in the drain of an abandoned building—his attraction then to mysticism and his friendship with Nikolai Petrovich—his encounter with Leslie's music—all of that, Gilbert believed, issued from a puddle that he'd glimpsed without so much as a second thought. A puddle in the desert, that was where it all started...

"There are puddles in the desert, you know."

This didn't make much sense to Leslie. "What?" he said.

"Why we're drawn to the desert. Isn't that the subject? At first, I didn't realize it was because of the puddles. Arthur, the guitarist, was in the passenger seat of the Caravan. His groupies, Melanie and Celia, were in the back seat."

That was how Gilbert's story began.

"Arthur? Who's Arthur?" asked Leslie.

"A musician like you. Just a guitar-slinging hippie, but his songs had soul. I first heard him at the Clark Hotel in downtown L.A. He got to me. Particles of sound, entering my body. I'd just gotten back from 'Nam. I was knocking about aimless. He asked me if I'd be his manager. Hardly knew each other. It wasn't so much a choice. He had this way of asking, you see. It was my duty to abide by him, he put it in some such way. What an arrogant way to ask a favor of a man, and that was one condescending expression. He was an asshole, not much fun to be around. Somehow, led by his music, under managerial pretenses, I tumbled from town to town, a wanderer in the deserts of this West. Arthur picked up girls in the towns, obviously underage girls, inviting them on the Caravan. I guess I was also his personal chauffeur. I was younger than you are now."

The desert landscape hadn't changed since then; as they hit Barstow, the freeway forked into I-40 and I-15 just as he remembered.

PARADISE

Gilbert told Leslie about the scene he'd witnessed twenty years ago. It was less a story than a straightforward description of a landscape.

On that night in June of 1973, he was driving the Caravan through the Mohave Desert, heading north on I-15. Suddenly, puddles glinted in the white moonlight to the east. He looked up at the stars and the half-moon nestled among them. Seeing that there wasn't a single cloud in the sky, he figured a squall must have blown through earlier that day. He was captivated by the small patches of water scattered across the sand. After driving further, he saw that some of them were big enough to be lakes, though these would never be found on any map. Less than a day old, they blurred together in the horizon like a distant waterline in a sea of darkness. He pulled over to the right and stopped the car.

"Hey, what's the deal?" Arthur asked.

Gilbert pointed ahead with his chin. "Those puddles out there."

"So what? Let's blow this joint, man."

Though they'd known each other for two years, Gilbert was still unaccustomed to Arthur's arrogance. Arthur was a stifling person to be around, and his unpredictable nature would have tested anyone's patience. And yet, Gilbert found himself unable to just shed off his love for Arthur's music. It was like a drug.

Gilbert got out of the car and began walking toward the shores of the lake.

"Gil, where are you going?"

Arthur got out of the car and chased after him.

The water's faint surface blended into the line that sky and earth formed. When there was no reflection, it was impossible even to see that the water was there.

When Gilbert halted, so did Arthur. From the darkness behind them came the vulgar laughter of the two girls. Both Melanie and Celia were minors, and both were high on marijuana.

There by the lake, Arthur said in a different tone of voice, "Let's camp here tonight."

It was a whimsical suggestion. The irritation was gone from his voice—instead the water's enchantment. Gilbert, of course, agreed.

And then, later that night, he saw it.

Having lost all of its stored heat from the daytime, the desert was extremely cold. It was after midnight and Gilbert was shivering in his blanket on the ground. He got up, thinking he might warm up in the Caravan. Their bonfire had already been reduced to embers, but it still crackled, sending small sparks into the sky. Celia was sleeping soundly like a cat, curled up at his feet, but he didn't see Arthur or Melanie. He was about to look for them when he noticed them not far away, by the lake's edge, holding one another, their bodies glowing red as though warmed by the earth's heat. They stood there in their embrace reflecting the dying flames. Arthur's body, which always seemed slender and frail under his clothes, gave off an aura of immense strength against the backdrop of the night sky. Even his too pale skin, in the firelight, shone with a dark reddish hue exuding life. The vitality of life. The vivid scene struck Gilbert as beautiful. The water would be gone by morning and, in his enchantment, Gilbert could almost see twinkling particles of water rising off the surface. His senses were coming unhinged—or rather, the scene was burning itself into his mind. The half moon illuminated only a low overgrowth of bushes and revealed no fleshy plants. Arthur stretched an arched leg, brushing a few pebbles into the water. In the occasional passing headlights, Arthur and Melanie looked like cacti intertwined at the arms. Cacti, fleshy and covered with thorns—if you sliced them, a clear liquid seeped from the slits...

Gilbert stopped his story here and looked at Leslie, who was hanging on his every word.

"Then what? What happened to Arthur?"

Gilbert returned his eyes to the road and stretched his legs. "He disappeared," he said.

"Disappeared?"

"Yes, he literally disappeared."

"How?"

"When I woke up the next morning, he was gone. Simple as that."

Gilbert never did meet Arthur again. How Arthur disappeared was still a mystery to him—and the same went for why he disappeared. Gilbert had been left in the middle of the desert bereft of all sense of direction. The music that had lured him out into the desert had vanished, swallowed up by the earth with the night's end. That morning he could only stand there in a daze, unable to take his eyes away from the spot where Arthur had disappeared.

"And Melanie?"

"Only Arthur disappeared. Well, actually, that's not entirely true. The puddle disappeared, too. A puddle big enough to be a lake disappeared overnight. Can you believe that?"

"Sounds like a fairy tale."

"Exactly. When the water disappeared, Arthur's music departed along with it."

"I see." Leslie nodded, at last realizing the point of Gilbert's story.

Arthur, his music, and the strange events of that night in the desert had left an indelible impression on Gilbert. The sudden disappearance of a person inevitably left lingering doubts as to the cause, the reason. Some sort of answer as to where he or she went was necessary for one's peace of mind. Gilbert had had no choice but to search for the past that the desert had swallowed up within it.

"When the underground lake was discovered six months ago, I knew I had to see it for myself, and when I finally did, all those memories came flooding back. It was as if the water had seeped through the sands, taking Arthur's music with it, ending up in a vast lake deep below the earth."

"I understand now."

"But do you really? That was a very personal experience."

"So is everyone's. Me, I have no idea where my passion comes from. But you, if I may say such a thing to a prominent mystic, seem to know exactly where your passion comes from."

Gilbert began to laugh as if he'd heard the funniest thing in the world. He liked Leslie all the more for his latest remark.

The mystic pointed ahead with his chin. "Look..."

It was about ten o'clock and they were approaching a town. Both of them were tired and had spoken enough for the day. Thinking it time to check into a motel, Leslie slowed down and looked for a VACANCY sign, but he found it hard to shake the images of Gilbert's story from his mind.

6

Flora woke up at six the next morning. As she was combing her hair after her shower, she looked closely into the mirror, contorting her face into various expressions. She smiled, raised her eyebrows, puffed out her cheeks, and rubbed her eyes, trying to figure out how best to present herself to Leslie.

Just before seven, she went down to the front desk, where a mustached Mexican greeted her with a courteous smile.

"Your rental car is waiting for you out front," he said, handing her the keys.

"Thank you. I'll have it back by tomorrow."

As soon as she walked out the door, however, she stopped dead in her tracks. There was a yellow sports car out front. A two-seater Datsun, it was the only car out there. Still grasping the key, she went back inside, wondering who'd made a mistake, she or the motel.

"Excuse me, but didn't I tell you what kind of car I wanted?"

The man opened his eyes in an exaggerated fashion. That there was something wrong was clear from Flora's expression.

"No, not really..."

"Oh..."

Flora thought back to the night before. She *had* been weary from her trip; maybe she'd made an oversight.

"Didn't I say I wanted a car for the desert?"

The man sighed and shook his head, his actions seeming more rehearsed than genuine.

"I'm sure that's what I asked for," Flora said, only slightly relieved it hadn't been her mistake. "So what's that car out there?"

The desk clerk's face darkened as he realized he'd misunderstood her. He figured she meant driving on a freeway across the desert, not *into* the desert in a 4WD. He'd assumed wrongly because she was a woman, but Flora was partly to blame for not having made sure.

She explained that she wanted an off-road vehicle that could handle the sands.

"So you'd like a jeep or something...?"

"I don't really care about the details, just as long as it can get me to where I need to go."

He signaled with his hand to wait a moment and made a few calls. Then, covering the receiver with his mouth, he asked, "Can you wait until ten o'clock?"

If she left at ten, she would never make her appointment.

"I need it as soon as possible."

After trying a few more places, he gave up.

"I'm so sorry about this, ma'am," he said, looking away sadly. "You'll have to wait until ten. The rental car office doesn't open until then and none of the other places that are open have any four-wheel-drive vehicles available."

Flora looked at the clock. At this rate, she wouldn't arrive in Springerville until after three, but she had no choice now. She could never reach the cave in that Datsun, which meant she wouldn't be there to watch him work. She gave up and went back to her room to wait.

Leslie stopped his car in front of the Springerville Post Office right on time. After telling Gilbert he was going to mail a postcard, he stepped out of the car and went towards the door, scanning the parking lot for any signs of Flora's car. He had no idea what Flora looked like or how old she was. He didn't even know the type of car she'd rented, but he was sure he'd spot it. Considering how inspired he'd been just by hearing her voice on the phone, he was sure his sixth sense would alert him when he saw her in person.

But she wasn't there. The only two cars in the lot both had Arizona license plates, and Flora's was more likely to have a Texas plate. Hoping she was just running a little late, he decided to wait for ten more minutes. Any longer would seem a bit much just to send a postcard. Leslie thought maybe she'd gotten lost or held up at work and wasn't able to catch her flight.

When Flora didn't show, he gave up and went back to the car. As he and Gilbert made their way towards the desert, Leslie kept checking the rearview mirror. He couldn't stop thinking about her. He watched for signs of her car in the dust clouds behind them. No one was following them. Flora's voice echoed in every part of his being. He let up on the gas, reluctant to move on, but had to go where Gilbert directed him. When at last they went over a small hill, the long highway disappeared behind them, leaving them surrounded on all sides by desolate land. She would never find them now. Leslie took his eyes away from the rearview mirror and looked ahead.

7

"All right, we're here," said Gilbert, pointing to their right. "Park over there."

Leslie did as he was told and shut off the engine. The sudden silence was refreshing. He surveyed the landscape, but saw only desert. This wasn't as he'd imagined it. The spot was impossible to locate without Gilbert's guidance.

He then noticed that the ground sloped downward into a basin, pockmarked with small outcroppings of stone. The bottom was covered with clay, above which some clear water had collected.

Gilbert pointed to the bottom. "This bowl-shaped formation is called a doline," he explained.

Once they'd stuffed all their essentials into rucksacks, Leslie and Gilbert scuttled down into the basin like insects. When they reached the bottom, the gaping cave entrance awaited them. Gilbert started the generator in front of it, sending power through the cord that ran into the cave and igniting the vast darkness within. They would have nothing to fear now.

The entrance itself was not all that big, but was at least high and wide enough to walk through without bending down. Once inside, it opened up to a steep, staired passageway that was much larger than the entrance led one to expect. Leslie went down back first, wrapping the guide rope around his hands to keep from slipping off the rocks.

The light pouring in from the outside world softened and gradually faded away, the desert sunlight now replaced by an equally intense darkness. A freezing cold draft prickled their skin.

Though their helmet lights weren't strong enough to reach the ceiling, Leslie was able to see the deep gray layers of sediment curving like waves along the roughhewn walls.

When they reached what looked to be a dead end, Gilbert pointed out a deep, black crevice in the wall, and the rope in their hands indeed led into it. Gilbert went down first. The rock grew steeper further in and narrowed to a width just ample enough for one person to fit through. The sedimentary layers were clearly visible now; an unimaginable number of years were written into the neatly distinct strata.

Leslie was finding it hard to breathe. It wasn't that there wasn't enough air. Looking down and scanning the layers on the rock wall, he was feeling faint from the passage of time, of epochs. These things were visible as he looked up and down. A blast of air had ruffled the pages of the book of history towards the past, so rapidly, that Leslie was losing all sense of time. *Beringia*. More than the name of his composition, it was the northern corridor crossed by his ancestors. It was a picture of the entire cycle of a people, indeed of all life birthed upon the planet. Leslie wondered what marked the passage of an era and why rock stratified at all. When his body someday rotted and returned to the earth, he hoped to become a part of these layers.

Large floodlights on a rock ledge struggled against the darkness to illuminate their way. Leslie and Gilbert stood on the ledge in silent awe before this microcosm of creation. The artificial light was tinged a faint blue, casting indistinct shadows in the far reaches of the cave. From the ceiling stalactites hung like icicles while here and there from the cave floor stalagmites poked out, the two connecting into thick columns like at some ancient Greek palace done in the Ionian style. Flow stone made jellyfish patterns like a waterfall on the walls. Curly outcroppings seemed to defy gravity with the help of an eonic draft. The smooth surfaces of the tabular stalactites resembled a silk curtain. Gilbert gave Leslie a crash course on the various kinds of limestone. These were natural sculptures, masterpieces whose artist was Time. While everything appeared frozen, the process was going on even now. Drops of water were trickling through the desert sands above and forming new extensions even as they stood there. Too slowly for the eye to see.

"Shall we proceed?" said Gilbert. It was only because he had been here before that he was much calmer than Leslie.

Rope in hand, they scaled the ledge until they reached the level floor below. Each step sent a flurry of rocks into unseen pits. Gilbert seemed sure about where he was going, but Leslie couldn't imagine that this mysterious realm came to an end. It was like wading through the grain fields of the midwest; no matter how far they went, the same landscape confronted them.

Leslie stopped for a moment and asked, "How far are we going?"

"It's just ahead... We won't be able to go any deeper, you'll see."

Leslie looked out into the dark expanse before him, and, sure enough, after taking about a few dozen steps, he realized Gilbert had spoken truly. It wasn't so much the darkness but the breathtaking transparency that had fooled him. Leslie's right foot splashed in water, and before he knew it, the lake was spread out before him.

Shining light on the water's surface didn't help him see where the water ended and the air began. The light seeped with ease into the water and bounced off against the bottom. Light was an artificial ray violating this virgin sea. Slipping through the particles of water, hitting the smooth rocks at the bottom, it brought into relief random patches of the lake.

"Let's rest here."

Perhaps feeling his age, Gilbert's breathing had been getting slightly irregular. Here at last, they sat on the slick rocks.

Gilbert took out a cup and a bottle of whiskey from his rucksack, diluted it with a little water from the lake, and drank.

"You want some?"

Leslie took the cup and downed just a mouthful.

He let out one awestruck sigh after another. He swiveled and craned his neck to take it all in. This was beyond words. He was sure he would be inspired by this. If he ever had any doubts as to why Gilbert wanted to bring him here, they were gone now. Time by the million, a world of pitch darkness, the origins of the universe, absolute stasis. This space was indeed contiguous with his *Beringia* symphony.

Gilbert explained to him, in simple terms, how this place had formed.

Millions of years ago, it had all been ocean floor. The water was replete with drifting life-forms such as sea lilies, foraminifers, and fusulina, as well as crinoids, coral, and shellfish. When these died, they sank and accumulated along the ocean floor. Then, after countless years, intense pressure, coupled with chemical reactions, solidified the calcium deposits into limestone. Such a plateau was pushed above water when the continents shifted and collided. The same also caused the formation of mountain ranges, which intercepted the moist ocean winds, turning interior areas into arid deserts. When it did rain in the desert, the water seeped underground through cracks in the limestone. The carbonic acid in the water dissolved the limestone, forming, over untold millennia, elaborate patterns and the world they now beheld.

Leslie rose to his feet and took a few steps as though to check his footing.

He was impressed by all this, but not because the place used to be underwater. Most populated land was once the bottom of a vast ocean. What intrigued him was that this subterranean environment was essentially a burial ground for countless animals. The unfathomable amount of time it had taken to create these rock formations meant an equally unfathomable amount of corpses to form them. Leslie had never seen a sea lily, nor even an illustration of one. He could only guess from the name that they were shaped like their namesake flowers. He imagined thousands of colorful lilies wavering at the bottom of a deep, dark sea.

Once Gilbert finished his brief explanation, he kept quiet. It was clear that Leslie was even more awestruck by this place than Gilbert himself. The mystic didn't want to interfere with the artist's inspiration. Gilbert looked at his watch. They'd already spent two hours getting here. Now was the time.

Leslie scooped up some water into his hands and drank it. He bent down to pick up a pebble on the bank, when suddenly he saw pebbles rolling at the lake bottom. Given that there was no draft, Leslie was startled. Then he heard it—something crawling on the pebbles. A splash sent ripples across the lake's surface.

"Gil!" Leslie had stepped back.

"What is it?"

"There's something moving down there."

Another splash.

"Look!" Leslie turned his light towards the noise. There was nothing. However, the surface broke into a V, indicating that something was swimming through it.

"It's just an animal," echoed Gilbert's voice. "There must be plenty of them. They've probably always lived here."

"But I don't see anything."

"Exactly. Think about it. Not a single ray of sunlight has ever found its way in here, but that doesn't mean nothing can live in this environment. I'm sure that, in the process of acclimating themselves to the darkness, their eyes degenerated—and they've probably become colorless or even transparent. They compensate for this with a highly developed sense of smell and touch. At any rate they've survived."

How pointless! Leslie thought. A creature without a discernible shape! What business did it have to exist?

"They're simply living according to nature," Gilbert said. "They have a food chain and subsist in this totally self-contained society. They're no different from organisms who live aboveground."

Yet another splash.

"Sound. The only proof of their existence," Gilbert noted.

Sound only... echoed Leslie in his mind. *Why, just like me...*

A time would come when the only proof he'd ever existed would be the music he'd written.

The splashing stopped and echoed into silence. The creature showed a faint glow in its body and dove deep into the water. Leslie didn't know at this time that the light radiating from the creature was actually a residue from his own flashlight.

Sounds were spiraling in Leslie's body. He quickly pulled out his notepad. He took out the stone pendant hanging from his neck, grasped it in his left hand, then gently opened his fingers. The red deer was ready to leap. Whenever he composed anything, he felt he could never pull it off unless he was being watched over by the deer. This thin, flat stone was the only memento handed down to him by his father and grandmother's ancestors. It had the power to stir up from the depths of his cells the dreams that humanity dreamed when it was still young.

The sounds came, from afar. His music did not form in his body. From outside him it came, from a terrible distance indeed, charging. He could barely let it flow through his pen. He couldn't begin to describe in words this music that was coming to him now. Afraid that he was going to miss notes, he cursed himself that he couldn't take them down faster. It was a sublime experience that seemed unrepeatable to him. If, in truth, nothing beyond this was attainable for him, then perhaps he would never again be moved to compose. It wasn't his nature to accept reproduction on a regressive scale.

After half an hour, the flood of sound had receded. Leslie looked up at the cave ceiling, cradled in a pleasant fatigue. Gilbert was obviously reluctant to break the silence, so Leslie spoke up first.

"I'm done, Gil."

"How did it go?"

Leslie simply closed his eyes and made as to chase after the music's echo.

"I get it, your expression says it all. I wish I could hear it, too."

"Gil, I can't thank you enough for this."

And indeed Leslie wanted to thank Gilbert from the bottom of his heart for hatching such a crackpot idea. The composition would never have come without the sight before him. Without Gilbert, the music would never have been born.

"I'm looking forward to hearing your piece in concert."

Gilbert rose to his feet and approached Leslie. At that moment, the floodlights on the ledge blinked slowly. Thinking the generator might be shorting out, Leslie stood and backed away from the lake. They heard water sloshing around and the ground began to shake violently. By the time they realized it was an earthquake, it was already too late, and in the flickering light they saw the ground split at their feet, throwing Leslie and Gilbert into greater darkness. The two of them fell, along with the water of the lake, into the crack.

As gravity pulled them down, their bodies tumbled with the torrent, slipping down a jagged limestone cliff. Their fear snowballed in the dark air. They could see nothing in front of them. They shielded their heads and screamed at the top of their lungs, but their voices were drowned by the roar of the water with a force that nearly knocked out Leslie's senses. The fall felt like an eternity, but was over in a matter of seconds.

Leslie realized what was happening to him when he felt himself drop from the natural slide into a large hollow. Thinking his body would smash into the rocks below, he was sure that he was done for, and every memory of the past thirty-four years passed before his eyes.

The descent was so swift, he nearly lost consciousness. Leslie heard the sound of a waterfall. He couldn't tell whether he was remembering it or if he was hearing it. It reminded him of summer, though this hardly seemed appropriate given where he was.

As if ripping apart his delusion, Leslie's body was shocked into awareness when it hit water, which then filled his mouth and gushed into his stomach. He'd fallen into another lake. He stopped breathing and closed his eyes, his body spinning around in the current. Unable to tell up from down, he went into a panic. He was one step away from losing it, when suddenly he realized: *If I just keep still, my body will float up naturally.*

This was only common sense, yet it required superhuman nerves. Many people had killed themselves trying to resist the very forces that would have saved them.

Leslie concentrated as hard as he could and let the water carry him upward. As soon as his head broke the surface, he coughed and breathed in the suffocatingly cold air.

"Gil!...Gilbert!" he cried out. Leslie had felt Gilbert's body banging against his when they fell, so he had to be close by.

There was a groan and the sounds of arms struggling against the water.

"Gil...are you there?"

Leslie swam towards Gilbert's voice and groped around until his left hand touched a sleeve.

"You okay?"

Gilbert managed a weak moan in response. Leslie took him by the waist as he continued to tread water.

Try as he might, he could hardly see anything. He knew he had to find a way out of here as soon as possible. He didn't know how much longer he could stay above water. The cold alone would kill him if he didn't take action soon, but he was more worried that Gilbert's condition was critical.

He knew he needed to get up onto the bank, but there was no way to tell which way to go. He started swimming randomly, and just when he thought he was going the right way, his fears got the better of him and he lost the will to go on.

He heard the waterfall again. It was real after all. Leslie tried to locate it, but to no avail. Gradually, the sound began to fade, as if it were moving away from him, which indicated the water was diminishing. Leslie was able to pinpoint the waterfall's sound with his extraordinary hearing. He began swimming for it.

The presence of a waterfall meant there was a good chance a cliff would be close by. If he could find a rock to grab onto, it would help him stay afloat. And if they could just make it up along the waterfall, there had to be a crack leading outside. But the violent current was fading into a mere trickle. Leslie held onto Gilbert, swimming with all his might to make it before the trickling faded and he lost its position.

And then, he reached the stone. He grabbed its craggy surface with his left hand and pulled himself out of the water, feeling around for a safe place. When he found one, he pulled Gilbert out onto it. Though he'd just narrowly escaped death, he hardly counted it as a victory just yet. Leslie's body trembled. He had no idea how much time had passed since they fell into the crevice. Maybe this was the end. No, it *was* the end. He was much more afraid of the moments leading up to death than death itself.

Leslie put his fingers between the stalagmites and tried to form a mental picture of his surroundings. The stone at his feet was smooth and he had to be careful not to slip back into the water.

Once he calmed down a little, he realized after careful thought that there was no way to escape on their own. The only hope was if someone knew he and Gilbert were here. In other words, Flora. But they were in the middle of the desert, a place marked on no map. It wouldn't be easy for Flora to find without a guide. Still, Leslie called out Flora's name. Springerville was within reach, only twenty miles away. She was already on her way; she had to be. He'd already been worried that she hadn't shown up as planned, but he tried to convince himself that she'd flown in to El Paso, at least. In light of his desperate circumstances, this shred of hope was indispensable.

Though he didn't see it reaching out, he felt Gilbert's feeble hand upon his knee. Leslie grabbed it tightly.

"Everything's going to be okay, Gilbert. We'll make it out just fine," he said, touching Gilbert's shoulder. The sensation of warm, slimy skin made Leslie uneasy. He didn't know where the wound was, but as he feared, Gilbert was losing blood.

"Leslie...Leslie..."

Gilbert's hoarse, disembodied voice threaded the stalactites, bouncing everywhere into distant echoes.

"Leslie, there's something I want to ask you..."

Leslie leaned in closer in the direction of Gilbert's voice.

8

Flora reached Springerville via Route 180 at exactly 3 pm and checked into the first motel that she saw, the southernmost. She was certain it was the first motel sign Leslie would see on his way back from the cave, too. He should have no trouble finding her.

It was a small, one-story motel, but was quiet enough. She walked into her room and opened the curtains to let the air in. She checked the refrigerator, only to find nothing in it. Flora put a hand to her chin and muttered to herself that she should go to the supermarket later.

That's when she felt it. Reeling from the rumbling beneath her, she instinctively grasped the fridge door. She hadn't been in an earthquake for a long time. She'd been through her fair share during her childhood in San Diego, but this was her first since she'd moved to the East Coast. After four quick jolts, the earth settled, but Flora's heart was still pounding. She thought she smelled rotten vegetables, but realized it was probably just from the open fridge. Suddenly a series of scenes flashed through her mind at dizzying speed. A terrible premonition that something great was coming. Without context, she heard ocean waves and smelled the tide. Dogs were barking in the distance. She also heard birds flocking into the sky. Brightly colored flowers bloomed and withered, tips of palm leaves glinted with sunlight. The silhouette of a black boat being pulled towards the shore, a forest of dim metal rods pointed towards the sky. Her chest tightened at these images before they were blotted out completely by a surge of intense emotions beyond anger or fear...a seething of the cells and blood.

Flora snapped back to reality.

What was that?

She braced herself against the wall, her eyes alert and her breathing quick. Why would she suddenly think of the ocean in a desert town like this? She could only imagine that the visions had been triggered by the earthquake.

It was strange: an ocean and an island covered with palm trees.

Why?

She drew near the window and looked out towards the desert in the east, blinking a few times to clear her eyes. Her vision had changed. She encountered not the indifferent sands she'd driven through to get here, but a landscape, indeed a *feeling*, she'd once known before. A feeling that spoke to her.

Something terrible is coming...

Flora continued gazing into the east, knowing that Leslie's cave was only twenty miles away.

She was suddenly worried about him. He was still underground right now, which meant he was probably in trouble. For the moment, she hesitated. As long as she didn't know the exact location of the cave, there was nothing she could do to help him. Besides, she'd been in stronger earthquakes before, so there was no reason to be too fatalistic. While she'd been confused by the tropical imagery, she rationalized it away with a little careful thought. Flora waited for her heart to return to its normal pace. Assuming that things had gone as planned, Leslie and Gilbert would be arriving in town around 4 pm.

She decided to wait until nightfall. After ordering take-out, she sat eagerly with the key to the jeep in her hand. Whatever fears she had about the situation, all Flora could do now was wait.

9

Leslie heard a voice calling out to him, but in the mounting darkness it took on an alien quality and served only to compound his fears. Gilbert whispered with the guttural voice of a demon: "Leslie...Leslie..." Leslie couldn't take this anymore. He imagined creatures without substance, slowly but surely coming near—insects crawling all over him by the thousands, eating him alive. His body itched painfully everywhere. Something burrowed into his shirt. He thrashed around, trying to shake off the feeling. The voice called to him again: "Leslie...Leslie..." Now it wasn't Gilbert, but a fierce noise that pierced him, like fingernails on a chalkboard. Leslie stood up and screamed to make it go away, and suddenly the voice changed from a hoarse whisper to a comforting woman's song. The cold silence returned. It was the same voice he'd heard on the phone. Flora's voice.

"Leslie..."

She was calling to him, so close, he could almost feel her. The thought brought him relief. As if by magic, his pain disappeared and the darkness grew a touch lighter. The voice stopped suddenly and Leslie realized it had all been in his head. His heart calmed down and he finally answered the real voice he'd heard.

"What is it, Gil?"

Gilbert held Leslie's shoulder in silence. They had lost all sense of time. Leslie knew he had to keep Gilbert talking so he wouldn't fade on him. The weight of the darkness seemed to lift, then returned with full force.

"Hey, Gil. Gil... Did you just say something?"

Leslie shook him awake. The older man's breathing was irregular. Leslie's eyes darted back and forth.

"I was just calling your name..."

"Yes, I know."

"The piece you just composed. Would you say it is...something you created?"

Thinking the shock of the fall might have impaired Gilbert's state of mind, Leslie asked, "What are you talking about, Gil?"

"Sorry, maybe I wasn't clear... I'm not a composer, of course, so it's hard for me to articulate this... There's obviously music in this space...it is undeniable...but an amateur like me would never be able to pick up on it. And yet, an accomplished artist like yourself is so in tune with it... Do you know what I'm saying?"

This time, Leslie knew exactly what Gilbert meant, because he'd thought about the exact same thing. For him, music did not come from within, but was rather something that passed through him from afar. In his previous compositions, Leslie had taken music that was universal and rendered it into a notated score. Now, more than ever, he felt like a mere vehicle for this entire creative process.

"You're right, Gil. I guess you could say that I hear the voices in this space."

He wasn't trying to be arrogant. It was simply his privileged experience as a composer. Such people were chosen to translate the whispers hidden all around us...

"I've always thought...there are two types of geniuses," said

Gilbert raspingly. "Discovery and creation. A scientific genius discovers the laws of the universe through the inspiration of his intellect. And artists create using that same power... At least, that's how I see it. But sometimes I think that creation is not unlike discovery... True creation means bringing forth something new, but perhaps it's beyond us humans... You understand?" Leslie answered by squeezing Gilbert's hand. "...Perfect beauty is a natural component of the universe. As a composer, you have the power to discover that and recreate it... I wanted so much to hear what you heard...the music in this subterranean space...but it's impossible now..." Gilbert coughed violently. "I'm sorry it came to this."

"Gil, like I said before, I'm in your debt. This place is filled with music. It resounds with wonderful melodies."

"Yes, and you have...discovered them."

Leslie then heard something. It sounded like dripping at first, but his keen ears told him it was a living thing, like a fish jumping out of water. Leslie strained his ears and tried to locate the sound. As he listened, he realized it was coming from more than one location. The sounds of animals swimming in the lake were growing louder.

"They're here, too," said Leslie.

Even the faintest sounds reached his ears. He couldn't help think that, if he stayed down here long enough, he would turn into one of them, translucent and sightless in an isolated world.

"Flora!" he cried out, to halt his delusional thoughts. If there was one thing he knew for sure, it was that this place was infinite. His voice was swallowed completely by the gloom and made none of the echoes one would expect from close limestone walls. He called out again.

"Gil. This lake must be as big as an ocean."

Gilbert wheezed in pain, unable to answer.

Leslie searched his clinging wet clothes for a flashlight, but of course found nothing. He wasn't a smoker, so he didn't even have a lighter on him, not that it would have helped much. And yet, for reasons he couldn't explain, the sheer expansiveness of this place put him at ease.

Gilbert started coughing again. Leslie patted him on the back.

"You want some water?"

Gilbert laughed.

"I think I've had enough water for today."

Leslie's hand was touching Gilbert's wound. A gash on his left side was bleeding profusely. Leslie applied as much pressure to it as he could, but it refused to stop. Gilbert had been pierced by a sharp rock during the fall and Leslie didn't know how much blood he'd lost already.

"I'm done for..." whispered Gilbert through a fit of coughing. But Leslie wouldn't let him go that easily. Hope could help one pull through, and in this case, their only hope was to wait for outside help. He told Gilbert about Flora.

"...and when she sees we haven't come back, she's sure to come looking for us. We just have to stick it out. We'll get through this. Okay, Gil?"

Gilbert laughed weakly again. He reached for Leslie and grasped both of his hands.

"Leslie, you're a good person, and I thank you... But I'm ready for this."

It seemed Gilbert thought Leslie had made the whole thing up just to comfort a dying old man in his last moments.

"No, really, Gil. I'm serious. I feel terrible for hiding it from you this whole time, but Flora's sure to be on her way already. Okay, Gil...? Gil...?"

Gilbert's answer was late in coming.

"So you have never...met this woman Flora?"

"...No, never."

Gilbert laughed at this, thinking there was no reason why a person they'd never even met would care enough to come rescue them.

"Just trust me on this one, Gil. I guess you could say Flora is...well, the 'one.'"

"And how do you know?"

"Because when I heard her voice on the phone, I felt it deep down."

"...How?"

"I lost interest in other women."

This time, Gilbert didn't laugh.

"Your body knows the truth... Maybe you *have* met before... That, too, is a kind of...discovery."

Just then, Leslie felt a stirring in the air. It wasn't wind, but a shifting of the elements. He felt it on the backs of his hands, on his wet cheeks. He could hear it—something was coming their way. The water rippled and sloshed against the limestone around them. Leslie instinctively felt around for something to hold on to. When he found a protruding rock, he pulled Gilbert's body upright.

"What's going on?"

"Can't you hear it? That noise, listen."

He propped Gilbert's body against the rocks and held on to them with Gilbert in between. Leslie strained his ears and, from the sound alone, knew he had to act fast. He felt the lake rising, and soon the small waves grew to a booming rush of energy, as if the creatures of this cave were once again disturbing the waters. The noise grew closer. Leslie feared that he couldn't endure whatever was approaching in the darkness. He unconsciously stopped breathing, grabbing the rocks with all his might.

In an instant, water was all around him. His body was buoyed upward, but he held on to the rocks. He was submerged from the neck down, and countless creatures squirmed by his neck, leaving a slimy sensation on his skin. The waves drew back suddenly, leaving them in eerie silence. Leslie closed his eyes, his lips trembling from the cold.

I can't take any more of this! he wanted to scream. He couldn't handle a surprise attack. His body kept shaking.

Gilbert exhaled, proving he was at least alive, though Leslie was worried because the intervals between his breaths were growing longer and longer.

"Gil...What was that?"

"A tidal wave...from the earthquake."

Leslie couldn't believe it. A tidal wave down here? Was this place really that big? He'd read that tsunamis from earthquakes off the shores of Peru took twenty-three hours to cross the Pacific. Judging from that, this was not a lake, but an ocean. Leslie felt he'd seen everything now.

"Leslie...get out of here," Gilbert urged.

"I want to, but how are we going to do that?"

"No, I want *you* to get out of here. I know you can. Just do it for me."

"For you?"

"Yes... You see, this whole situation...reminds me of when I was stuck in that drain...I wanted so much to get out...but I was helpless. In my fading consciousness...I heard the agitations of the city. The last thing I remember was the feeling of my body floating in the shallow rainwater at the bottom of the drain. When I came to...I was in a bed. I didn't know if I'd made it out on my own...or if someone had rescued me...but at least...I was in the outside world again. I wouldn't want you to miss out on that feeling because of me...so get out while you still can."

Leslie felt uneasy and wondered if Gilbert was deranged. He was growing more incoherent, expending his last remaining strength to convey his message.

"You've seen the rock layers at the entrance to the cave... Ever since life has existed on this planet...countless generations have come and gone in an endless cycle... You could say there's no meaning to any of it. The formation of this limestone...as I said before...was made...from corpses that accumulated at the bottom of the sea... And now, I will become one of them. It is...my fate. But you...you will return to the outside. Even if there is no purpose to any of the endless repetition...you must go... There's a point...in living!"

Leslie was irritated that Gilbert was wasting his breath on this, because it was only natural to want to get out of this place. Who in their right mind would ever want to rot away in such a wretched place?

"Tell me, Gil. How am I ever supposed to find a way out

when I can't see a damned thing down here?"

"The world works in...mysterious ways."

"Like I haven't heard that before."

Gilbert gave a long pause.

"Leslie. Have you forgotten...the ability that you possess? I...haven't. I have seen it...with my own eyes...during the rehearsal...of *Beringia*...when you...singled out...that one imperfect sound...the cellist. Your ears...aren't normal. You can pinpoint a sound's source exactly...whatever its source."

These words sparked something in Leslie. Then, as if in response, the sound of dripping water entered his ears. It awakened his senses so much that he could almost see it. Then, as if a haze were clearing, it condensed in one direction. Its clear echoes scattered above Leslie's left ear before being swallowed up in the underground lake.

"I hear it, too..." croaked Gilbert. "But I can't tell which direction it's coming from... But I know you can... It must be coming from...the crevice we fell into... Quickly now...find it...before it fades away."

Leslie focused his attentions on the noise. He moved his outstretched hand 45 degrees to the left, then up 60 degrees. His left index finger shot out, pointing to the exact location. That would be his way out.

"Gil, it's just as you said. I can't see it, but I know where it's coming from, so let's go together..."

"Don't be foolish. If you have any sense...you'll go on without me and send a search party for me...later."

"Gil..."

Gilbert's breathing turned into heavy wheezing.

"It's okay, Leslie... No one knows...how the world works... But...you...can get closer... Tear away the veils, one by one! Now is the time to move on... It will become clear."

With those final words, the darkness grew heavier.

Leslie brought his ear close to Gilbert's mouth. He was no longer breathing.

"...Gil...Gil?"

The splashing of subterranean creatures disturbed the silence, but this only intensified Leslie's loneliness.

"Hey, Gil? Answer me," he said with tears in his eyes, but the only thing to answer him was the sound of water. He wondered how much longer he could stay here before he went crazy. Though he was a man of tough nerves, he couldn't handle this.

Before he knew it, Leslie had removed the pendant from his neck. He'd grown so used to this image of a red deer since he was a child, that even now its contours floated clearly before him. As he closed his eyes and thought of the deer, its redness grew deeper, front legs poised for the sky. This image had run through his music, bolstered his will to live, and influenced everything he did.

What should I do?

The answer was simple. He had to face things and prevail. There was no other way.

Leslie hung the pendant around Gilbert's neck and folded Gilbert's hands over it. If Leslie was going to leave him behind, the least he could do was to offer this protection. Even if the pendant was no longer with him, the red deer's spirit would continue to guide him.

Leslie stood up and fumbled around until he encountered a wall of jagged limestone. The protrusions were sturdy enough to hold his weight. He found a dent above his head and pulled himself up, searching for the next foothold. After he managed to climb a few steps higher, he realized there would be no way to reach the crevice. If the precipice somehow curved inward near the top, it might provide enough leeway. Leslie knew he had to keep climbing. But even if he went through all the trouble, at the risk of injury, would anything come of it?

Without warning, the rock he was grasping in his right hand snapped off. Just as he was about to fall, Leslie thought fast and pushed off the wall with his feet as hard as he could to propel his body into the water.

Leslie fell many times in the coming hours. His feet were blistered and bleeding, but he was more worried about the brittle rock than his injuries. Every time he fell, he was overcome with the same fear. What would happen if he fell onto the stone? If he knew for sure that his efforts were futile, he wouldn't risk his own execution so many times. As things were, he couldn't just sit and wait for death to take him. Like Gilbert said, it was all about clarity.

After climbing countless times, there was another earthquake, this one a little stronger than the first. Twice it pealed through the cave. The force of it threw Leslie from the cliff. He was certain this time would be the last.

10

Flora awoke with a start from a light sleep, her body rigid with fear.

Another quake.

Not ten seconds later, she felt the land tremble below. It was exactly like the earthquake the day before. Flora grabbed the clock on the night stand. It was 4 am. She was about to let her hand fall when the exact scene from yesterday unfolded in her mind. The scent of soil and of tides, the ocean, a tropical paradise, waves crashing on shore, the masts of a ship swaying against the sky. An unshakable feeling that something was coming—something magnificent and terrible. Flora smelled sweat. For the second time now, she was seeing things she'd never experienced. But even more strange was the fact that she'd foreseen the earthquake. And this time, the images didn't leave her completely. One lingered in her head more vividly than all the rest. A large animal with antlers. A red deer. A megalith covered in ivy.

Flora jumped from the bed in shock and ran to the bathroom. She tore off her pajama top and gazed at her birthmark in the mirror, at last realizing what it meant. She raised and lowered her shoulder, the deer dancing on her skin from her movements. Her brain was suddenly flooded with memories. She began to weep without reason, knowing only that she was changing into a different self.

The desert outside her window was beginning to lighten with the coming of dawn. It was already clear to her what she had to do. After waiting all night for Leslie's arrival, it was the earthquake that had finally shown her the way.

Go. East. To the desert.

Spurred on by the red deer, she got herself ready. Leslie was in trouble, and Flora knew she was the only one on earth who could help him.

She pulled out the map from her bag. She knew the cave's approximate location, but nothing more. She could easily get lost if she simply went traipsing around in the desert. Having no other options, Flora hopped into the jeep and drove. The eastern horizon emerged from the night's last traces, separating gradually into land and sky.

She turned the wheel and looked in the rearview mirror. She heard a voice inside her.

I will fight everything that surrounds me.

A familiar, powerful voice, fading with the sound of ocean waves.

Flora shouted hysterically as she drove up and down the road.

"How the hell am I ever going to find this place?!"

She knew how unforgiving the desert could be and knew also how insane it was to explore it without a concrete plan. When she finally gathered enough courage to veer off the road, the land was completely flat, devoid of dunes she'd hoped to use as landmarks. Flora stopped the car. She left the engine running and got out. The refreshing morning air helped cool her temper. It was then that, by chance, she caught sight of a small river gushing from a fissure in the east. Once Flora saw this, she knew the underground lake couldn't be far away. She grabbed her map from the car and managed to find it: Little Colorado River. She followed it upstream with her fingertip until it hit the north-south border of Arizona and New Mexico. She remembered Leslie's words:

......The underground lake is right on the Arizona-New Mexico border.

The murmuring of the river was pleasing to the ear. The water was also carrying something unseen—a passion that spoke to the very core of her being.

Flora knew this river could stem from nowhere else but the underground lake. If she followed it for twenty miles and found nothing, she would at least have a clear path back. This minimized her chances of getting lost, and she would have plenty of water on hand.

Let's go!

Flora traveled east along the river, certain that the cave entrance would be waiting for her at its source.

11

Leslie poked his head above the water's surface, bathed in the deluge from above. The trickle's volume had increased due to the earthquake and, from this, Leslie knew the way out must be somewhere near. Having only his instincts to rely on, he looked around in the pitch-black darkness. He drank some of the falling water to quench his thirst as he fought to understand every detail of this subterranean world. Even so, this was a place shrouded in mystery, where not even an eternity would provide clues. Perhaps the struggle was the only meaningful thing down here.

Leslie climbed up onto the rocks, heading for the crack from which water poured overhead. He hauled his body up onto the ledge, no longer caring if he slipped or not. He was afraid, but nothing more. The cliff was uneven and difficult to scale, and though his strength was fading with every attempt, Leslie refused to give up. Putting one foot carefully above the other, he ascended the rock. The red deer danced in his mind, encircled by Flora's strangely familiar voice.

Flora stopped the jeep exactly twenty miles up the Little Colorado River. She didn't see the cave entrance anywhere, but noticed something yellow glinting off to her right in the early light. It stood out vividly against the dark blue sky. Flora drove towards it and soon realized that the light was coming from a gold-colored pickup truck. Knowing this could only be the truck they'd taken from L.A., she felt an overwhelming sense of relief. They were close, she could feel it. Despite her joy, she was still aware of the real danger Leslie and Gilbert might be in, a possibility that overshadowed her relief. The empty truck told her they'd been in the cave the whole night.

Flora pulled up alongside the truck. There were a few polyurethane gas containers and coiled ropes in the truck bed. She stepped out of the jeep and took a look around. She saw the doline and walked down to the generator, which had fallen over, perhaps from the second earthquake. Flora followed the weather-resistant cord with her eyes. It led into an opening that was much smaller than she imagined. It was so small that, had she not seen the truck, she would easily have missed it.

Found it at last.

Flora bent over and peered into the cave, calling out Leslie's name. Her voice was immediately swallowed by the darkness. After receiving no answer, she tried again, but to no effect.

She assumed that the generator's purpose was to light up the cave—leaving the interior in darkness now. Leslie and Gilbert were surely lost with no way out. It was past 5 am.

She glared at the generator as though that would force it to offer up its secrets to her. She took off the cap to the mounted tank and looked inside. The acrid smell of gasoline entered her nostrils, indicating there was still some left. Because one of the legs had broken and the thing sat at a slant, the fuel wasn't reaching the carburetor. Flora grabbed the generator with both hands and tried to pull it upright, but it wouldn't even budge. This was clearly an impossible feat for her. The carburetor needed gas.

Flora ran up the slope, pushed a gas canister from the back of the truck, then kicked it down into the doline. She used so much of her strength just pushing it that, by the time she got to the bottom, she was already tired out. She collapsed onto the tan earth and looked up, panting at the reddening sky. Her T-shirt was soaked with sweat. Flora looked dolefully at the container. She would need to haul it up as high as her chest in order to pour the gas properly. She closed her eyes and prayed.

Give me the strength to lift this thing.

The container weighed practically as much as her, so how was she ever going to pour in enough gas to fill the generator? It seemed utterly impossible. Unable to endure the thought of losing something so precious to her, she wanted to just run away from it all. She quickly became afraid to touch the container.

Impossible, impossible! Just like her grandfather's stories of crossing the Pacific by raft. And yet her desire to make the impossible possible grew stronger, reviving her vision of unknown waters.

Fight! Fight whatever stands in your way!

Again, she heard that voice, so distant yet so familiar. A voice she'd never heard in real life. The voice from a distant past, a long-lost memory of astounding courage.

Flora stood up and put her hands underneath the container. She had to believe she could lift it, with the strength of three men.

I have to bring him back.

Bring back whom? Her dead son? Or was it Leslie...? Yes, Leslie. The man who'd saved her from death just when she was at her breaking point. It was her turn now. She had to save Leslie. Only then could she recover her child with him. She had to make up for everything that she'd lost. She knew there was no logic to it. Why did she feel so compelled to save a man she'd never met? But it was that voice who told her to find him, the very source of her power.

Flora gathered as much strength as she could and pulled up with a force that went beyond her wont. She lifted the container above the generator.

Gasoline poured out with a chugging sound. Seeing that the tank was overflowing, Flora came to her senses and fell back, spilling gasoline all over her shirt. Her face was wet—with tears or perspiration, she couldn't tell. The gasoline on her chest vaporized in the heat, leaving a cool, pleasant sensation behind. Her arms were numb. She wanted to just lie down from exhaustion, but she stood up and pulled the lever a few times to start the motor. The pistons began moving up and down loudly and mirage-like fumes came out of the exhaust pipe. Once she saw that the machine was working again, Flora quickly followed the cord with her eyes, as if she could see the electrical current ooze through inside it. She pictured a pale glow inside the cave...

Flora stood before the entrance and checked her supplies once again. She was lacking a few things, but there was no time to go back now. Two bundles of nylon rope, a searchlight, dry-cell batteries, some food and water just in case. The bats clustered near the entrance made her uneasy. Flora slipped inside quietly, so as not to disturb them.

She followed the lead rope as it stretched unbroken like a long snake into the darkness. The generator-powered lights slanted upward and were spaced far apart. The light they offered was diffuse at best, so she had to rely on her flashlight to navigate the long stretches between them. She lost her footing and stumbled many times on unseen rocks.

She passed through a narrow crack into a vast space. At first, she thought this was where the cave ended, but when she looked around, she noticed that the rope was still stretching ahead. Leslie and Gilbert weren't here. Flora pressed on past the floodlights and was awed to see just how deep this place went.

The floodlights gave no indication of a final wall, but there were no lights beyond this point, suggesting this was as far as she could go. Once her eyes grew accustomed to the dark, she slowly scanned the bottom of the hall a few times. There was no moving light, but she happened to notice a faint glow down and to the right. She cried out before she even guessed what it might be.

"Leslie!"

The light didn't move and there was no answer. With so much space to explore here, she could only imagine what unspeakable things might have happened to them. Fear of the unknown overpowered her. This space had an atmosphere all its own and she was fascinated by it, even intoxicated despite the situation. Certain it was Leslie down there, she gathered up the courage to scale the cliff to reach him.

She shuddered as she climbed down, not because of the descent itself, but from the thought of how she was going to haul an injured full-grown man up the cliff by herself.

The dim light she'd seen from the top of the cliff was hidden by the shadows of rocks and impossible to see now. Flora guessed its direction and started walking towards it. Just when the darkness ahead threatened to swallowed her completely, the light became visible again. She quickened her step and cried out Leslie's name.

The light was from the headlamp on Leslie's helmet, but he was nowhere to be seen. The drained battery made it flicker. Overtaken by a feeling of ill omen, Flora turned off the lamp before it went extinct on its own. There was sheet music scattered about and, thankfully, because there was no draft, it hadn't been dispersed. She picked the sheets up one by one and shined her flashlight on them. The notes were grouped into clusters and written more freely as they went along. Flora had no doubts as to the brilliance of what she was holding in her hand. This was composition guided by inspiration, a surrender to something outside the body where only the voices of the heavens were heard. It seemed Leslie had achieved what he had come to do. Of the ten manuscript pages she gathered, only one seemed incomplete, any further writing presumably having been stopped by the earthquake and the blackout that followed.

She called out to him again, moving her flashlight in an arc, and scouted the area. She heard the faint sound of water dripping. When she shined her flashlight in the direction of the sound, the light glinted off something glasslike. And there it was: the underground lake. She then spotted a long, thin crack running along the bank. Flora stood at the edge and cast her light into the abyss. A few meters down, stalactites made it impossible to see any deeper. Once again, she looked up. The scattered manuscript, the dying headlamp, the rucksack left on the rocks, and now the crevice, opened like a fresh wound, through which water was dripping into the bottom of darkness. If this rift was a result of the earthquake, there was only one logical conclusion. Leslie and Gilbert had fallen into it.

"Leslie!"

Flora knelt at the edge, calling his name over and over again.

At that precise moment, Leslie was stuck on the cliff. The steep precipice curved gradually as he went up and now bent back over his head. His way was blocked. He could hear the waterfall right above him, but there was no way to reach it now. The thought tore at his heart and he let out a cry of anger.

So I never find it after all.

His arms and legs went weak. It would have been so easy to just throw his body into the water. There seemed little point in trying anymore. Already at the limits of his fatigue, he was going numb with pain. Just when he'd lost his will to live, he heard a faint sound above him.

For a moment, Leslie broke away from his pessimistic thoughts and strained his ears. It wasn't bats or falling rocks. The sound was filled with warmth. It wove its way through the intricate spaces between the limestone until it rained down from the gaps in the ceiling. Though difficult to make out, it didn't take long for Leslie to realize what it was: a woman's voice. He then heard words. His name. It had to be Flora. He called out to her as loudly as he could, but his voice was absorbed by the vast mass of water, and he worried that it might not reach her through the crevice. But he kept yelling. If he didn't, Flora might think he wasn't where he was and move on to a different spot.

In fact, Flora didn't hear him. She was on all fours at the edge of the crevice, peering into the depths below, but sensed nothing to indicate that he was down there. Even so, she knew he had to be, and the lack of response frightened her.

Flora trusted her intuition and got to her feet. She took out the rope from her rucksack and tied it to the base of a rock. She then fed the remainder into the crevice, when something occurred to her.

If he fell in, the rocks must have determined which way he fell. I ought to know where I'm going instead of just climbing into the crack.

She found what she was looking for in Gilbert's rucksack: a waterproof flashlight covered in sturdy plastic. It was heavy and had a new dry-cell battery in it. Flora tied it tightly to the end of her rope and lowered it into the crevice.

The flashlight clattered as it slipped down the cliff face, disappearing into the gloom. Flora lowered the rope further, letting gravity guide it along. She could tell from the feeling of the rope that the light was slipping down a fairly steep and uneven path. When she had just several feet of rope left, it stopped trembling and began to slip straight through Flora's hands without resistance. She soon realized what this meant. At the end of the slide was nothingness. Just how far had Leslie fallen? The weight fell faster and the rope just kept going out. Twelve feet, fifteen feet...

Her knees were shaking from fear, her throat dry. How could anyone survive such a high fall? Without knowing that a large lake was waiting at the other end, Flora hoped the light would hit the bottom soon. When the rope went taut, she drew it towards her a little before letting it fall again. Still, no resistance. She had no doubt that the light was suspended in mid-air. The distance of the fall was more than fifteen feet, but she didn't know how much further it went down. Flora was consumed by despair, yet somehow managed to keep her bearings.

PARADISE

A light appeared unexpectedly from the crack above Leslie's head. It was the first light to ever enter this space since its creation. It fell smoothly down, stopping about six feet above the water. The flashlight was tied to the end of a rope, piercing the clear water's surface with sharp rays of light as it swayed gently back and forth. If only he could grab it, he'd be pulled to safety.

I'm saved.

This unexpected helping hand came so suddenly that the strength nearly went out of him. Leslie marveled at the immense promise that a mere ray of light proffered.

After what seemed a long time, the still waters erupted. Touched by their first light ever, aquatic creatures who had lived their entire lives in darkness began to stir. These transparent life forms had the ability to absorb light into their bodies, reemitting it in milky white radiation. Once they were ignited, the light seemed trapped inside them, never to fade until their deaths.

The glow spread from one creature to the next, rippling outward from the center below the dangling flashlight. Only then did Leslie see the lake for its true size. Countless little lights dotted this sea like stars. The air itself began to glow a faint green, outlining a gently curving horizon above the water line.

Leslie turned around, still holding onto the rock, and looked out around him in a daze. At that moment, he forgot his predicament and felt as if he were in a dream where heaven and earth had changed places right before his eyes. But there was no time to immerse himself in beauty. He remembered where he was: about twenty feet above an underground lake, clinging to a rock wall, the only visible connection to safety the slender rope dangling from above.

Leslie eyed the light-source carefully and judged it to be indeed a tall man's height above the water. If he swam out beneath it, it would still be out of reach.

His position, however, afforded him a clear view of the layout below, and he soon noticed a wave approaching from a few hundred feet away.

Flora held the rope taut and looked through her rucksack. She took out the other bundle of rope to tie them together, hoping it would give her sufficient length. Her hands trembled at the thought that it might not be enough.

The water undulated higher and higher, rising as it reached the middle of the lake. The tidal wave was coming back.

Leslie suddenly thought of a solution.

I must borrow the water's strength.

The wave was coming towards him and he would probably only have one chance at this. He turned toward Gilbert's peaceful face below in a final farewell and jumped into the lake, swimming out towards the rope. Then, as he tread water directly under it, he waited for the wave to come, hoping it would push him high enough. The water was eerily still for a brief moment, then the wave came rushing in, crashing against the rocks, sending thousands of the glowing creatures into the air. Leslie tried his best to stay in position as the water lifted him higher. He lost sight of the flashlight when the water swallowed it. He flailed wildly until he grabbed hold of it, and floated up.

Just as Flora was bending over, about to untie the rope from the base of the rock, it suddenly sprung to life. She fell back in surprise, then got up and grabbed the rope, her hand trembling with anticipation. It was Leslie. He was hanging from the rope. She could feel his body weight, and it filled her with joy. She tried with all her might to pull him up, but he was too heavy for her.

For a long while, Leslie swayed at the end of the rope. The flashlight was securely tied, which put him at ease. Even as he savored the thought of being rescued, he looked down at the lake again, only to see an even bigger wave approaching at considerable speed. Judging from the height of the preceding wave, he was sure he'd be able to reach the ceiling this time, but was afraid he might have trouble holding on to the rope. He tried pulling himself up to take refuge in the crevice before the wave came. If he could just reach it, he'd be able to climb up from there with ease.

His body shook from the intense air pressure as the wave blinded his entire field of vision. He managed to pull himself up into the crevice just in time. Specks of light floated all around him. The water not only ran up along the diagonal face of the limestone to touch the ceiling, but pushed into the gap, into its every nook and cranny, shooting Leslie's body upward. It was then that he realized what was happening. This was a quickening inside the earth—the earthquake and the tsunami were labor pains. This had happened to him before. Fluid pushing him out, birth and breath, blinking in the brightness of the outside world.

Once she heard it, Flora braced herself for another earthquake. The sound shook the rock beneath her and came towards her with tremendous speed. The rope suddenly slackened. She coiled it around her arms, keeping an eye on the crevice for any signs of Leslie. She covered her ears from the deafening noise. Just then, a massive wall of water shot up before her, filling up with glowing white dots as her headlamp shone through it. Among them Flora glimpsed Leslie's body. It was only for a moment, before the violent torrent came crashing down on her head. The water surrounded and immobilized her, but she never let go of the rope connecting her and Leslie, wrapping it around her legs and waist as she tumbled in the cascade. The outpour became a wave along the hall floor and paused momentarily. Leslie and Flora poked their heads above the water and took a breath, pulling the rope towards each other. The water now began to pull back into the crevice. Flora made it to the rock base where the rope was tied and clung to it. Then she spotted Leslie about twenty feet ahead of her. He wasn't swimming, but standing with his head barely above the surface. Before the current could pick up speed, Flora pulled on the rope to lessen the distance between them. She turned her back against the crag so that the pressure of the water pinned her against it, freeing up her arms to tug the rope. Leslie, unable to stand his ground, was being drawn back into the crevice. Flora pulled the rope with all her might.

Leslie's body swerved off course just as he seemed about to reach Flora. When he found the floor and braced himself, it was right by the crevice; only the rope was keeping him from being sucked back into the dark space below. He stood there, poised at the edge of the crack, as the water flowed past him. Particles of light in that intense pressure left lukewarm sensations as they shot past him. The cave creatures were ending their first journey to a higher world and returning like a meteor shower across the night sky to their former habitat.

As the water lowered and the current weakened, Leslie at last sobered to the reality of his rescue. He started wading towards Flora in the knee-deep water.

She was leaning against the rock and coughing up water, her legs outstretched for support. Leslie saw that she was about his age. Her long, dark hair, which resembled a Native American woman's, clung wetly to her cheeks, revealing the roundness of her face. She had smooth brown skin and blue eyes set in slightly recessed orbits that made her look pretty. When she looked up at Leslie, water dripped down her forehead into her eyes and rolled down her cheeks as larger drops. Their gazes locked. Not taking his eyes off her for a moment, Leslie took one step, then another towards her. She was here. The one he'd been waiting for. He was seeing her for the first time, so why did his soul cry out with such longing?

A long-forgotten legend, a destiny buried within every cell of his body, resurfaced now. Leslie felt it with both shock and joy. This was fulfillment.

Just then, a familiar-looking sheet of paper floated forth from behind the crag. His score. Though the notes had already faded beyond recognition, Flora instinctively reached out to glean it like some sacred object. When it slipped through her fingers and started drifting toward the hole, she gasped and looked at Leslie's face. He shook his head and laughed, as if to say, "I couldn't care less."

The red deer pendant and Leslie's music were both gone now. Flora didn't know that her birthmark was also disappearing. That very same marking, which only a few hours before had revealed its true form to her, was about to fade, its work complete.

Leslie looked stronger. Stronger compared to what, Flora wasn't sure—the photographs she'd seen of him, perhaps, or memories from some forgotten past. His body was covered all over with markings of a life that had struggled to prevail. His palms were bloodstained, but he betrayed no pain as he hobbled toward her with no little dignity.

Leslie knelt down beside her. For a long time, they stared at each other without a word. Nothing would have come out had they tried to speak. Flora grabbed his arms tightly. In the distant glow of the floodlights, her lips seemed to be trembling from the cold.

He wrapped his arms around her shoulders to warm her. They drew closer, their eyes unwavering.

Of course, the two of them knew nothing of each other's past—that ten thousand years ago, their ancestors had become separated in Asia, going their respective ways on northern and southern paths, crossing to the birthplace of the sun. Not knowing, they yet felt the force. One by one, their cells were rekindled with ancient passion.

They stood up, emerging from the shadows of the crag, and looked around them. The water had almost completely disappeared into the crevice, but some of it remained in small puddles, and in them were left a number of the glowing creatures. Flora and Leslie watched as one of them turned around in its little basin like an underwater firefly. These puddles were tiny compared to the vast sea below and Leslie felt pity at the sight of the trapped creatures. But they, too, were no doubt ready to move on, to evolve anew as creatures that held light within them.

Leslie tried to remember the music he'd composed, but it too seemed to have washed away in his mind. Only the main motif remained, nebulous like the memory of a dream growing distant with time. He only remembered how wonderful it had been—the only thing about it, it seemed, that he would never forget.

He held Flora's shoulders and hobbled towards the cave entrance. As they approached the light, they heard the noise of the generator.

It was already well into morning. They climbed up to the edge of the doline and were greeted by a fiery jewel glittering in the cloudless eastern skyline. As they squinted into the glare, they saw the figure of an antlered deer leaping towards the orb. An illusion, no doubt—but both of them knew, without exchanging a word, that they'd witnessed the exact same thing.

The desert was cool in the morning air. The landscape resembled the Asian earth that their ancestors had once inhabited.

The desert...

The road had been long, but they had returned at last to their beginning. Now into a new life, they were about to take their first step.

THE END

ABOUT THE AUTHOR

Koji Suzuki was born in 1957 in Hamamastu, southwest of Tokyo. He attended Keio University where he majored in French. After graduating he held numerous odd jobs, including a stint as a cram school teacher. Also a self-described jock, he holds a first-class yachting license and crossed the U.S., from Key West to L.A., on his motorcycle.

The father of two daughters, Suzuki is a respected authority on childrearing and has written numerous works on the subject. He acquired his expertise when he was a struggling writer and househusband. Suzuki also has translated a children's book into Japanese, *The Little Sod Diaries* by the crime novelist Simon Brett.

Paradise is Suzuki's fifth novel to appear in English. His current work in progress is *Edge City*, a novel of "quantum horror." He is based in Tokyo but loves to travel, often in the United States.

READ

From one of the world's greatest graphic novels to epoch-making horror, from epic fantasy to histories that read like novels, Vertical brings you Japanese authors who write for the world.

For upcoming titles, visit our website at

Ashes

Tanaka is an aging yakuza gangster experiencing a mid-life crisis.

"In his forays to seedy dives and upscale French restaurants, Western signifiers take on an Eastern feel… Kitakata delineates yakuza rituals, where the traditional hacking off of one finger is no longer sufficient punishment." *Village Voice Bcach Read*

1-932234-02-0 , $23.95/$29.95
224 pages, Hardcover

The Japanese noir trilogy by the don of hardboiled,

KENZO KITAKATA

"The spirit of James M. Cain's novels hovers over *Winter Sleep*, a bleak but compelling slice of deadpan noir."
– *The Seattle Times*

Winter Sleep

Nakagi is an ex-con with a talent for abstract art. In his mountain cabin far from the noisy city, he tries to eke out a life of solitude, but when the art world insists on his return, violence erupts.

1-932234-13-6
$14.95/$19.95, 288 pages, Paperback

The Cage

"Manager Takino" runs the local supermarket, but when someone attempts to blackmail his store, the old yakuza gangster in him will chafe against the bars of the cage he'd put himself in. Once he leaves the cage, he can never go back in.

Publication sponsored by the Japanese Literature Publishing Project.

978-1-932234-24-4/1-932234-24-1
$14.95/$21.00, 232 pages, Paperback